The General's Guard

Charles M. DuPuy

Praise for the EZ Kelly Series

Praise for *Easy Kill*

"EZ Kelly is the next, great kickass heroine."

—EmKay Connor, Award-winning Author

Praise for *Saving Melissa*

"There are few things that cause panic and concern in the law enforcement community than kidnapping. When the victim is a young girl and sex trafficking is suspected, then the gloves come off. Charles DuPuy's *Saving Melissa* will keep you pinned as the main character, EZ Kelly, does what the cops can't."

—Joseph E. Mosca, Author, *Scorpion Wind* and Retired Sergeant, Florida Highway Patrol

"A well-orchestrated plot. A fourteen-year-old girl has been abducted and the race is on to find her. *Saving Melissa* is a real page turner and difficult to put down."

—Flo Parfitt, Author of Daughters of Evolution series

"The characters are intriguing and well-developed. The heroine, EZ Kelly is one tough lady who can hold her own with seasoned investigators. From the beginning, this read is action-packed."

—Floy Turner, Special Agent Florida Department of Law Enforcement, Retired and Best-selling Author of *Behind Her Miami Badge*

"At its heart, *Saving Melissa* is a modern literary homage to Magnum P.I. that entrances you with a kick-ass female lead in the everglades of Florida. Readers will be enthralled by Charles M. DuPuy's action, its suspense and mystery while watching EZ Kelly save the day."

—Nathan Hopp, Author of *The Adventures of Peter Gray*

Advance Praise for *The General's Guard*

"*The General's Guard* is an interesting story with a unique protagonist. Women have been special operators for many years and experiencing a story where one is the protagonist lends a fresh look to a common theme. EZ Kelly comes across as a refreshing take on an old theme."

—D.M. Herrmann, Author of the John Henry Chronicles military series

"Charles DuPuy writes a tantalizing love story between two soldiers that are caught in the cross fire of life's unexpected twists and turns!"

—Elizabeth Visgar, United States Army Veteran

"EZ Kelly (don't let the name fool you), a former Special Forces soldier and now a new travel agent, accepts a mission to scout out an island retreat for her agency. With the promise of sun and fun, the mission quickly takes an unexpected turn when she meets up with a former Commanding Officer General McKelvy. None of what happens after this chance meeting remotely resembles paradise. Fast-paced, action-filled, and unexpected turns abound, especially for EZ who comes quickly to the realization that her strength in training will most likely be what keeps her alive. With women being allowed into the coveted ranks of Special Ops, EZ's character was made more real to me. Kudos to Mr. DuPuy for breaking the mold! Given the opportunity, I could've read this book in one sitting!"

—Susan Teti-Finnegan, Natural Health Consultant

The General's Guard

An EZ Kelly Novel

Charles M. DuPuy

Green Bay, WI

Publisher/Executive Editor: Brittiany Koren
Copy-edit: Callie Trautmiller
Cover Art Designer: Ed Vincent/ENC Graphics
Interior Layout Designer: Amit Dey
Ebook Interior Layout Designer: Amit Dey

Category: Mystery/Suspense

Description: A young travel agent finds more than what she's bargained for when she takes her first all-inclusive paid trip to a luxury resort in the Dominican Republic and meets her old commanding officer.

Hardback ISBN: 978-1-951375-69-0
Paperback ISBN: 978-1-951375-71-3
Ebook ISBN: 978-1-951375-72-0
LOC Catalogue Data: Applied for.

First Edition published by Written Dreams Publishing in July 2022.
Ebook Edition published by Written Dreams Publishing in July 2022.

Green Bay, WI

Published in Green Bay, Wisconsin. Printed in the United States of America.

Books by Charles M. DuPuy

Easy Kill
Saving Melissa
The General's Guard
Say the Word
Rescue Man

*This third EZ Kelly novel is dedicated to my beloved wife, Janet.
She stands by me through thick and through thin,
offering encouragement to me at all the right moments.*

Chapter One

Tuesday, January 24ᵗʰ

I leaned back, my hands resting on my spanking new pale blue pantsuit. My blonde hair, secured in a high ponytail, provided a cushion for my head. The Delta jet lost altitude and flew along the southern coast of the Dominican Republic, low enough so I could gaze down from my tourist class window seat at the seemingly endless white sand beaches and turquoise waters beyond, though we were too high to identify any landmarks in detail.

As I stared down at the brilliant ocean water, I saw dark shapes that could have been schools of sharks idling along. I wondered what it would be like to swim amongst the sharks. I'd heard conflicting tales, some with happy endings, others with unpleasant ones. Like any predator, whether on land or in the water, hunger had to play a part in the level of aggressiveness they displayed. A well-fed lion could be a big pussy cat. A well-nourished shark could be curious, playful even. The problem was, how to tell when the brute had eaten its last good meal? Add to that the potential danger their wildness presented and it ended up being a coin toss: heads you win, tails you lose. Minutes later, I concluded swimming with dolphins made more sense.

The jet banked to the left and swept inland, then banked right.

Almost there, I thought, a picture in my mind of the invitation that had triggered this trip. It arrived in the mail at my and Holly's new travel agency, typed on heavy bond stationery designed to impress and catch the eye. It was addressed to: EASY HOLLY DAY'S TRAVEL.

Holly, a seasoned veteran travel agent, knew at once what it was as she passed the envelope over to me, a knowing smile erupting on her cherubic face. Puzzled, I took it from her extended hand, ripped open the envelope and read the letter.

We cordially invite one of your travel agents to spend three all-expenses paid days with us at El Mar Placida, our new all-inclusive five-star resort situated on Punta Cana's spectacular white sand beaches on the southeast coast of the Dominican Republic. Included in your package is a round trip flight from Atlanta to Punta Cana, limousine transfer from the airport to our resort,

*and all meals and beverages during your stay in one of our luxu-
rious swim-up suites that includes your own private plunge pool.*

*We are confident you'll love your visit with us so much that you
will return home and urge your customers to visit us.*

I set the letter down. "You should go, Holly."

"Nonsense," Holly said. "I've gone on lots of these junkets. It's your
turn, EZ."

"I'm still a greenhorn travel agent. You should go," I repeated.

"That's exactly the point. The experience will propel you forward, make
you a super star agent. End of discussion."

"It does sound like an incredible junket," I said, accepting my fate
as graciously as I could. I knew that free trips like this one, offered by
travel destinations in exchange for good words passed on to the travel
agent's customers were one of the perks. It had caught my attention when
I first considered becoming an agent. They came from hotels, resorts, even
chambers of commerce, as a cost-effective way to promote their businesses.
It was an old, tried-and-true system: "I'll scratch your back if you'll scratch
mine." It worked well for everyone.

The letter raised two questions in my naïve mindset.

"What's a swim-up suite, Holly?"

"I've read about them but never experienced one first-hand. If it's what
I think it is, you go from your suite right into a canal. You climb down into
it or jump in if you're more adventurous, and swim along in the canal to the
main pool where there are swim-up bars. When you've had your fill, you
swim back to your suite. Oh, and you'll need a bathing suit," Holly added,
grinning widely.

"I knew this little junket would end up costing me dearly. I guess I can
use the bathing suit in the plunge pool, too," I countered.

"Oh, I think you could go skinny-dipping in your plunge pool," she
offered, her eyebrows dancing suggestively.

"Okay, now tell me what a plunge pool is, Smarty." I made my own
eyebrows dance the mambo.

"They're like oversized hot tubs filled with warm water. You plunge in,
lollygag around for a bit and climb out. They're for soaking and relaxing,
not meant for exercise. Unless you're accompanied in it by some handsome
hunk," she added.

"There was no mention of handsome hunks in the letter," I shot back.

"Some things are better left to your own devices," said Holly, a wry
smile taking over for her tiring eyebrows.

"Too bad Paul couldn't come with me, but it's a long way from
Afghanistan," I said, a little wistful.

Holly, sensing my mood change, said, "Look at it as a scouting mission.
If you like it, you can recommend it to Paul when he gets home."

She knew only too well from our previous conversations that Paul
was the long-time love of my life, and he was nearing his final tour in

Afghanistan as an U.S. Army Special Forces soldier. His discharge date was fast approaching. For me, though, it wasn't fast enough.

"Yeah, okay. I'll treat it like a reconnaissance mission," I said, reflecting back on my own time as a Special Forces soldier in Afghanistan.

"There you go," said Holly, smiling. "It's settled, then."

"You won't need my help on the home front while I'm off on this junket?"

Holly gave me a look that said it all.

"I know. You've been running things by yourself for the last four years," I said, the respect for her showing up in the sound of my voice.

"Not quite four years. Mister Mitchell, the dead creep who started the travel agency, did his share of the work at the outset. Then, as you know, he got into dealing with young teens, selling them as sex slaves. He lost interest in the travel agency after that," said Holly, a grim expression dominating her countenance.

"He got what he deserved."

"Amen to that, and good riddance," agreed Holly.

"So, what's my next step?" I asked, steering our conversation back to the trip.

"You can write a snail mail letter, or you can fire off an email note, or you can phone them. I've always thought that a phone call offers a more personal touch."

"Phone call, it is. This'll be my first phone call to accept an offer of a free trip. *EZ Kelly, Travel Agent.* I love the sound of that," I added.

"Me, too, EZ. I'm tickled beyond belief that you've come on board with me. We're Don Quixote and Sancho Panza. Nope. They're has-beens and they're both men. How about we're Wonder Woman and Etta Candy? Together, we'll win the day," said Holly. Her genuine smile added the exclamation point to her thoughts.

The cabin intercom came to life, dissolving my thoughts of what had brought me here. "Ladies and gentlemen, and children of all ages, this is the captain speaking. We are on our final approach to Punta Cana International Airport." I could sense a smile working its way through his professional voice. "In anticipation of our touchdown, please raise and lock your tray table, and return your seat back to its upright position. Thank you."

Following the message, passengers moved to follow the captain's request while the flight attendants went along the aisles to ensure that the orders hadn't fallen on deaf ears. Moments later, the captain came on again to say, "Flight crew, please prepare for landing."

The crew responded by taking their seats and buckling themselves in. I peered out the window at the ground racing up to meet us. Houses and commercial buildings rushed by below, and then we were over open land, the jet dropping quickly. I drew an anticipatory breath as the jet's wheels contacted the tarmac and the engines were reversed to slow the plane's speed. I exhaled slowly. Another successful landing. We'd get to walk away and live another day.

"Welcome to Punta Cana, folks. Please remain seated with your seat belts fastened until we reach the terminal," said the calm, steady voice of the captain.

Most of the passengers complied with his request. I heard a few seat belts being released early, and I couldn't help wondering what would happen if the captain had to ram on the brakes unexpectedly.

The plane came to a stop and the *fasten seat belts* light winked off, silently signaling that we could release our seat belts and begin retrieving belongings from the overhead bins. I released my belt and smoothed the light cotton material of my pantsuit, pleased that the three-hour flight hadn't caused any major wrinkles. I sat, pinned in by the two passengers seated in my row, my eyes sweeping over the men and women crowding the aisle. They all pressed forward in their eagerness to disembark.

I searched each face, an old habit I would never discard, despite having scrutinized every face when I boarded. I knew there were still people out there who would love to see me dead, but I didn't see anything unexpected. Having been a major player in the destruction of a child sexual exploitation ring, I maintained a high level of awareness of those around me at all times.

At last, it was my turn to scooch over and stand up, then retrieve my bulky purse and matching light blue jacket from the overhead bin. That done, I began the slow shuffle down the aisle to the exit door. An image came to mind of a herd of mindless cattle lumbering along towards their preordained fate.

A portable ramp had been deployed at the exit door. I followed the passengers ahead of me down the ramp steps to the tarmac and to the waiting buses, the bright, humid tropical sun making me squint. I glanced around as I strolled to the waiting bus and noted that some of the arriving planes had the privilege of deplaning via ramps that led directly into the main terminal. I wondered if straws were drawn to see which planes got the privilege.

The ride to the terminal took less than five minutes. Though I considered the distance perfect for stretching out my muscles by walking, I guessed the disabled and less athletic passengers around me might complain if there was no bus service.

When my turn came, I climbed down out of the bus and moved along with the flow of passengers into the terminal. The air inside was seriously chilled, an effort to appease passengers unused to the noonday sun, maybe.

I followed the directional signs that led to the baggage claim area, made easy by the glut of passengers already heading there. Arriving, I waited with the other passengers for my suitcase to be spit out of the conveyor. I would have carried my bag on the plane if it wasn't for my lockback knife. No way could I get through security with it on me, but checked bags were a different story. I'd heard stories of people who checked bags through with their handguns stowed inside. If a random search found them, the Customs inspectors made life miserable for the owner, and their firearms were confiscated. My lockback knife was a part of me, and it'd saved my skin more than once. It was small and evaded detection. As the saying goes, I never left home without it.

With my suitcase trailing behind, I moved on to the security checkpoint, my eyes busy sweeping everywhere for anyone taking the least interest in me. I did the slow shuffle once more, and finally reached the uniformed Customs and Immigration officer who asked for my passport and the nature of my visit.

"Pleasure," I told him as I passed my passport over to him.

The officer stamped my passport and held it out to me, and I was suddenly unencumbered, free of lines and jostling. The glass doors to the outside beckoned me. Without hesitation, I pushed through, prompted by the sign leading to ground transportation. Bright sunlight again flooded my vision, and the fragrance of tropical flowers bombarded my senses.

The invitation letter from El Mar Placida had promised transportation via limousine, but I was prepared to settle for anything with four wheels and an engine. I searched the area to my right, and then to my left, keenly aware of how exposed I'd become, standing out in the open.

I spotted a young Hispanic man who was dressed in a dark chauffeur's uniform. He held a sign with my name printed on it as he stood beside a big black limo. Relieved, I hurried up to him.

"I'm EZ Kelly," I told him, offering him a smile.

"Welcome, Miss Kelly. I am Fidel, your driver. Allow me to take your bag," he said, all formal, reaching for my suitcase.

I handed it off to him and watched as he opened the trunk and stowed it inside, then reclosed it. He returned to my side and opened the rear door of the limousine for me. I peered inside, squinting to see in the relative gloom, and spotted a man sitting on the rear seat.

Alarm bells rang in my head. I turned back to the driver, expecting a confrontation, but my surprised expression was met by a disarming smile. He sensed my discomfort and hurried to explain. "This is Mister Donohue, Miss Kelly. He is a fellow travel agent," he explained.

"I promise not to bite, as long as you promise not to scratch," said Mister Donohue, an easy smile on his face.

"I scratch as a last resort," I said, and offered up a canned smile as I bent to climb inside. I opted to take the seat facing him rather than sitting next to him.

Once I was seated, he reached his hand toward me. "Hi, I'm Roger Donohue, from Charlottesville, Virginia."

I took his hand, not surprised at his limp grip. "EZ Kelly, from Valdosta, Georgia."

"Now that's a first," said Roger Donohue, leering broadly at me.

"What's that?" I asked, puzzled.

"It's not every day that a woman I've just met announces that she's easy," said Roger, his eyebrows lifting.

Dork!

"You wouldn't believe how many times I've heard that line, Roger. I wish I could say it's bright and fresh, but it's not," I said, my eyes leveled on his. I watched the animation leach from his round, pudgy face.

"Is everything good back there?" asked Fidel from the driver's seat, sensing tension.

"We're good, Fidel," we confirmed as one.

"*Magnifico!* Enjoy the scenery as we make our way to El Mar Placida. Our journey will take us a half of an hour, depending on traffic," he told us, as he looked at us by way of the rearview mirror.

As the limo began moving, Roger tried again. "Let's start over, if you're willing. That was a sophomoric comment I made, and I apologize."

"Apology accepted," I said, nodding at Roger.

"Thank you. I'm a travel agent, and I assume you are, too."

"You assume right. I'm fairly new on the scene, having come up through the ranks. I cut my teeth in a hotel lobby, tending the check-in counter and graduating to agenting local tours. Now I'm working in an agency in Valdosta," I explained.

Roger listened politely. When I'd finished, he told me he worked in the agency founded by his father in Charlottesville. "We get a lot of college students who come in looking for something better than a week of beer and barfing in Florida. This new resort sounds like something I could sell to the more affluent students," he concluded.

"It does sound unique. I'm looking forward to my visit," I replied, by way of making conversation.

I looked out the side window. We were on the airport access road, lined with palm trees and a variety of ornate tropical plantings. To me, it wasn't much different than a drive along many Miami roadways, but to a tourist from the north it would doubtless have a greater impact on their visual cortexes.

"Now that's the kind of scenery I've been looking forward to," said Roger, confirming my thoughts. I smiled and nodded at him in confirmation.

I closed my eyes and an image of Paul appeared. If only he could have been here in the limo with me instead of dorky Roger. He was being discharged from the army today, though I hadn't known that at the time of booking the trip. I wished I could be back in South Carolina to meet him, but the freebie trip to the Dominican resort got in the way. Canceling at the last minute would've been bad form. The last thing I needed as a novitiate travel agent was a stain on my reputation.

Once the limo left the access road, the scenery changed. The drive took us north on RD-3, which turned rural quickly. There were a few scattered houses, mostly one-story ones with metal roofs to protect them from the occasional downpours, but they were widely spaced on open, undeveloped land.

I knew from my internet search that Punta Cana was a relatively recent tourist destination. American investors had bought 30 square miles along the Dominican Republic's eastern shore in 1969. At the time, there were a few scattered coastline fishing villages, but no roads gave access to the area. By 1984, the airport became operational, and improved roads gave access to the shoreline. Real commercial development began in earnest soon after. There are still shoreline areas yet to be developed, and El Mar Placido took advantage of one of those.

My daydreaming was interrupted by Fidel announcing our arrival. "We are turning into the entryway to El Mar Placida just now," he told us with a smile by way of the rearview mirror.

Fidel drove along a wide entrance road with more exotic tropical plantings along the way, all carefully trimmed and meticulously maintained. At length, the driveway turned to the right and passed under a large portal at the entrance to the main building. Fidel brought the limo to a stop and leaped out to open the door for us.

A chastened gentleman now, Roger beckoned to me to be first out. I nodded my thanks and exited.

I was stunned by the intricate beauty of the entrance. No expense had been spared. The portico soared upwards a good three stories, and the building's façade shimmered with hundreds of roughly cut blocks of sparkling minerals set amongst lesser blocks of red, yellow and brown stone. The effect was stunning. It beckoned me inside with the promise of more spectacular beauty beyond.

"Nice," said Roger, standing by my side.

I hadn't formed words to express what I saw, but 'nice' didn't come close. "You got that right," I said, trying to sound casual.

"If you will follow me, I will bring your bags to the reception desk," said Fidel. He had taken our two bags from the trunk and beckoned for us to follow him.

My eyes moved from the sweeping façade to the entrance doors where I saw more opulent finishing touches. The two huge glass entry doors were easily twenty feet tall. Fidel walked towards them, our bags trailing behind, and they swung open without a sound, a motion sensor responding to his approach. I couldn't help shaking my head in wonder. Roger, at my side, nodded in agreement.

I stepped through the outer doors and into a spacious vestibule, the tall walls on either side covered by a 3D map of the Dominican Republic, a gold star marking our location. Thirty feet ahead stood another set of tall glass doors. Cool air enveloped me.

As we moved to the center of the vestibule, the outer doors silently closed behind us, followed by the equally silent opening of the inner doors. It all worked flawlessly to conserve the cool air inside.

The thought was swept away by the spectacle of the lobby. The lobby of the Adriatic Hotel in Miami, where I cut my teeth as a budding travel agent, was all I had for comparison. I saw at once that there was no comparison. For starters, the ceiling soared upwards at least four stories, with multiple mobiles suspended above me, subtle lighting interspersed to highlight them. The floor was polished travertine marble with intricate designs leading the way to the reception desk. The walls were hung with distinctive paintings portraying scenes of life in the Dominican Republic, and above the paintings, in the towering space above, were oversized tapestries, some with designs showing people, others depicting outdoor scenes. Scattered around the immense floor area were groupings of low tables and upholstered chairs, places for guests to rest and converse, whether going or coming. I noted a group of six men sitting in a circle around one of the glass-top tables, but I couldn't make out their features from a distance.

Dazzled by all the luxury, I followed along behind Fidel as he led the way to the huge polished marble reception counter. I saw ornate designs cut and fitted together on its surface. As I neared it, I realized that it portrayed a beach scene with gentle waves breaking on the shore. I stared in wonder at its intricacies. The artist had put it all together with a variety of different colored and carefully cut stone. I also guessed that it had cost a pretty penny. Clearly, no expense was spared. I made a mental note to mention the incredible designs in the lobby to my potential customers.

* * *

"Welcome to El Mar Placida, Miss Kelly. I'm Donna. We've been expecting you," said a trim, attractive young Dominican woman from behind the counter. I looked up to see a woman about my own age smiling in welcome.

"How did you know who I am?" I asked, surprised.

"Ah, that is easy. Fidel announced your arrival when he brought in your bag," she replied, again smiling warmly.

"Of course. Fidel is very good at what he does."

"Thank you for your compliment. I will be sure to pass it on. May I see your passport?"

I removed my passport from my handbag and gave it to Donna, who took it and opened it to the first page, glancing at my picture and the brief information. "We will place it in the concierge safe during your stay here as a security measure. If you need it during your stay, you only have to ask and we will retrieve it for you."

"That's fine. One less thing to worry about," I said, nodding my approval to her.

"Are you right or left-handed, Miss Kelly?"

She had surprised me again. "Right-handed. Why?"

"We need to attach your color-coded wristband. It identifies you to our staff as a premier guest. By showing it, you will be extended every courtesy. All your drinks and meals are provided free of charge to you, and any alcoholic beverage you choose will contain nothing but the finest alcohol available. The wristband also serves as your room key. By placing it in front of your suite door's lock, it will open the door for you."

"What a great idea," I said, amazed at what a simple wristband could do.

"Yes, it makes our guest's stay here so much less complicated. Everything's built into one little band secured to your wrist. It's waterproof and suntan lotion proof, too," added Donna, a quirky smile spreading over her round, pleasant face.

"Now I see why you asked me what hand I use most," I said, returning the smile, holding out my left wrist.

Donna deftly attached the light green wristband, then used a pair of scissors to cut off the extra material. "There you go, Miss Kelly." She put the scissors away.

I checked out the wristband and was pleased with its snug fit. It would be unlikely to snag on anything.

"You will be staying in suite number 16, Miss Kelly. We call it Suite 16, an age we all look back on with nostalgia," said Donna, her smile widening with her little play on words.

"I like it," I said, grinning at her humor.

"And now for the, ah, business part of your stay with us. Miss Haversham, our marketing director, will be meeting with you and the other visiting travel agents for a breakfast and orientation tour tomorrow morning at eight o'clock. The breakfast will be at the Oceania Restaurant, which is out the front entry door and to your right. Miss Haversham requests that you be on time. She will explain the resort concept to you while you enjoy your breakfast, and then she'll take you around and show you all the amenities of the resort. Do you have any questions?"

"I can't think of anything right now," I said.

"There's just one more thing, Miss Kelly. As a guest of the resort, you are forbidden from offering gratuities to any of our staff, for whatever reason. The staff knows that you are here as a guest in order to promote the resort to the world, and they understand that you won't be offering them any tips. And with that, I will summon Ramon to escort you and your bag to your suite. Is there anything more I can do for you at this moment?"

"No. Everything's good, Donna. Thank you for your attention to all the details."

"You are quite welcome," she said. She tapped a desk bell that trilled softly.

A young Dominican man dressed in a crisp, white shirt and white trousers hurried forward to my side. "Welcome to El Mar Placida, Miss. My name is Ramon. It is my pleasure to escort you and your luggage to your suite." His face wore a well-rehearsed smile.

"Thank you, Ramon." I returned the smile.

Ramon picked up my bag and led the way across the lobby towards my suite. Halfway across, a man's voice cut through the air.

"Hey, soldier! What brings you here?"

I recognized the voice instantly, despite the fact it had been, what? Two, no three years since I'd heard it last. I turned towards the figure who stood facing me. "Hello, General McKelvy. I could ask you the same question," I fired back.

"I'm glad to hear you've still got that smart mouth, Sergeant Kelly. Come. Join us for a moment," he said, beckoning me over.

I glanced at Ramon who had stopped, waiting for me, raised my eyebrows and shrugged my shoulders, then turned and strode toward McKelvy. Ramon, getting it, moved to the side and stood by my bag, waiting patiently.

"How did you recognize me, General?"

"I pinned a medal on you, Kelly. I remember."

"You have a good memory," I said, taking in the other five men seated with him. They were all dressed casually in shorts and short-sleeved sports shirts. Their pale arms and legs told me they hadn't spent time in the sun yet. I noted that all their wristbands were blue and wondered what they were entitled to.

"It's not General any longer, Sergeant Kelly. When I retired, I went back to being Walter McKelvy again," he said, a lopsided grin on his lean, weathered face. At the same time, he reached his right hand out to me.

I accepted his hand and did my best to match his firm grip. "It's not Sergeant Kelly any longer, either, General McKelvy. Folks just call me EZ Kelly," I fired back at him.

"Yeah, I remember that name now. I always wondered what kind of trouble it got you into over the years," said McKelvy, his left eyebrow lifting with the question.

"No trouble I couldn't handle, sir, thanks to my dad's instruction from an early age," I replied levelly.

"Tell me about him." It came through as more of an order than a request.

"He was Special Forces, too. When he realized the kind of trouble I might face because my name got shortened from Esther Zane to EZ, he taught me everything he knew to protect myself."

"Kelly, huh? What's his first name?"

"Sean, sir."

"You're kidding! You're Sean Kelly's daughter? No wonder you handled yourself so well in combat."

"Sounds like you knew him back then," I said, intrigued. I searched the general's face for signs of a con. No con came back at me.

"Hell yeah, I knew him. Trusted him with my life, more than once. You talk to him, tell him Mad Mac wants to know how they're hangin'."

"Mad Mac, huh? Where'd that come from?" I asked, curious about the nickname.

"Your old man'll tell you," said Walter McKelvy, a twinkle in his eyes.

"That'll speed up my making the call to him," I said, grinning at him.

"Hey, look, Kelly. I didn't mean to hold you up. Go get settled in, check the place out, and come on back for more, if you want," said McKelvy, apologizing.

"I'll come back on one condition, Sir," I replied.

"And what's that?"

"You drop Kelly, call me EZ."

"Okay, on one condition of my own. Drop the 'sir.' I'm a civilian now, like you. First name's Walt."

"Fair enough, Walt. See you in a bit." I did a quick wave at him and his group who had been following along with their eyes during my exchange with General McKelvy, then rejoined Ramon.

Ramon gave me a broad smile and turned to lead me to my suite. I fell in next to him and said, "Thanks for your patience, Ramon."

"It is nothing, Miss. It is my pleasure, waiting for you. Your suite is not far," he said, gesturing down the long hallway with his free hand.

I took in the impressive hallway, replete with what appeared to be original works of art hanging on the walls. I took a Fine Arts course in college as an elective, which had given me an appreciation for the masters. Though I doubted I was passing any masterpieces, I could see the bold strokes and artful detail that marked them as creations of talented artists. I made a mental note to check them out more closely later.

"Here we are, Miss," said Ramon. He stopped in front of an impressive tall wood door that I guessed was fashioned from mahogany. He motioned for me to hold my wristband next to the locking mechanism. As I did so, I heard a subtle clunk and Ramon swung the door inward with a well-rehearsed flourish.

I stepped through the doorway and stared in disbelief at what I saw. My previous exposure to a suite had been at a hotel in Cleveland. I guessed that two of those suites would have fit inside this one, with room to spare. I giggled at the pun I'd made internally.

Ramon followed me into the room and began a running commentary of the suite's features, most of which I missed as I gawked in wonder at the opulent setting. Arrayed before me was a towering lounge area. I guessed it had to be ten feet up to the sculpted ceiling, shaped like a cloister with curved arches meeting at the highest point. The walls were a pale blue. I wondered if I'd been given this suite because the walls matched my pantsuit. Another giggle escaped me.

"…and if you'll follow me, I will show you your outside amenities," spoke Ramon with a sweep of his arm at a door on the far side of the room.

I followed.

When Ramon opened the door, the tropical sunlight swept in on me, accompanied by the scent of a thousand tropical flowers. I followed Ramon outside onto a small, private patio. There was a glass-topped table and four padded chairs ahead, and to the right a ten-by-ten tile-lined enclosure filled with clear water: my plunge pool, I guessed.

The patio area was surrounded by high stucco walls that shielded me from my neighbors. Bougainvillea and other bright tropical plants broke up the wall and added color to the area. Natural-looking tile covered the ground.

"And over here is your private entry to the water channel," said Ramon as he stepped over to a full-height door in the wall to the left of the table and chairs. He opened the door and beckoned me forward.

I looked out on another small patio area, complete with its own table and chairs, and beyond it was the water channel. An ornately tiled table held a small stack of folded clean towels. A basket next to it was set to accept used towels.

I spotted a set of four steps that led down to the water at the same time Ramon pointed them out to me. "If you enter the water and swim to the right, you will reach the main swimming pool and its swim-up bar. There is a place by the swim-up bar where you can climb out and access the restaurant and its menu of snacks and sandwiches."

Hearing this, I realized how hungry I had become. Breakfast seemed like a lifetime ago. "What if I swim to the left?" I asked Ramon with a gesture in that direction.

"Ah, that will lead you through two smaller pools and past two other restaurants, and ultimately to the main pool. It was designed that way so that guests who get confused can go either way to get back to their rooms." He didn't mention an overindulgence of alcohol as a reason for confusion, but I guessed that could be one of the reasons.

I turned around to get my bearings and saw that the door to the water channel was clearly marked with my suite number in bold letters, obviously designed so a swimmer returning couldn't miss it. I also saw the same locking mechanism on the door that would respond to my wristband.

"Thanks for the tour, Ramon. I can take it from here."

"Oh, yes, yes, of course! If you need anything, you only have to call the front desk. Will there be anything else?" His wide black eyebrows raised in question.

"No, Ramon. I am only sorry that I can't give you something for your trouble."

"No trouble, Miss, I assure you!" He backed through the door to the patio, then through the door to the suite proper, me following him.

As a final gesture towards orientating me, he swept his right arm at a large mahogany door on the right side of the main lounge area and said, "Your bedroom and bath are through that way. I have placed your suitcase there by the door," he said, pointing.

"Thank you for your thoroughness, Ramon. I'll put in a good word for you with the management."

"You are too kind, Miss!" he said as he backed to the entry door and made his exit. I heard the click of the door shutting tight.

Aah! Alone at last, I breathed and kicked off my pale blue low-wedge heels. Then I peeled off my jacket and stepped out of my pants, arranging them carefully on a nearby overstuffed chair. I stood in my bra and panties, surveying the room and its open space. Decided on an area, I moved into my daily exercise routine.

I started out slowly, concentrating on stretching and limbering my body after its confines on the plane and after. Once I felt loose and my muscle tone returned, I began my more strenuous movements, which included leaps (over furniture), rolls (on the carpet) and lunging and sparring with invisible antagonists. A full twenty minutes later, slightly out of breath, I chose an open area and did my wall climb. I ran at the open wall, leaped and planted my right foot as high up as I could, then pushed off. My body arched backwards and did a complete flip in midair, and I landed on my feet with hardly a sound, facing the wall once more. I did that maneuver three times, taking pleasure in landing within a foot of my original touchdown site, and then I modified my wall climb. This time, I rotated my body as I pushed off and landed facing the opposite direction. I repeated this move twice more, landing within a foot of my original touchdown each time.

Might as well save a little energy for later, I thought while wiping the dampness from my brow with the back of a hand. I sauntered into the bedroom feeling lithe and loose and found the bathroom.

Ignoring its opulent granite counters and gold sink fixtures, I opened the glass shower door and spun on the water controls. A thick jet of water rewarded me. I grabbed a pale blue bath towel from a gold towel bar while the water turned warm. Then I stepped out of my panties and dropped my bra before moving under the warm cascade, making no effort to keep my hair dry.

I soaped up using the resort-provided body gel. The soothing scent filled my senses and added to the relaxation of the shower. "I must've died and gone to heaven," I breathed, inhaling the subtle fragrance. Lilac? Lavender? I wasn't sure, but I luxuriated in the aroma.

Done, I shut off the water and stepped out onto the brightly colored bathmat and picked up the towel. After wiping my body dry, I finished with a vigorous tousling of my dripping blonde hair.

"It's time to go exploring in my new bathing suit," I announced to the empty bathroom.

Hearing no objections, I padded out into the huge bedroom with its elevated king-size bed and set my suitcase on the caddy at the foot of the bed. Opening it, I dug down and found my bathing suit. I held it out in front of me, appraising it for the umpteenth time. Holly had reassured me that it wasn't too risqué, but I still had my doubts.

"What the hell," I told myself as I stepped into the lower half and tugged it upwards. It covered what it needed to cover. My belly button showed, but there was a reasonable amount of red and blue checkered fabric below it to protect my modesty. I put the bra portion around my chest, fastened it, and tied the strap around my neck. I searched for a mirror to check the results.

The full-length mirror on the bathroom door confirmed that I still had it. My shoulder-length blonde hair contrasted nicely with my slightly tanned face as my clear blue eyes winked back at me. I smiled and the mirror returned the favor. I eyed my small, upturned breasts, reassured that my bathing suit presented a modest display of my attributes. I checked out my trim waist, flaring hips, and straight, muscular legs. "Lookin' good, EZ," I whispered to the smiling image.

Confident that the new packaging was doing what I paid for it to do, I hurried out onto my patio and approached the plunge pool, swirling my hand in it to test the temperature. I smiled, feeling the comforting warmth. I swung effortlessly over the edge and dropped into the warm water with hardly a ripple. I submerged completely, then porpoised briefly, luxuriating in its enveloping embrace. Now I knew what a plunge pool was all about. I liked it.

"Time to explore." I swung myself out and onto the terraced surface, water dripping from my glistening body and scant suit. I stepped carefully to the exit door, aware of the potential for slipping on the surface made wet by my antics, and opened it wide, then closed it behind me. I scanned the canal in both directions.

No other guests were anywhere to be seen.

I took the steps down to the canal where a short ladder was provided for the less adventurous. I ignored it and leaped in, my legs held loosely under me in case it was shallower than expected. My feet barely grazed the bottom as my body came to a stop. With my legs fully extended, my face above the surface, I guessed the depth at about six feet. The water temperature was the same as in my plunge pool. No doubt the canal water circulated through it as well.

Turning right, I dogpaddled along the canal, my eyes taking in the brightly colored tile lining both sides. I swam past other suites on both sides. No occupants were in sight. I wondered if the rooms were vacant, or were the occupants elsewhere? New resort, the word not out yet. "I'm part of the task force to change that," I whispered to the silent canal.

The canal widened ahead of me. I'd reached the main pool. Irregular in shape, it was constructed of smooth concrete and inlaid tile. Entering it, I glanced about and spotted three other swimmers, all lolling about and enjoying the warm water. I looked left and saw the swim-up bar Ramon had mentioned. I breast-stroked for it.

A thin young Dominican man standing behind the low bar turned and offered me a smile as I approached. I stood up and made my way to one of the low round stools surrounding the tiled bar.

"Welcome, young lady," he addressed me with his deep bass voice as I sat on one of the stools.

"Thank you. What is your name?" I asked him.

"My name is Ramon," he said.

"What a coincidence. The man who showed me to my room is Ramon as well."

"It is no coincidence. All the men on staff are named Ramon," he explained.

"Really? How could that happen?"

"The management wishes to make it easy for the guests to remember our names, so they have us all respond to the name Ramon."

"So, Ramon isn't your real name then," I said.

"Exactly. While I'm at work, my name is Ramon," he said, smiling broadly.

"What is your name when you aren't at work?" I pursued.

"It is Antonio. But you must call me Ramon when I am working," he said emphatically.

"Of course, Ramon."

"Thank you, young lady. Now, what can I get for you? Perhaps a fresh Dominican rum punch?"

"Only if you call me EZ instead of young lady," I said, smiling impishly.

Ramon/Antonio glanced about, and reassured that nobody else was within earshot, said, "Since we are private, I can do that. EZ," he added.

"Thank you. Do you have any fruit juice? Plain, that is?" I asked.

"Of course! This is the Dominican Republic! I have papaya juice, mango juice, pineapple juice, orange juice, all of them fresh," he explained.

"Yum! Make me a papaya-mango-pineapple-orange juice cocktail, please."

"No rum, young— I mean EZ?" he said, catching himself.

"No rum. Maybe later," I said, nodding at him.

"No problem."

Ramon/Antonio set a large glass before me and poured a small amount of juice from four different glass carafes that he plucked from their icy baths, one after the other. Done, he swirled the juices together with a bar spoon.

I reached for the glass.

"Do you want some ice mixed in?" he asked.

"No, it looks perfect the way it is." I raised the glass to my mouth and took a hearty gulp. The combination of fresh tropical juices swirled over and around my taste buds, sending rivulets of pleasure through my mouth.

"Good, no?" asked Ramon/Antonio.

"Good, yes," I confirmed.

"Nothing like fresh fruit juice," he said, grinning.

"You are so right. Now all I need is a plate of fresh fruit for my lunch."

"If you like, I can have the restaurant above bring you whatever you wish. I have their menu here," he said as he plucked a plasticized menu from between two rum bottles and set it on the counter before me.

"What a great idea," I said and scanned the menu.

"Many customers prefer it this way," he told me.

"Oh, there it is. A tropical fruit plate. Perfect, Antonio." I handed back the menu.

"That's an easy one. Nothing to cook," he said. He picked up a phone behind him, tapped out a three-digit number, and spoke softly for a moment. He turned back to me.

"It will be here in no time, EZ," he said in a confidential way, with a glance around to assure himself that no one was within earshot.

"Thanks, Antonio," I replied, smiling at his caution. I continued sipping my juice, fully immersed in the complex tastes. I had enjoyed fresh juice when I lived in Miami, but I couldn't remember anything as good as this. *A little touch of heaven.*

Between sips, I asked, "Have you always wanted to work at the resort?"

"My cousin works at the police station. I thought that might be interesting," he said.

"Oh, what department?" I asked.

"The lab," Antonio said and grabbed a bar cloth to wipe down an area of the bar.

A waiter dressed in white arrived before I'd finished my juice and set a plate of fresh fruit in front of me with a small flourish.

"Thank you, Ramon," I said to him, a smile making my mouth dance.

"Enjoy, young lady," he replied.

I was tempted to ask him what his real name was, but one of the swimmers was wading up to the swim-up bar, and I thought better of it. I turned towards the swimmer, my eyes sweeping over him. It was an old habit, drilled into me since I'd sat on my daddy's knee. Ex-Special Forces, he told me to always check out someone coming towards me. Keep yourself *one step ahead of a possible enemy.* It had served me well.

I saw a middle-aged man whose full, sagging gut bore testament to his excesses and lack of conditioning. He saw me looking and said, "Hiya, pretty girl. I'm Steve," as he extended his fleshy hand towards me.

I took it, tempted to squeeze it until his eyes watered, but decided not to create a scene. I gave it a cursory squeeze instead. "Hi, Steve. My name's EZ." From experience I knew I got more of a reaction if I simply said 'I'm EZ.'

Steve's face looked blank a moment, and then he recovered. "My pleasure."

I felt his eyes assessing my breasts and then he glanced down at my fruit plate.

"Hey, Ramon. Mix me up a rum punch and lemme see the menu, okay?" he said, shifting his attention to the real business at hand.

"Yes, Sir!" replied Ramon/Antonio. He set a menu in front of Steve and went about putting together Steve's rum punch.

I went to work on my fruit plate. I recognized pineapple, mango, papaya, banana, chunks of coconut, cantaloupe, and slices of a star-shaped fruit I hadn't had before. I tried a bite and found it had a great flavor all its own.

"Ramon, what's this?" I asked, pointing at the unknown fruit.

Ramon glanced at my plate and said, "That's carambola, young lady. It is also called star fruit. You like it?" He looked at me expectantly.

"It's delicious. Thanks."

"It's no trouble, young lady. Any time."

I turned my attention back to my plate, relishing the unique flavors of each individual bite, only dimly aware that Steve had ordered a double cheeseburger and fries and was gulping down his rum punch while waiting.

I savored the last bite and reluctantly set down my fork. "That was incredible, Ramon. I'll be back for more tomorrow," I told him as I stood.

"I'm so glad you liked it. I await your arrival tomorrow."

I waved farewell and began the easy swim back to my suite. As I moved along, I chuckled softly at the image: EZ off on an *easy swim.*

Chapter 2

Tuesday, January 24th

With my hair dried and held with a scrunchie in a ponytail, I dressed in tan capris and a pale yellow blouse. Then, I left my suite and moved purposely towards the lobby, automatically sweeping my surroundings with well-practiced eyes. The hallway was empty. I reached the lobby and was surprised to find General McKelvy and his five buddies still ensconced in the same place. The only addition was that each of the five men had yellow legal-sized pads in front of them, with pens in hand or on their pads. Curious to find out what they were up to, I approached them.

Walt saw me and smiled, waving me over. I stepped up to the group.

"Hey, EZ, welcome back! You look like you belong here now," he said, appraising my casual attire.

"I had a swim and some lunch, so I feel like I belong, too," I responded, doing my best to sound nonchalant to the man I knew as General.

"Good, good. Let me introduce my associates here." When he spoke, all five men got to their feet, their attention on me, some smiling, some with serious expressions.

"You men act more like a team than a bunch of guys on vacation together," I said, sizing them up.

"That's a sharp observation, EZ. Meet Bob Hixon, the treasurer. Very important guy," said Walt.

I reached out to shake Bob's hand, noting his neutral grip. "Hi, Bob."

"Next is Jim Bennett, my pollster," said Walt, indicating a sixtyish tall man to his right.

"Nice meeting you, Jim," I said, extending my hand to him.

"And next is Tony Marino who's in charge of scheduling," said Walt, pointing to a tall, heavyset man who looked to be in his forties.

"Good to meet you, Tony," I said, shaking his extended hand.

"And this is Kim Boucher, head of publicity," said Walt, with a wave towards a wiry man I guessed to be in his fifties and about my height.

I moved to shake Kim's hand. "My pleasure," I said.

"Last but not least, meet Peter Spaulding. Pete's my media man," said Walt, gesturing towards a fiftyish man, short, stocky, and with energetic eyes.

I stepped over to shake his hand. "Nice to meet you, Peter," I said.

"There, now, EZ. Can you remember anyone's name, after all that?" asked Walt, a sly smile on his face.

"Let's see. That's Bob Hixon, the treasurer, and next to him is Jim Bennett, the pollster, who's next to Tony Marino, in charge of scheduling, and then Kim Boucher, head of publicity, and last but not least, Peter Spaulding, your media man," I said, with a nod towards Walt.

"Jesus, EZ. How'd you do that?" asked Walt, a surprised expression on his face.

"I paid attention," I said, making light of my eidetic memory.

"Well done! Let me grab a chair for you. Join the group!" said Walt.

"I'll get one," I said. I turned to pull a chair from a neighboring table and into the circle. The men shuffled their chairs about to make a space for me.

Once we were all seated, Walt asked me, "Got any idea what we're all about here?"

"If I had to guess, I'd say you're thinking of running for office," I said, looking at Walt.

"Not much gets by you. I like that. Fact is, this is my presidential exploratory committee," Walt explained.

"Like in, president of the United States?" I asked, eyebrows raised.

"Exactly. What do you think?"

"You mean, I could be sitting next to the future president of the United States?"

"If everything goes well, yes," said Walt, a shy smile on his rugged face.

"Are you a Republican or a Democrat?" I asked by way of making conversation.

"Neither. I'll be running as an Independent. I think both the Republicans and the Democrats are too full of themselves, waste their time and our money on frivolous political issues, spend more time arguing with each other than in getting things done. I'll work to unite them from a neutral position, make them turn their focus from backstabbing to bill passing."

"That's a really cool idea. Think it could work?"

"If I make the decision to run, after we've had a look at all the ins and outs, it'll be up to me to *make* it work," said Walt, all serious.

"From what you've said, I can promise you my vote," I said.

"I'd like to have more than your vote, EZ."

"What do you mean?" His statement raised my hackles. Was he making a play for me?

"After we talked earlier, I told the crew what I knew of you," said Walt with a gesture towards the other five. "They agreed with me that we should offer you a job."

"Thanks, but I have a job. I'm a travel agent now. I was invited here by the resort management so I can tell my clients what a great vacation place this is," I explained. At the same time, my hackles eased back down, but my curiosity moved to take their place.

"Good for you, and I wish you all success. What I'm proposing is short-term. I need someone I trust to cover me, be my security person. If I declare myself as a candidate, the Secret Service'll take over and you'll be out of a job," Walt explained.

"I don't know why you need security, someone to protect you. At this point in the process, you're one of the unknowns, excuse my bluntness, so who could want to harm you?" I asked, looking directly at Walt.

"That's the thing. I'll be going up against the Washington elite, the 'swamp' as it's called, and I've been advised by more than these five men that there are people out there who don't take kindly to someone declaring himself a candidate who hasn't come up through the ranks. *Their ranks*," Walt added with a head nod. "And then there are the unhappy warriors who have it in for me for abuses, real or imagined, that occurred during my long military career."

I gave him a knowing look. "Do you think they could cause you bodily harm?"

"There are stories," said Walt, not elaborating.

"You mean unwelcome candidates have been attacked?"

"There are stories," Walt repeated.

"How *serious* are the stories?" I pursued.

"You know the old Jimmy Hoffa story, right?" he asked.

"Sure. Teamster, vanished without a trace. Rumors are out there that he's doing his part to support a bridge abutment in Jersey," I said, recalling Dad's story about Hoffa.

"There have been candidates who have vanished, candidates who ignored the old guard's way of doing things," said Walt.

"That kind of violence would require more than one attacker. Sounds like you need a team, not little old me standing guard. Have you tried to hire one?"

"No, the potential threat came to our attention this morning. I'm thinking you'd have a hell of an advantage. They'd never think an attractive young woman could take them down," said Walt, his eyes appraising me for a reaction.

I shrugged. "Does it pay well?" I asked, trying to lighten the mood, a sly smile playing on the corners of my mouth.

Walt turned to face his treasurer. "What do you think, Bob?"

"In all seriousness, Walt, we all agree that the threat is real, and if we're putting EZ's life on the line she should be well-compensated," Bob replied.

Walt turned back to me and asked, "So, what do you think your life's worth?"

"I got around three thousand a month when I was playing soldier in Afghanistan. That works out to around a hundred a day. Somehow that doesn't seem like enough, if what you're telling me is true," I said as I watched Walt's face for a reaction.

Walt returned my expression with an equal one of his own. "I wouldn't insult you by offering you your Army Sergeant's pay, EZ. What do you think, Bob?" he asked the man in charge of finances.

"You want my honest opinion, we should pay her five hundred a day, minimum, and add room and board to that. And if she runs into trouble, which is to say *you* run into trouble, then we can raise it. Your life is worth every bit of that. No, that's not true. It's worth more," said Bob, his facial expression confirming the seriousness of his words.

Walt looked at me. "That sound okay to you?"

"It sounds more than fair. Understand, though, that I've got two more days here, and a lot of tomorrow is already taken up with talks and tours of the resort. I won't be able to cover you while I'm doing that," I said, my open hands held out to my side as I spoke.

"Fair enough. I'll try to stay out of trouble until you're done being a travel agent," said Walt. He tried out a smile that I figured he'd be using during his long campaign.

"I sure hope you'll stay safe without me. How long do you think it'll be before the Secret Service takes my new job away?"

"We hope to wrap up the exploratory committee work within a week, ten days max. If I throw my hat in the ring, you'll be out of a job by then," said Walt.

"So you're saying ten days max, right? I need to tell my business partner of my change of plans."

"Yep. Ten days should be more than enough time. Do you want us to secure you a weapon?"

"I've got a weapon," I said, patting my right pants pocket.

"It doesn't look like the bulge of a handgun," said Walt, peering at my right thigh.

"Nope. It's my trusty lockback knife. It's seen me through the good times and the bad," I said with a nod of my head.

"You decide you want something more powerful, let me know. I can get it for you."

"Thanks. Things change, I might take you up on that. Meanwhile, let me make a couple calls and I'll let you know after that."

"We'll be here until six, when we break for dinner, and we'd love to include you," said Walt.

"Sounds good," I said, standing. I gave the group a sweeping wave and turned to go back to my suite.

* * *

Back in my suite, I made the first call. "Hey, Dad. Do you know someone who calls himself Mad Mac?"

"Where'd you hear that name?" Dad fired back, curiosity brimming in his question.

"From the man himself. He's here at the same resort I've come to check out," I said, settling into the soft upholstered chair in my suite's main room.

"That tough old sonofabitch! How'd he know I'm your old man?"

I explained, leaving no details out. "When he was my Regional Commander in the Stan (military slang for Afghanistan), I never had much contact with him, but he remembered me. Today he recognized me across the lobby, which impressed me, after all that time."

"Yeah, I remember he had a sharp mind, and he could kick some ass. That's how he got his nickname. We went on a lot of missions together, back in the day. He saved my butt more than once," he said. "He's a general now, isn't he?"

"Yeah. He told me you saved *his* butt more than once," I said.

"That's how it was. We looked after one another. But you know that. You were in it, too," he said, referring to my time in Afghanistan.

"I hear you, Dad. Think you can keep a secret?" I asked, changing the subject.

He chuckled. "As long as it doesn't bring harm to anyone. Shoot."

"General McKelvy is exploring running for president."

There was a long silence, and I was on the brink of asking Dad if he was still there when he said, "Huh! I think he'd make a great president. Of these United States, right?"

"Uh huh. The one and only."

"Well, you tell Mad Mac that Killer Kelly wishes him the best. I'll be rooting for him," he said.

"Killer Kelly? How come you never shared *that* nickname with me before?" I asked, trying to sound hurt.

"Hell, EZ, if I shared everything with you, we'd have nothing new to talk about." I could feel his sly smile come through the phone line.

"Remind me to tell you what *my* nickname is someday," I countered.

"Good one, little darlin'. I look forward to it."

"McKelvy wants me to be his security person while he's exploring the idea of running," I said, changing the subject once more.

"That sounds like a cushy job."

"I thought so, too, but that's not what he and his team think. He's running as an Independent, and the good old boys in Washington don't like the likes of him horning in. He's not looked on as a member of their team, so they consider him to be unpredictable, a danger to their well-established way of doing things," I explained. "Oh, and he says there's a couple of skeletons in his career closet who'd like nothing more than to do their part in blocking his presidential run," I added.

"Correct my last comment. Cushy doesn't apply in this situation. Who's working with you?"

"I'm it, Dad."

"You really know how to put the worry on me, don't you?" he fired back.

"You shouldn't worry. You taught me how to defend myself."

"And you were my best student, EZ. That doesn't mean I can't worry about you. That's what dads do," he said.

"I know, and I love you for it," I said simply.

"I hear Paul's mustering out. Any idea when he'll be home?"

"It depends on the flight schedule from Kandahar. I'm thinking tomorrow or Thursday."

"I'll call his dad. He should know by now."

"There you go. I'm jealous you'll see Paul before I do," I said. The words caught in my throat as I thought about how much I missed him.

"I'll tell him you said hello," he said. Dad the diplomat. He could read me like a book.

"Thanks, Dad. How's Mom?"

"Your mom's doing well. She has far less pain and skin issues on her new psoriatic arthritis meds. She's resting now or I'd give her the phone."

"That's good to hear. Give her a hug and tell her I love her."

"Will do."

"I love you, too, Dad."

"Stay safe, EZ. Love you back. Bye."

I hung up, thought a moment, and called Holly at her home phone, seeing it was already past closing time in Valdosta. She picked up on the third ring.

"Hey, Holly! It's me," I announced.

"Hi, Me, what's up? You decide you're never coming back?" said Holly. The light tone in her voice buoyed me up.

"Where do I start?" I began. I collected my thoughts and told Holly about meeting General McKelvy at the resort, filled her in on my connection to him, and told her he was exploring a run for the presidency and asked me to be his bodyguard for $500 a day.

"Wow, EZ, you don't waste any time, do you? Can you fit all that in and still meet your obligations for your free trip?"

"I've got the grand tour and lecture tomorrow morning, after which I'm free to do as I please for the next couple days," I told Holly.

"How long does this bodyguard thing last?" she asked.

"If McKelvy decides to run, Secret Service takes over. If he decides not to run, he won't need a bodyguard any longer. He said he'd make the decision in the next week to ten days."

"Okay. Now break it to me gently. Why does he need a bodyguard?"

I grinned. "How did I know that you'd ask me that?"

"You've just as much as told me that you could get your sweet little ass killed, am I right?"

"You know me, Holly. I can take care of myself."

"Against what kind of odds? Why don't you get your boyfriend Paul to join forces with you? That might give you a fighting chance if the fit hits the shan," she suggested, using an old play on words.

"Great minds think alike. I was thinking the same thing. I'm having dinner with General McKelvy and his team, and I'll ask to make Paul part of the deal."

"Good. I'll still worry until you call to say it's over and you're heading back to Valdosta and your humdrum life and all in one piece," said Holly, the humor back in her voice.

"Thanks for understanding, Holly. How's our travel business doing, by the way?"

"Your contacts at the FBI continue to book through us and pay the bills," she said.

"That's good. This is a beautiful resort. I can't wait to tell our clients about it."

"Another reason for you to come home safely, EZ."

"Right you are. Talk soon."

"Stay safe. Talk soon."

As I set the phone in the cradle, I thought about hidden cameras and microphones. Carelessness had nearly cost me my life in Cleveland, and I didn't want that happening again. I added electronics to the list of things I planned to discuss with the general.

* * *

"Ah, welcome back, EZ," said General McKelvy as I strolled up to the now-familiar group in the lobby seating area. As I approached their table, my eyes were everywhere else, searching for someone, anyone who seemed out of place, maybe paying a little more attention than they should be to Walt and his team. I saw no one who fit the bill. Relieved, I sat down in the chair I'd occupied before.

"It looks like nobody's moved a muscle since I left," I commented, watching faces for a reaction.

"We've been glued to our seats, waiting patiently for your return," said Walt, an easy smile gracing his weather-worn face.

"If you're trying to make me feel important, it's working. First off, Killer Kelly sends along his greetings, wishes you well in your campaign," I said with a subtle smile directed at McKelvy.

"Ah, yes. Mad Mac and Killer Kelly. We made a hellova team, though I doubt I can use references to it in the campaign," said McKelvy.

"Oh, you can probably drop it out there, but in a sanitized version," I said.

"I'll mull it over. You may be right. Anyway, your use of the name 'Killer Kelly' reassures me that you are the daughter of the same Sean Kelly, and someone to be trusted."

"Thanks for putting your trust in me, sir. There's one more thing. Since I've never been known for subtlety, I'm requesting that you include Paul Miller as part of your security detail." I watched McKelvy's face for a reaction.

"That name sounds familiar. Do I know him?" asked McKelvy, his eyes boring into mine.

"He's Special Forces, too. Been in Afghanistan longer than I was. He's on his way home now," I said.

"How do you know him?"

"It's a long story. We were in high school together. His dad was a SEAL and taught Paul all his tricks. We sparred together throughout high school, and I've kept in touch with him," I said, leaving it at that. "He's trustworthy."

"I vaguely remember him. I'm sure I'll know him when I see him," said McKelvy.

"So, you approve of adding him to your security team?"

"So, it's a team now? Yeah, I think two of you together have a better chance of neutralizing any threats. That okay with you, Bob?" he asked, turning to his treasurer.

"Makes perfect sense, Walt. I had my worries about Miss Kelly stopping any attacks single-handedly. Besides, I'm guessing she may need to sleep every once in a while. We'll pay him the same as Miss Kelly, with your approval," said Bob.

"I approve!" said Walt. "Now, what do you say we go get some chow?"

Kim Boucher spoke out as they all got to their feet. "We may have to work on your slang expressions, Walt. Most Americans call it dinner, not chow," he said good-naturedly.

"Hell, I've called it chow for so long now, I don't know the difference."

We moved off together, Walt taking the lead, something I guessed he'd been doing all his life. I fell in next to him as we passed through the lobby and took the far-right corridor. Walt's five advisors followed behind, chatting with one another as they worked to keep up with Walt's long strides.

"Where are we going, Walt?" I asked him.

"To one of the five restaurants in the resort. It's called Fruit of the Sea," he replied as he continued his brisk pace.

"Oh, good. I had thoughts of a nice steak," I replied while watching Walt for a reaction.

He never wavered. "You can get them there, no problem. Tuna steaks, swordfish steaks, maybe more."

"Sounds like you know your way around the resort pretty well," I said.

"Yeah, I reconnoitered soon as we got here. An old habit. Makes getting around easy."

"I get the official resort tour tomorrow morning at eight, starting at a restaurant called Oceania," I said.

"Great breakfast place," said Walt, his summary short and to the point.

"Are you worried about a possible threat?" I asked. I didn't add "to your life."

"I gave up worrying about things out of my control years ago. Now that you're aboard, I'm sure I'll be fine. Here we are," he said, pointing out the restaurant sign ahead.

I followed his forefinger to the entrance of Fruit of the Sea. A large plate glass window had the name of the restaurant etched into it, with colored illustrations of a variety of fish surrounding it. The large glass entry door had been secured in its open position, beckoning diners to enter. Walt led the way, coming to a halt in front of the maître d's pedestal.

"Ah, good evening, sir. Do you have a reservation?" the well-dressed host asked, a warm smile resting easily on his long, mustached face.

"I do. It's in the name of McKelvy for five, and as you can see, we are six now," said Walt with a gesture at all of us surrounding him.

"That is not a problem, sir. Give me a moment to have another table setting added." He turned and spoke briefly to a waiter, who hurried off to do his bidding.

While waiting, my eyes scanned the area around us. Everything appeared normal. The restaurant seating area lay ahead of me. I could see linen-covered tables with upholstered armless chairs surrounding them. Each table had a floral centerpiece of tropical flowers and two bright porcelain candleholders, each with two white candles waiting to be lit once the diners were seated. I saw five occupied tables, widely spaced to provide the occupants their privacy. None of the table's occupants paid me or our group any attention.

"I hope you like seafood, EZ," said Walt, as his eyes danced over the restaurant and its occupants, duplicating my own search.

"I do. When I lived in Miami I even went so far as to catch my own fish dinner from time to time," I told him, making a gesture of reeling in a fish.

"Nothing like fresh seafood. Hard to get in Afghanistan," he quipped, filling in the lull while we waited for our table.

As I turned back to him to reply, the waiter returned, and with a welcoming gesture, invited us to follow him to our table.

We followed along single file, Walt leading the way, to a table set for six on the right side of the restaurant's large room. My eyes swept the occupied tables as we made our way, and I was relieved to see no interest, no recognition by any of their occupants to our passing. Their meals and companions held their total attention.

Walt chose a chair on the far side of the table, and I scooted in to claim the chair next to him. It put my back against the wall, offering me a full view of the room and its occupants without having to turn in my seat. It allowed me to see any threat and be ready to take immediate action.

The waiter handed each of us a large ocean-blue menu that was tied together in the middle with a gold braided cord. With the menus passed out, he recited the specials for the evening. When I heard him say 'pan-seared tuna steak' I set my menu down in front of me, my decision made. His list completed, the waiter asked if there were any questions. Nobody spoke up. Walt asked if anyone needed more time, and the men's heads either shook side to side or they said no.

Following his cue, the waiter smiled and took out his order pad and pen. "What would you like, Miss?" he asked, directing his question to me, giving me obeisance as the only female.

"I'll have the pan-seared tuna steak, Ramon."

"Excellent. And how do you want it cooked?"

"Seared gently on both sides, please."

"Ah, perfect! It will remain pink in the middle that way. It comes with seasoned rice and a garden salad, or you can change that."

"No changes. It's all perfect."

"Very well, then. And you, sir?"

The waiter continued around the table, getting everyone's orders. Done, he asked if anyone wanted wine or another beverage. Walt and his entourage ordered beer or wine. I ordered iced tea.

"I will bring your drinks right away," announced the waiter, and he turned away from the table.

Walt glanced at me, a puzzled look on his face. "I thought you'd only got here. How'd you know the waiter's name?"

"You'll get a kick out of this, Walt. Every male waiter here answers to Ramon. The staff thinks it's a way of making the guests feel more at ease. Easy to remember."

"How'd you figure that out?" pursued Walt, his brows lifting with the question.

"The man who led me to my room was named Ramon. I didn't think anything of it at the time, but when I got to the swim-up bar at the main pool and asked the barman his name, he said it was Ramon. Thinking it was a big coincidence, I told him the man who showed me to my room was named Ramon, too. He said every man on staff has to use the name Ramon, so guests only have to remember the one name."

"That's pretty impressive investigative work on your part, EZ," said Walt, a smile emphasizing his words.

"Curiosity, is all," I replied, making light of it. By way of changing the subject, I asked Walt what rooms they were in.

"We're in suites 6, 8 and 10. Next to each other, but not connecting. Bob and I share 6, Jim and Tony share 8, and Peter and Kim are together in 10. Where are you?" he asked me.

"I'm in suite 16," I said, a smile tracing its way across my face.

"Ah, 'Sweet Sixteen and Never Been Kissed,' right?"

"There you go. And there've been a lot of other songs commemorating the event, too," I said.

"Oh, yeah! Neil Sedaka wrote and sang, 'Happy Birthday, Sweet Sixteen.' Before my time, but who hasn't heard it?"

"True. I looked it up once. Everyone from B.B. King to Ringo Starr, including Judy Garland in 1938, Glen Campbell, Chuck Berry, Aretha Franklin, right up to Green Day in 2017. Do you remember Billy Idol's 'Sweet Sixteen' from the eighties? A totally different sound. Same song title, different lyrics."

"You don't have a problem remembering things, do you EZ?" said Walt. He was stopped from saying more by the waiter returning with the drink orders.

Moving unerringly around the table, he set down wine and beer, plus my iced tea, precisely in front of each of us. He disappeared as quickly as he arrived. Everyone took an exploratory sip, and conversations resumed.

"Back to business for a minute, Walt. As I said, I'm tied up with travel agent stuff starting at eight tomorrow morning and then I'll get the grand tour of the resort for as long as that takes. While I'm tied up with all that, please keep a low profile. I wouldn't want something to happen to you when

I'm not around to help," I said, my face a reflection of how serious I took my new position as his security detail.

"Will do. We'll all be going to Oceania for breakfast, maybe see you there, and after breakfast we'll all head back to Jim and Tony's room. We'll powwow there until you come back, okay?"

"That works for me," I said. Though tempted to say something to Walt about his using the word 'powwow' in public, I chose not to. *I'll mention it to Jim, get his reaction.* Nowadays, everything said was either racist, misogynistic or xenophobic, or so it seemed.

Further conversation was interrupted by the arrival of our meals. Our waiter carried one tray while a second waiter followed him with another one. Three meals were on each tray.

I took the opportunity to sweep the room with my eyes for anything, anyone out of place and visually checked out the second waiter while dishes were deployed. The original waiter set my tuna steak platter in front of me with a smile and a flourish, then presented Walt's plate before him in the same well-rehearsed manner. Once all of our meals were in front of us, the waiter asked us if we wanted anything else. Heads were shaken and hands picked up forks, ready to attack the mounds of seafood that lay before us. Silence once more took charge.

I broke off a dainty chunk of my tuna steak with my heavy silver-plated fork. It was bright pink on the inside.

"Just the way I like it," I said to Walt before guiding the first morsel into my mouth.

"Enjoy!" he said as he attacked his own plate of a seafood medley with his own brand of gusto.

* * *

After saying good night to the team and confirming with Walt that I'd see him at 8 the next morning, referring to Jim and Tony's suite number, not the hour, I made my way to my own suite. I hadn't seen anybody who looked out of place or acted suspicious, but I kept up my level of alertness, nonetheless. Old habits die hard. I remembered my concern for bugs, the electronic kind, and decided to search my suite. Cameras and microphones had become so miniaturized that I knew my chances of spotting any were slim, but it was worth a try. Besides, it was just past eight and I was a long way from being tired, even though I'd already put in a lengthy day.

I held my wristband to the lock front and heard the satisfying grinding clunk of the door mechanism opening. When I pushed open the door and stepped inside, all my alarm bells went off at once. It could have been something in the air that didn't belong there, wasn't there before.

Dropping onto my left knee, I plunged my right hand into my right pants pocket and closed it on my lockback knife. I withdrew it and flicked it open with a swing of my hand while my eyes searched the dimly illuminated room for the source of danger. I made out the fuzzy outline of someone sitting rock-still in one of the upholstered chairs.

"Who's there?" I asked, doing my best to sound forceful but struggling with the effort.

"It's me, Antonio, Miss EZ," came a shaky voice from the shadows.

"Antonio? From the pool?"

"Yes, Miss EZ, and I suddenly think that I've made a terrible mistake in judgment."

I stepped back to the open door and hit the light switch, illuminating the room and Antonio sitting hunched over in the chair. I closed the room door, my eyes locked on him, while folding my knife and returning it to my pocket.

"What do you mean?" I asked, my voice returning to normal.

"At the pool, when you asked me for my real name and then gave me your name, I thought…"

"You thought I wanted to have a romantic relationship with you?" I said, completing his statement.

"Yes! Yes! I'm such a fool. How can you ever forgive me?"

I ignored his plea. "How did you get into my room?"

"My sister is a, what do you say, a chambermaid. She has a passkey card to all the rooms so she can go in and make the beds, change the towels, clean the carpets. I told her that I needed to get into your room to meet with you. She understood what I was about, and she gave me her passkey card," he said, holding up the card for me to see.

I refrained from rolling my eyes. "Yes, Antonio, you made a mistake. Perhaps part of the fault is mine. I simply wanted to be friendly towards you. Nothing more."

Antonio struggled out of the chair and began moving towards the door. "I am so sorry, Miss EZ. This will not happen again!"

"Sit back down, Antonio. Please. I have some questions I want to ask you before you go."

Antonio sat down without hesitation, and I parked myself in the adjoining chair facing him.

"How many of those passkey cards are there? Do you know?" I asked, holding his eyes with mine.

"The exact number, I don't know. All the chambermaids have one, and the front desk surely has one in the event that a guest loses the wristband," he said.

"How many chambermaids are there?"

"In all, perhaps ten, maybe fifteen. I can ask my sister. She will know," Antonio hurried to offer.

"The exact number isn't important. Do you think your sister would open a room door for a guest?"

"She might, if the guest had lost the wristband and couldn't get into his room," said Antonio.

"How would she know if the guest belonged in the room he wanted to get into?"

"Ah, I see what you mean. I believe that her training included an identification of the guests, and if she didn't know if the guest belonged to the room, she would send him to the front desk for the passkey," he said. He maintained eye contact with me as he spoke, an indication that he was trying his best to be honest.

"A good answer," I said, all the while thinking how easy it would be to con a chambermaid into opening a door, perhaps even bribing her to do so. A hundred dollar bill could be very persuasive, I knew. Especially if it represented more than two weeks' pay in the Dominican Republic.

"Can I go now?" His voice trembled. He came close to begging.

"One more question, Antonio. Have you seen any guests here in the past couple days who look like they don't belong, maybe look like tough military types instead of the usual tourists?"

"Only you, Miss EZ. Your trim and muscular figure caught my eye right away," he said, a shy smile fighting to show itself on his face.

"Thanks for the compliment. Will you tell me if you see anyone like that among the guests?"

"Yes, yes, of course I will! Is it all right if I go now?" he asked as he got back on his feet.

"Yes, Antonio. I look forward to seeing you again, at the pool," I said pointedly.

"And I as well. Thank you for your understanding of my terrible error of judgment."

"I have already put it in the past. Good night."

"Good night, Miss EZ." He let himself out and pulled the door closed behind him. The lock clicked home.

I stared at the closed door. It surprised me to think that Antonio had reached the conclusion that I lusted after him. I concluded that my friendliness at the pool bar must have given him the wrong idea. What surprised me even more was how easily he'd arranged to gain access to my suite. Suddenly the privacy and protection the lock on the suite's door provided was gone. I needed to keep that in mind, not only for myself but for Walt and his team as well.

I put the upsetting scene with Antonio in a memory hole and turned my attention to a search of my suite for cameras and microphones. I climbed reluctantly from the plush chair and stepped back to the entry door where I began my search. I moved slowly and methodically around the room, checking what I considered to be the most obvious places where cameras or microphones might be hidden. I moved slowly, trying my best to seem casual, acting like the curious tourist checking out her fancy digs in case I missed a camera and my image reached beyond the room.

When I had completed the circle and found nothing, I felt better, and worse. Better because I'd put the effort into a search. Worse because I found nothing. I shrugged it off and decided to go for a swim. It was barely eight-thirty and I had the adrenaline surge from Antonio's surprise visit to burn off.

My two-piece bathing suit was still damp from my noontime swim, so it resisted my efforts to pull the bottom half into its proper position. Persistence paid off. The top put up far less of a fight.

I stepped out onto my private patio and opened the second door that led to the canal while I searched for other swimmers. I was relieved to find none. I closed the second door and eased myself silently into the warm water, careful not to make a splash. The temperature hadn't changed since my earlier dip. I guessed it to be in the high seventies. It felt wonderful.

Alone, I made my way silently to the left, knowing that suites 6, 8 and 10 lay that way. Looking up, I saw pale, milky light illuminating each suite number. I passed 14, 12, and came to suite 10. It looked no different from my own suite's entrance, save for the different illuminated number. No sign of Peter and Kim.

I moved on to suite 8 and heard nothing, saw nothing. Jim and Tony weren't outside.

One more, I thought, as I swam silently along. As I neared suite 6, I heard a splash in the water ahead of me. A strong swimmer clawed the water, distancing himself from me. Had to be a man. The thrashing of the water and the speed the swimmer moved away from me said 'man' all the way.

Instinct kicked in and I began swimming after the retreating swimmer, but a memory surfaced and stopped me in my tracks. Special Forces training in the water. My instructor had said: *watch out for someone swimming noisily away from you. Could be a trap. You go for the retreating swimmer and a hidden second one jumps you. Game, set, match.*

I stopped and tread water, motionless, my eyes wildly searching for a second man as the swimmer thrashed his way out of sight. I saw no one in the water, but a sinister thought came to me. What if someone was lurking out of the water, poised above me on one side or the other of the canal, ready to leap on me? I wished I'd thought to tuck my lockback knife into my bikini bottom. I felt exposed, vulnerable.

I decided that the best option would be to play dumb, act like I'd been surprised in my evening swim and make a hasty retreat, pretending to be frightened by the situation. Anyone watching would conclude I'd been swimming idly along and got scared when the swimmer splashed away from me. Or so I hoped…

I reversed my direction and swam back towards my own suite, varying my stroke from breaststroke to side stroke so I could watch my back. I swam past the water access to suites 8 and 10, then stopped to tread water by suite 12. If anyone was following me, I wanted to know it before I got to my suite. I didn't want anyone to know where I climbed out.

An idea came to me and I acted on it. I climbed the steps to suite 12 and stopped by the door, dripping water around the base. Then I reentered the water without a ripple and swam to suite 14 where I repeated the same process. I eased back into the water and made my way to suite 18, bypassing my own, and climbed out. I paused by the door, my eyes searching for any movement in the water, any sound betraying another swimmer.

Hearing and seeing none, I reentered the water and swam silently back to my suite. I used my wristband to unlock the door and quickly entered, then closed the door behind me. If anyone followed me from a distance, there would be a watery trail at four exit points, not one, making it impossible to tell which exit I'd taken.

I grabbed a towel from the table and dried off, then reentered my suite. Once inside, I stripped out of my swimsuit quickly, toweled my hair damp-dry and dressed, putting on capris and a flowery blouse. I slipped my feet into sensible sneakers and retrieved my cell phone. Then, I called Walt. He answered on the second ring.

"What's up, EZ? I thought you'd be here by now." His caller ID had given me away.

I explained what had happened, told him I wanted to check out his patio area.

"I'll be at the door when you knock one time," he said. The line went dead.

I inched the door to the corridor open and looked, listened. Nobody in sight. No voices reached me.

I stepped out and pulled the door closed behind me, then hurried down the corridor to suite 6, alert to anyone coming or going. Reaching the door without incident, I knocked once.

Walt swung it open and beckoned me inside without a word.

I spotted Bob sitting in one of the upholstered chairs, a glass of amber liquid held in his hand, watching as I made my entrance.

I nodded to Walt and Bob and went directly to the suite's patio door. With my lockback knife opened and held in front of me in my right hand, I pulled open the door and stepped swiftly outside, my eyes sweeping the area as I did so.

All was quiet. The pale light that shone on the suite's identifying sign illuminated the patio area sufficiently enough that if an intruder was lurking there, I'd spot him. Or her. The only concealed area was the space between the plunge pool and the outer wall. I inched my way along it until I could confirm all was clear. No one hid there.

As I searched the area close by the outer wall, I spotted a dark, irregular stain on the tiles. Advancing slowly, I peered down at it, trying to make sense of what it was. I bent down and placed my fingers to it. They came away wet, with no color to them. Water.

I looked up at the wall and saw wetness at the top. Water had run down the side in lazy streaks. No question about it. Someone had scaled the wall from the canal side and eased himself down to the patio floor where more water had dripped from him, making the pool of water I'd discovered.

I turned abruptly and reentered the suite.

Walt watched my return, a puzzled look on his face. My expression must have given away my concern.

"Have either of you been out there since coming back from dinner?" I asked them, hoping the answer was 'yes.'

"Nope. We've been sitting here going over the finance picture," said Walt, answering for both of them.

"If that's the case, we have a problem. Someone climbed over your outer wall and left a puddle of water where he stood on the patio floor," I said. I allowed that to sink in for a moment, then went on.

"The good news is, he didn't have a master key. Otherwise, he'd have burst through your hallway door rather than climb the wall from the canal."

I shoved a chair around so it faced both men and sat down. I had their full attention. I told them about my swim and how I had surprised someone outside their suite. "The splash that got my attention could have been caused when the intruder leaped from the wall back into the canal. It had to have been a man. The splashing that the getaway made was far from ladylike."

"What're you thinking?" asked Walt when I'd finished my story.

"I'm thinking there's truth to your speculation. Whether he intended to harm you or simply deliver the message that you're vulnerable is the big question," I said, watching both Walt and Bob for a reaction.

"Which do you think it is, EZ?" Walt's piercing gray eyes bored into mine.

"Seems like a lot of time and trouble for someone to swim to your outer suite and climb over the wall if all they planned on doing was putting a scare in you. A simple phone call could do that, save a lot of time and trouble," I said.

"You've made your point. What do you suggest we do now?" asked Walt.

First, I think I should camp in here for the night. If your visitor, maybe visitors, come back, I can surprise the hell out of them. I'll also call Miller, see when he can get here," I added. Calling him Miller seemed appropriate, though I'd always thought of him as Paul.

"Don't forget, I'm pretty good at handling myself, too, or at least I used to be," said Walt, finishing his statement with a grim smile.

"I know that, Walt," I replied while taking out my cell phone and tapping Paul's number. I listened to two, three, then four rings, and came close to disconnecting when I heard Paul's voice.

"Paul Miller," came his strong voice through the miles between us. I could hear the thrumming of jet engines.

"It's EZ, Paul. Where are you?"

"Hey, EZ! I'm about thirty thousand feet above the Atlantic Ocean, on a course for Pope Field at Fort Bragg. ETA is an hour, give or take. You planning on meeting my flight?"

"Not exactly, but I want to see you ASAP." I explained my situation to him in as few words as possible.

"General Walter McKelvy? Really? Of course I'll help. He's one hellova soldier and an even better commander. I'll figure out how to get there fastest," he said.

"Hold on a sec," I said into the phone and turned to Walt, who watched me intently.

"What's the fastest way for Paul to get here from Bragg?"

Walt gave me the name of a general at the base. "Tell Paul to say Walt McKelvy needs a favor. He'll get him here at top speed, or I'll have some ass-kicking to do," he added, smiling.

I relayed the information to Paul, who breathed, "Man's got some good connections. Thank him for me, EZ. I'll call when I'm in the air to the Dominican."

"Stay safe, Paul. See you soon." I got a small catch in my voice as I said the last.

"You, too, EZ."

The sudden cessation of jet engine noise signaled the end of the connection. Turning to Walt, I said, "He'll call me when he's airborne to Punta Cana. Meanwhile, I'm camping in your living room. I want to be here if the mystery swimmer comes back."

"You sure? The sofa doesn't look all that comfortable to me."

"I've spent the night on far worse. Anyway, I have to be on my toes if we have a visitor. Or visitors," I added ominously.

"I'll get you a blanket and pillow from my bedroom closet. Least I can do," he said. He walked purposely into the main bedroom. I heard a closet door open, then close, and Walt was back, blanket and pillow in hand.

"Thanks, Walt," I said, taking them from him and dropping them on the large floral-covered sofa. I'm going to scoot back to my suite for a minute. First, though, I'll check your patio once more, in case our friend came back."

I moved to the door that led to the back patio and flicked on the outside wall light, and at the same time I opened the door a crack and peered out. No movement. I swung the door wide and stepped out, my eyes everywhere, my senses tuned for any surprises, my knife open in my right palm. Once again, I couldn't visualize the space behind the plunge pool.

With surprise on my side, I dashed out onto the patio and scanned the area behind it. Nothing. No one. I examined the entire area, looking for new puddles, anything that hinted at the return of the intruder. I saw nothing.

Satisfied, I hurried back inside, conscious that if the intruder saw me, I would become a target as well.

"All clear," I announced to Walt and Bob. "I'll be back in a flash. Listen for my single knock at the door."

I cracked open the corridor door and searched the hallway for people, movement. Seeing none, I stepped out and closed the door behind me, then moved casually toward my own suite. There was nobody else about, though scattered conversations reached me from the lobby area.

When I swung my door open, I knew I was in trouble. My instincts weren't wrong.

The light from the table lamp I'd left on shone on a male figure sitting in one of the two padded armchairs. He'd turned the chair to face the door. My first thought that Antonio had come back was quickly dispelled when I saw the man glaring at me.

"Shut the door. Make a move and I'll kill you," he said in a voice both soft and charged with threat. The pistol he held in his hand emphasized his point.

I pushed the door shut behind me, never taking my eyes off the man. "Who are you and what do you want?" I asked, adding a tremor to my voice to make me sound timid, afraid.

"Come over here and sit down," he commanded, waving his pistol at the vacant armchair facing him.

"Really, sir, I'm fine where I am," I said, keeping the tremor in my voice to persuade him that I was far from being in control.

"Okay. I'll shoot you where you stand, then. My pistol has a suppressor on it. Are you familiar with suppressors?" he asked in the same soft voice.

"N-n-no, I'm not," I lied, tremoring away.

"A suppressor silences my pistol. When I shoot you, it'll make hardly any noise at all. You'll be dead, and there'll be no sound to alert anyone that I've shot you. Get the picture?"

"I better sit down," I said, a small whimper punctuating my last words.

"A wise choice," the man said, his voice staying soft, but far from soothing.

I crossed over to the vacant chair, my eyes taking in the intruder. He was dressed in dark trousers and a light blue polo shirt, so unless he brought his clothes in a waterproof bag, he hadn't come in by way of the canal and my back patio. That meant he'd used a passkey. Antonio and his sister came to mind.

Trembling for effect, I sat down in the empty chair while I took in his features. I saw close-cropped brown hair atop a lean, hard face. His eyes had a vacant look about them. I couldn't tell color in the dim light. There was a wide, irregular scar running down the left side of his face, beginning below his eye and trailing down to his jaw. It produced a slight droop to the left side of his mouth. I guessed ex-military, maybe Ranger, maybe Special Forces like me. My right hand rested on my knife concealed in the pocket below it.

"There, now. That's better, isn't it?" he said in his irritatingly soft voice.

I didn't answer him. Instead, I stared at the man, my hands trembling in my lap, doing my best to show the man my abject fear of him.

"What's your connection to General McKelvy?" he asked suddenly, his cold eyes fixed on mine.

Time to play dumb.

"Who's General McKelvy?" I asked in my shaky voice.

"You know full well who he is. You've spent a lot of time with him and his, ah, friends. You even had dinner with him."

"Oh, you mean Walt? I just met him today when I checked in. He seems nice enough. His friends do, too. I accepted his invitation when he asked me to join them. You say he's a general? He never told me that," I added, keeping the tremor flickering back and forth in my voice.

"You're lying!" he said with sudden force, bringing his pistol to bear on me.

I recoiled in my seat, doing my best to play the terrified victim. "Why would I lie? I have no reason to lie," I whimpered. I saw that the pistol was a Beretta 9 mm semi-automatic handgun, probably an M9, maybe even government-issue. I noted the suppressor mounted on the muzzle. Quiet. Efficient. All business.

The man seemed to reach a decision. "Stand up. Let's take a walk out onto your patio, get some fresh air," he ordered, his voice soft, cajoling once more.

"Why? I don't want to go outside," I said, still with the tremor in my voice.

"I don't care what you want. I do, and you're coming with me. Understand?"

I nodded my head and stood with apparent difficulty, my knees shaking. I casually slipped my right hand into my Capri pocket, my fingers circling my knife, then withdrew it. I held the knife concealed in my palm, my hand resting at my side.

The man walked me to the patio door, pulled it open and pushed me through. His pistol never wavered from my head. I stood trembling by his side, doing my best to act like a terrified woman while considering my next move.

When the man shuffled me towards the door to the canal, I knew what he planned to do. Get me out there, check to make sure there were no witnesses, and put a bullet in my head. With the suppressor on his pistol, the sound would be minimal. My body would drop into the canal and the slight current would move it along, away from the crime scene, to be discovered later, maybe not until the next morning. Meanwhile, the man would be long gone by then. Mission accomplished: pointed message sent to General McKelvy to forget about running for the presidency.

Nearing the outer door, the man reached forward with his left hand to pull it open.

I took the opportunity to flick the blade open, locked and ready, and transferred it to my other hand, all in slow motion so I wouldn't alert the man. Unaware of my action, he grasped the door handle and pulled inward. It was hinged on the right. He let go of the handle and the door continued to swing open on its own.

"Come on," he said in his soft, reassuring voice, and moved me forward with his hand, the pale light cast by the wall light shining the way.

We stood together, side by side, while the man scanned the canal for activity. I did the same. I watched him look to the left, and then change his focus to the right. With his gaze directed away from me, I made my move.

I did two things at the same time. My left arm swung my knife around in an arc and slammed its three-inch case-hardened carbide steel blade into the man's exposed left temple, just ahead of his ear, while at the same time I reached my right hand around for the man's pistol hand.

My plan worked perfectly. The blade penetrated the man's brain, causing instant paralysis, and my right hand gripped his pistol and yanked it away from him, preventing him from discharging it and possibly having it fall into the canal.

Now it was time for the man to take a dive into the canal, a dive originally meant for me. I tucked his pistol behind my back and grasped his belt in my hand. Then I wrenched my blade back and forth to further scramble his brains before yanking it free from the side of his head. I slowly lowered his inert body to the tiled floor, being careful to position his bleeding left temple facing skyward to keep his blood from staining the deck. I carefully wiped my blade on the dead man's blue polo shirt, leaving a lightning bolt of blood along its back. I closed the blade and set my knife on his inert body, then checked his pants pockets.

I found what I was looking for: a hotel passkey attached to an ID tag. I pocketed it without examining it more closely. A further search of his pockets turned up no ID. A professional.

After I retrieved my knife, I inched his body forward and into the canal. He made a gentle splash, submerged for a moment, and then bobbed to the surface face down in the water. I noted with grim satisfaction the lack of any movement in his body. If he sucked in a spasming breath, it would be water, not air that filled his lungs.

"Have a nice swim, creep," I whispered through clenched teeth as the mild current moved the body along towards the main pool. Mindful of evidence, I searched the area for blood and found a few stray droplets. A knife wound to the temple, I knew, caused minimal bleeding. My dad had taught me well.

I turned away from the canal, secured the door and went back inside my suite to the bathroom. I set the knife in the sink and located the small bottle of peroxide I'd brought with me. After I spooled off a large handful of toilet tissue, I returned to the patio.

Kneeling, I scrutinized the area where I'd altered the man's plan to kill me, and carefully splashed a dollop of peroxide on each droplet of blood I found. I knew it was blood by the way the peroxide fizzed, contacting it. I wiped up each fizzing spot with the tissue.

After that, I poured more peroxide on each spot and watched for fizzing. No fizzing meant I'd cleaned up all blood traces.

I spent a good twenty minutes on my knees, searching for any missed blood droplets between the spot where I'd stabbed him and the edge of the canal. At last, I felt confident I'd found and dealt with them all. Standing, I closed the canal door and went back inside, bringing the suite door closed behind me.

Once more in the bathroom, I separated the bloody sheets of toilet paper into manageable clumps and flushed them, one clump at a time, down the toilet. When the last clump disappeared, I flushed the toilet one more time to be certain that the water bore no traces of his blood. Last, I rinsed my lockback knife in the sink and doused it with peroxide, a final step to assure it held no blood traces. Once dry, the knife went back in my pocket. I knew the peroxide would work on any blood left in the sink trap, too.

When I rinsed my hands with peroxide in the sink, I noticed they were trembling. I knew the cause: a surge of adrenaline from the physical conflict with the man who planned to kill me. I'd experienced it countless times. I knew it took time to burn it off, and the trembling in my hands told me I had an overflow of adrenaline released during a fight-or-flight conflict. Taking deep, cleansing breaths, I sped up the process. I began breathing deeply. Draw it in. Hold it a moment. Blow it out. Repeat as necessary until the trembles go away. Been there, done that before.

Back in the living room and calmer now, I searched for any evidence that the man had been there. I scanned the chair he'd sat in and saw nothing. While searching the area around the chair, my eyes picked up on the unmistakable imprint in the vacuumed carpet of a heavy person walking about. His footprints, not mine. I followed them as they led to the bookcase along the left-hand wall as bells sounded in my head. *Bugs. He'd planted bugs!*

I returned to the bedroom and retrieved my penlight. Back in the living room, I shone it around the bookcase where the man's footsteps stopped. When I spotted a mini-camera and listening device set on an ornate sculpture of a mother and child, I struggled to suppress a smile in case someone was watching me. A casual exam would have missed seeing them.

I plucked them up and carried them in my closed hand to the bathroom where I dropped them in the toilet and flushed, sending them along to join the bloody toilet paper. I wondered if the camera recorded the watery journey. Unlikely, I decided.

I knew there had to be a receiver stashed nearby, recording both visual and audio transmissions from the bugs. I'd need to find it before the authorities searched the suites and found it. The evidence on it could ruin my day.

First though, I needed to change my clothes in case there was blood on them. I stripped in the bathroom, setting my newly acquired Beretta M9 semi-auto pistol, complete with its suppressor, on the padded chair by the shower. I spread my blouse on the sink counter and saw two droplets of blood on the left sleeve. I soaked them with peroxide, then rinsed the spots under cold water. *And away goes trouble, down the drain.* I squeezed the water from the sleeve and draped the blouse over the back of a chair.

I followed up with an examination of my capri pants. I removed my lockback knife and the plastic passkey I'd taken off the dead man, setting them on the wide granite sink counter. My close examination of the pants showed them to be free of bloodstains, so I slipped back into them. I pocketed my knife and turned my attention to the passkey.

No question, it was identical to the one Antonio had held up, with one exception. The ID tag bore a photo of a young female whose name was Ina Dominguez. I guessed she was a chambermaid, but further sleuthing would find her out.

I pocketed the passkey and put on a clean blouse. I considered hiding my new Beretta 9mm handgun in the room, then decided against it. If someone broke in and tossed the place, they'd likely find it. I picked it up, pulled back the slide to visualize a round in the chamber, then ejected the magazine to check the load.

It was packed. Fifteen self-defense rounds. They were jacketed hollow points, designed to make a mess of whatever they hit. If the man had succeeded in shooting me, my head would've been seriously rearranged well beyond repair. Better him than me, I thought.

After reinserting the magazine in the M9, I unscrewed the suppressor and tucked the pistol in the small of my back and pulled my blouse down over it, hiding it from all but the most intense prying eyes.

The time had come to check the neighboring suites for a recording device.

With the chambermaid's passkey card clutched in my hand, I opened my hallway door, saw the coast was clear, and stepped out into the hallway, closing the door silently behind me. Reassured that I was the only person occupying the corridor, I moved to the entrance of suite 14 and waved the passkey card at the lock. I heard the metallic click as it opened. Tensed, I eased the door open, hoping the suite was unoccupied.

My prayers were answered. The stillness and sterility that faced me told me no one had moved in yet. It made for an ideal place to hide a recording device, especially by someone who had a passkey.

I closed the door behind me and flicked on the lights, which bathed the living area with a brightness I'd normally find obnoxious. Every available bulb was illuminated, making my search much easier. When I made a visual sweep of the vacuumed carpet, I spotted a set of heavy footsteps that made an impression in the otherwise-smooth carpet surface. They led to and away from a bookcase positioned along the left wall. Not surprisingly, it looked remarkably like the one in my suite. I followed the footsteps to it and spotted a duplicate of the mother and child statue on the bookcase. Behind it sat a miniature digital recorder. I grabbed it and made tracks for the door, anxious to be out of there. Flipping off the lights, I backed into the still-empty corridor and returned to my own suite without seeing a soul.

Once inside, I breathed a sigh of relief and then examined the recording device. It was eerily similar to ones I had used in the past. The small screen responded to my commands, and when I hit PLAY I saw an image of the man sitting in the chair waiting for my arrival, pistol in hand. The final image was of me approaching the bookcase in my suite and finding the bugs. A faint but distinct soundtrack accompanied the image. There were no other images on the recorder, confirming I'd found the only two bugs. A huge weight lifted off me. I'd dodged another bullet.

I hit the digital recorder's ERASE button and listened to the whirring sound as the internal drive was wiped clean. I knew an expert could likely access part of the images, but I had plans that would keep it out of any experts' hands. I hit PLAY to be sure it was wiped clean and watched the blank screen long enough to see that no images remained. As a final effort to render the receiver inoperable, I carried it to the bathroom, filled the sink with water, and dropped it in. When the bubbles ceased coming out of it, I drained the sink and took it out, allowing it to drip dry.

Time to update the general and his staff.

I pulled my suite door closed behind me and moved quickly to the locked chambermaids' closet. With the corridor empty, I used the passkey card to open the door.

Inside, I found the wheeled cart the maids used to pick up trash and resupply the rooms. I peered into the trash barrel and saw a few discarded items left from the previous day's rounds. I leaned down over the edge. It pressed painfully against my upper abdomen as I did so. I moved the trash items aside with my hand. With a space cleared, I dropped the recorder to the bottom and covered it up with the displaced trash. It would take an FBI-like mind to think of looking there. Or so I hoped.

Done, I backed out of the closet, closed the door, and moved casually down the corridor to suite 6. I knocked one time on the door, then waited. My wait was short. The door was quickly opened by Walt, who swung it wide and beckoned me inside. I hurried past him and he closed the door.

"We were worried, EZ. What took you so long?"

"Have a seat and I'll fill you in," I said. No doubt the serious expression on my face told the two men that something unexpected had happened.

Seeing my expression, Walt went back to his chair by Bob and sat down. I took the empty chair facing them, sitting slightly forward so I wouldn't dislodge the pistol tucked behind me.

"Go," said Walt, in true military fashion.

"I killed a man who was waiting for me when I opened the door to my suite. Here's the passkey card he used to get in," I said, holding it aloft to show them. Expressions of shock and surprise played across Bob's face. Walt's face gave away nothing. Years in the military had seen to that.

I explained in detail what had happened, finishing with how I disposed of the 'bug' receiver in the chambermaids' bin. "The man should be drifting by your back patio any time now, if he hasn't already done so," I concluded.

A long pause ensued.

Walt broke the silence. "So it's real," he said, his grim expression saying it all.

"I'd say so. He'd been watching me, us, long enough to suspect I was involved with your plans, and planned to kill me, I'm guessing for two reasons. One, to eliminate me from the picture, and two, to send you a message that you should give up any plans you have for running for president."

"Thanks to you, he fucked up on both," said Walt, which drew a fleeting disapproving look from Bob.

I guessed he was thinking language like that wouldn't get Walt elected. Then again, who knows? Maybe it would.

"I also got a nice sidearm out of the conflict," I said, withdrawing the Beretta from behind my back for Walt and Bob to see.

"Do you know how to use that?" asked Bob. He stared nervously at the pistol I held casually in my hand.

"I've fired a few rounds through this particular model," I replied as I returned it behind my back.

"That's an Army-issue model, Bob. When EZ says she's fired a few rounds, I'm guessing 'a few' means more like thousands of rounds. Right, EZ?" said Walt, his eyes on me.

I smiled and nodded in response.

"That makes me feel better," said Bob, the nervousness receding from his voice.

My cell phone ringtone broke the moment. I got out my phone and put it to my right ear after sweeping it on. "It's EZ," I announced, a non-committal response designed to confuse a wrong-number caller. I listened a moment, then looked at Walt and mouthed 'Paul' while I listened.

I said, "Sounds good, Paul. Call when you know your ETA and we'll go from there. See you soon. Bye."

I replaced my phone and turned to Walt and Bob. "Paul sent a message via the pilot to Bragg and your general friend there. He says the mention of your name got a positive response from him. Paul will meet the general when he lands, and as soon as he learns what arrangements are made to get him here, he'll call and let me know."

"Any idea what the timeline might be?" asked Walt.

"He's landing at Bragg any moment now. They've arranged a ride to meet the general," I said.

"With any luck, he'll get here by tomorrow morning," said Walt, nodding his approval.

Walt's statement brought out two reactions in me. First, I didn't believe in luck. Careful planning took the place of it every time. And second, the thought of seeing Paul, being with him again, made me momentarily weak in the knees.

"It's time we called it quits for the day. Bob, let's give EZ her privacy, here in the living room," said Walt, with a sweep of his arm at the awaiting sofa.

I took my cue and made a nest for myself using the blanket and pillow Walt had brought me earlier. I knew enough not to make things too comfortable, because sleep didn't play a part in my plans. Keeping watch over the possible next president of the United States didn't include sleep until Paul could get here and share the duty with me. I set things up with the pistol resting on the sofa arm in front of me, my body positioned so I could keep track of both the entry door and the patio door without having to move. From that point forward, I knew it was 'hurry up and wait' time, like so many sentry duties I'd been a part of in the army.

* * *

My cell phone vibrated at a little past two, startling me for an instant. Remembering who the likely caller was, the startle faded quickly.

"This is EZ," I said, my voice pitched low, not wanting to awaken Walt or Bob.

"Hey, EZ. It's Paul. You wouldn't believe the treatment I got here at Bragg. The general took care of everything. I'm a civilian again, the general got the PX opened so I could get new clothes for my vacation in the Dominican Republic, and he even arranged it so I can keep all my combat gear until everything's cleared up. Best part of all, he arranged a seat for me on a transport plane flying to Punta Cana. Leaves here in an hour, and it's a three-hour flight, they told me. It's a little past one now, so I should be there around five A.M.," he summarized.

"Add an hour. We're on Atlantic time, so you'll get here at six local time," I told him.

"That's good. Did you make a reservation for me at the resort?"

"No. We don't want to have any connection to you in case someone's monitoring the check-in desk. Here's the number to call to make your own reservation." I gave him the number from memory. "Book it for three nights, okay?"

"Got it. I should get to the resort by six-thirty, seven at the latest, sounds like. I'll call your room when I get to mine."

"Can't wait, Paul. It's been too long."

"You got that right. Get some rest, sweets."

"You, too, Paul."

He knew I wouldn't be sleeping. I hit END while my thoughts raced ahead. Paul and I would be together again soon. For better or for worse. I put my money on better.

I sat there for a moment with images of Paul dancing in my head. I let the dance go on for a while, and then I shook my head, clearing it, and settled in for the remainder of a watchful night.

Chapter Three

Wednesday, January 25ᵗʰ

At a little past six, the bedroom door opened and Walt stepped out. He was freshly shaved and sported a clean set of clothes. He was ready to face the new day.

"Good morning, EZ. How was it out here?"

"Never heard a thing," I said with a toss of my head.

"I'm sure it wasn't the best night you've ever had," quipped Walt, a boyish grin overspread on his weathered face.

"You're right. But it wasn't the worst, either," I said, recalling times in Afghanistan when I was the sentry for my team. Watching them sleep, comfortable in the knowledge that I watched over them, helped to keep me awake, alert to any danger.

"You think we had a 'one and done?'" asked Walt, a suggestion that no more attacks would come.

"No. When whoever's behind this gets word that their man failed his swimming test, I think they'll send in reinforcements," I said as I tucked a strand of stray blonde hair behind my ear.

"That gives us a couple hours of breathing room. You heard from Miller?"

"He called at two to give me an update. He said your general buddy pulled out all the stops for him." I told Walt everything Paul told me, leaving nothing out. Thank my unfailing memory for that. "He topped it off by arranging for Paul to be a passenger on a transport plane to Punta Cana. It was scheduled to land at around six, right about now," I summarized, checking my phone clock.

"Where's he staying?" asked Walt.

"Here, but I told him to make his own reservation. If someone's monitoring the reservation desk, I didn't want him connected to all of us. No sense making it easy for the bad guys," I said with a grim smile.

"You're right about that," said Walt.

"I'm heading back to my room to change and get ready for my breakfast meeting at eight. Paul should be calling any time now. I'll let you know as soon as I hear from him." I stepped to the hallway door.

"Thanks for watching over me last night, EZ. I appreciate it."

"Hey! That's why you're paying me the big bucks, right?"

"You know what I mean. I'll be waiting for your call. I'll also ignore you when you show up for breakfast at Oceania, in case someone's watching us," said Walt.

"Good point. See you in a bit," I said as I opened the door and scanned the hallway. Relieved to find nobody in sight, I closed the door behind me and sauntered to my own suite. I used the purloined passkey to open the door. Before I stepped inside, I drew the handgun from the small of my back and held it out front at the ready. If someone was waiting for me, I wanted to have the advantage.

I saw the patio door was closed, but I continued a thorough search of all the rooms to assure myself that I was alone. Finding no one, and seeing no signs of an intruder, I visibly relaxed. I stepped into the bedroom, and then I saw it. The red light on my house phone was blinking. A message? I picked up the handset and pushed the button to retrieve the message. Paul's voice greeted me.

"I don't know where you are, I hope you're okay," came the familiar voice. "I'm here in suite 14, so call me when you get this."

I noted that he didn't use my name. *Smart, Paul.* If someone intercepted his call, they couldn't know who he spoke to.

I dropped the phone in the cradle and rushed back to the door, my M9 tucked behind my back and concealed by my blouse. Finding the hallway clear, I moved silently to suite 14 and opened the door using my passkey card. When I swung it open, Paul was standing, facing me, an M9 of his own trained on me.

"Shit, EZ! How'd you open my door?" he said, lowering his pistol and visibly relaxing.

Instead of answering, I shut the door and rushed at him, my outstretched arms surrounding him in a long-overdo embrace. Paul tucked his pistol in the small of his back and returned the hug. We stood that way, locked together, enjoying the moment. I eased back far enough to search Paul's eyes and followed up with a long, passionate kiss. Paul responded with enthusiasm.

I broke the kiss and pushed back, knowing where this was going to lead if I didn't slam on the emergency brakes. Paul got it. "We'll put it in the bank for later," he said, grinning down at me.

"Pleasure delayed is pleasure doubled," I recited, not for the first time, adding a peck on his lips to seal the deal. I took his hand and led him to the comfortable lounge chairs where we sat, facing each other.

For the next ten minutes, I filled him in on all the events of the past day. Paul listened, interrupting me twice for additional information. When I was finished, I sat back and had a good look at him.

"Nice clothes, Paul. Your shorts and sports shirt, you'll fit right in around here. Hope you brought your bathing suit."

"You mean I can't skinny dip?" he asked, his eyebrows raised in question.

"If it was up to me you could, but I don't make the rules," I replied, my eyebrows joining in on the dance.

Then I forced myself to get serious. We talked strategy: who would do what to protect General Walter McKelvy, likely Independent candidate for the presidency. We both concluded we'd provide more complete protection by working independently of one another.

Paul would have solo duty while I did my travel agent breakfast and tour of the resort. After my tour was over, we'd both stand guard, but remain at arm's length from each other. An attacker, or attackers, wouldn't know there were two of us to contend with.

I gave Paul Walt's cell phone number and told him I'd call to tell him he had arrived. I got to my feet and moved to the door, then turned back to Paul. "I've got to get ready for my breakfast meeting. Walt and his team, six in all, will be at the Oceania Restaurant for breakfast, too. If you get a table near them, that'll give him the excuse to speak to you, maybe invite you to join them. An onlooker will think it's a casual thing, that you're not all in this together."

"Okay. Tell him I look forward to seeing him and his team," said Paul, joining me at the door.

"I will." I leaned into him and kissed him warmly. Backing away, I whispered, "That makes two deposits in the bank."

"I can't wait to make my own deposit," he murmured.

"Naughty, naughty. I love it," I whispered. I opened the door, checked to see the coast was clear, and hurried back to my own suite. I marveled over the coincidence that Paul was right next door to me.

Once inside, I phoned Walt and updated him. "When you see him sitting alone, it'd be natural for you to invite Paul to join you. You could chat it up, all casual," I suggested.

"Great minds think alike, EZ. Must be why I have such confidence in you." Walt ended the call and I hurried to make myself look presentable for my breakfast meeting.

* * *

I entered the Oceania at five minutes to eight, and immediately spotted the table for travel agents. Set off to the side, I saw nine chairs, five already occupied. A small placard in the center of the table confirmed it was reserved for the travel agents.

On my way to the table, I saw Walt, Bob, Jim, Tony, Peter and Kim at a table on the opposite side of the restaurant, and Paul by himself at a small table nearby. *Perfect.* My heart did a flutter at the sight of Paul.

I approached the travel agent table, leading the way with a warm smile. The smartly dressed young woman in the end chair saw me, stood to greet me. She matched my smile and said, "Welcome to El Mar Placido, Miss Kelly. I'm Rita Haversham." She extended her hand to me as she spoke.

I reached to shake it and was pleased to find she had a firm grip. "Thank you, Miss Haversham. It's my pleasure to be here," I lied ever so slightly, thinking of all that had gone on behind the scenes.

"Please, call me Rita," she offered.

"All right, Rita, but only if you call me EZ."

"Of course, of course. Allow me to introduce you to our other agents," she said, turning to face the table's occupants.

I listened to each name and reached to shake hands. I noticed the absence of Roger Donohue, the agent who shared the limo from the airport with me and wondered briefly where he was. I logged the four new names and faces away in my eidetic memory and sat down in one of the empty chairs that faced Walt and Paul, noting as I did so that a menu sat in the center of each of our place settings.

Rita Haversham remained standing and addressed the group. "It's just about eight, so we'll get started. Please select what you want for breakfast from your menus," she said, at the same time signaling a young waiter standing nearby, pad in hand.

I bet his name is Ramon. I almost giggled.

"While we wait for our food and beverages to appear, I'll give you my little talk about the resort and all its wonderful features," continued Rita. "Meanwhile, once you make your selections, tell our waiter, Ramon."

I must be psychic, I thought, smiling inwardly. I, like the other four seated agents, turned my attention to the breakfast menu. The selections were a cup of coffee short of incredible. I ignored all the eggs-bacon-sausage-home fries-pancakes-French toast-omelets dishes and found the fresh fruit plate. When my turn to order came, I emphasized coffee, black. Then, I sat back to absorb Rita's well-rehearsed talk and waited for breakfast to arrive.

I noticed the four other travel agents scribbled busily on pads set by their place settings, and I smiled, knowing my memory would make me the winner of any quiz Rita chose to throw at us.

As Rita finished her presentation, two waiters arrived carrying the breakfast dishes and a third waiter moved to take the plates and set them in front of the appropriate agents. All were served in a flash.

As I picked up my fork, I wondered again what had happened to Roger, the limo nerd. It didn't seem like him to miss out on a free breakfast.

My thoughts were interrupted when I saw Paul get up from his table and move over to Walt's table while Walt's group stood as one to welcome him. *Good.* The transfer looked innocent enough. Solo male diner asked to join a group of men. I turned my attention back to my plate of incredible fruit while Rita asked if there were any questions. I thought a moment, then raised my hand.

"Yes, Miss Kelly?"

"When we make a reservation for clients, should we call the resort directly or go through one of the internet booking services?"

"An excellent question, Miss Kelly. If you call directly, your share of the pie will be greater since you won't be splitting it with an internet booking service. Does that make sense?"

"It does, indeed. Thank you," I said, a warm smile creasing the corners of my mouth in response. I turned my attention back to the remaining fruit, savoring every mouth-watering bite.

As I speared the last remaining slice of mango, a Dominican man dressed in a light blue suit, tieless, collar open, approached our table and whispered into Rita Haversham's ear.

"Oh, my goodness!" exclaimed Miss Haversham.

The man whispered more.

"Well, certainly. I think that's the best plan," she said to him in hushed tones.

The man whispered a few final words and turned away, striding purposely for the exit.

Rita drew a breath, gathered herself and told us in a conspiratorial voice that a man had been discovered drowned at the entrance to the main swimming pool. She said the local police were on the scene to recover the body and do their investigation, so the pool and connecting waterways were closed for the time being.

"It appears that one of the other travel agents discovered the man. Have any of you met Roger Donohue?" she asked.

"Yes," I spoke up. "We shared the limo ride from the airport. Was he connected in some way to the man who drowned?" I forced an expression of shock, concern on my face.

"No, no, Miss Kelly. He was the person who discovered the drowned man, but there's no indication that he knew him. That certainly explains his absence from our breakfast meeting," she added.

"What a horrible discovery," said the agent to my left. "Glad it wasn't me who found him."

"It must have come as a shock to Mister Donohue," said Rita.

"It would shock any of us," I said, placing both hands on the side of my face for emphasis.

"We all need to put the nasty image from our minds," said Rita as she glanced around the table at the assemblage of travel agents. "We'll continue our tour, with a necessary detour to avoid the pool area. We have plenty of places to see, even though we'll be leaving the main pool out. Have any of you already been to the main pool?"

We all nodded in the affirmative.

"Well, you see, we don't have to go there anyway. Makes everything easier for me. I've arranged to have two golf carts take us around the resort. We'll stop at each point of interest and I'll tell you all about each one. Are we ready?" she asked, seeing that everyone's eating utensils had been set down.

We bobbed our heads in unison.

"Then follow me, and we'll begin the tour." Rita stood and led the way to the entrance, walking backwards for a few steps to assure herself that everyone followed.

I glanced at Walt's table as my group filed out. I saw Paul smiling and gesticulating to the others as he spoke. He'd chosen his location at the table with care. From where he sat, he had a clear view of the restaurant as well as the entrance. He'd spot any assault long before it reached the table. *Couldn't have chosen a better vantage myself*, I mused.

* * *

My tour of the resort as a travel agent took up three hours of the morning. Rita was thorough. We stopped at and toured each of the four other restaurants. There was El Gaucho, a restaurant featuring Argentine beef, prepared by either grilling or smoking and served in a variety of ways. La Trattoria served a wide variety of Italian dishes, with a different specialty each noon and evening. Fruit of the Sea, the restaurant Walt's team and I had eaten at the previous evening, presented seafood at its finest. Local lobster, conch and tropical fish were featured. The fifth restaurant, Rita told us, was by far the most popular. La Placida served a wide variety of food, served buffet-style, at breakfast, lunch and dinner, and guests were encouraged to refill their plates as often as they wished. Guests who appreciated getting a good bang for their bucks flocked there, Rita explained, a smile tracing across her bright face.

At each of the restaurants, we were presented with miniature plasticized menus. Rita explained that they could be shown to potential clients as a way of further selling them on booking a reservation at El Mar Placido.

We also visited the large, well-appointed health club, which, in addition to the treadmills, exercise bikes, ellipticals, inversion tables, resistance stations and free weights, included an area where men and women alike could be pampered with massages, facials, nail care, you name it, for a modest additional charge. I spotted a large open area of padded mats and wondered if Paul and I could find the time to practice our moves on one another. It had been a long time. Far too long.

The tour of the ocean waterfront occupied an hour of our time. Rita extolled the sandy beach and explained that bathers could walk into the calm surf well above their waists and not have to worry about stepping on anything sharp. She pointed out the variety of watercraft visitors could use. It included everything from paddleboards and kayaks to sailboats, and for the more adventurous, windsurfing boards. She swept her arm at the dark area well out from the beach and said the coral reef there provided an excellent area for snorkelers to explore. Finally, with a twinkle in her eyes, she gestured to an area away from the main beach and told everyone it was set aside for nude sunbathing. I watched one woman gasp, another smile coyly. The lone male stared wistfully in that direction.

Something for everyone, I thought, amused.

We moved on to the botanical gardens. "We'll all walk together through the gardens, and the golf carts will pick us up at the other end. Is there anyone who feels that the walk could be too strenuous?" asked Rita.

Nobody spoke up, so all of us followed Rita along a wide paved path through an incredible display of tropical plants. My senses were filled with a seemingly endless variety of fragrances from the flowering plants and bushes, and my eyes could scarcely absorb the spectacular beauty of the plantings. I wanted to stop and stare at each one, but Rita moved us along at a steady pace.

When we emerged at the other end where the golf carts waited, I knew I'd go back there for more, given the chance.

Once we had resumed our places in the carts, Rita announced we had one final stop.

"Our gift shop, we feel, is second to none, and we think you will all agree," she said as the carts carried us along.

We pulled to a stop in front of a large single-story building set back and to the left of the main one. Colorful banners placed on both sides of the inviting entryway waved gaily in the gentle breeze, and a bright sign above the doorway read 'La Tienda de Regalos.' Below it, a second sign declared 'Gifts for Everyone' in English, for the benefit of non-Spanish speaking visitors. We all climbed down from the carts and stepped inside, the air conditioning enveloping us.

Rita, I saw at once, was dead-on. The large open store offered everything from clothing, both casual and formal, to watches and jewelry, to cigarettes from every corner of the world, and cigars from Cuba and the Dominican Republic. There was a section devoted to fine liquors and wine, and another one with fine delicacies from around the world, all with prices to suit. French truffles and Russian caviar were included. The prices were in American dollars, with the price in Dominican pesos posted below.

I circulated through the gift shop, my keen eyes landing on one incredible item after another. I spotted a simple pale green sheath dress in my size, thought what an effect it'd have on Paul, looked at the price, and knew I'd never wear it. Disappointed, I moved on, passing the jewelry section for the same reason.

I need to take something back to Holly. My eyes swept the store for a gift both affordable and appropriate. *T-shirt? Get serious! A scarf? Maybe.*

I strolled back to the women's clothing section, passed the pale green sheath dress again and stopped at a rack of scarves tastefully displayed. One caught my eye. Everything about it screamed 'Holly.' I reached out, caught the tag, saw what it would cost me. *To hell with it. Holly deserves it,* I told myself. Rita's voice interrupted my thoughts.

"Can I see everyone in my party over here, please?" she said, holding up a slender arm for everyone to use as a landmark.

I let go of the scarf and hurried over to Rita, wondering what she had to say.

Once everyone was there, Rita smiled and said, "I hope you've all seen something in here that you'd like to take away with you. The price doesn't matter. We here at El Mar Placida wish to thank each and every one of you for taking the time from your busy lives to visit us. Our gift to you is our way of saying thanks. Please go and select your chosen token of our appreciation and bring it to the counter."

Oh my God! I thought, the realization of what Rita said getting through to me. I moved, trancelike, back to the women's section and lifted the pale green sheath dress from the rack. I held it out in front of me, turning it about, taking in its simple but elegant lines. *Oh my God!* I thought again as I carried it to the counter.

Rita watched as I approached, saw what I'd chosen, and smiled warmly. "That dress suits you perfectly, Miss Kelly," she said.

"Thank you so much for your generous gift. You must call me EZ. Everyone does," I added, returning Rita's warm smile with a blazing one of my own.

"I'd be delighted to call you EZ, EZ," she said, taking the dress from me. "Are you sure of the size?"

"I've been that size for as long as I can remember," I said.

"Well, if you find that it doesn't fit you, bring it back and get the next size down," said Rita, ever the diplomat.

I chuckled softly at her diplomatic choice of words while the clerk folded my new dress carefully and placed it in a suitable box.

With box in hand, I watched the other four bring their chosen gifts to the counter. The three women brought clothing items. The lone man held a box of Cuban cigars in his hand. Everyone wore a pleased expression. Life was sweet. For the moment.

Waiting, I wondered how everything was going with Paul and Walt's gang of five. I knew from comments Rita made to us at breakfast that the assailant's body hadn't been found until early morning. That meant that news of his death wouldn't have reached his employers until, say, mid-morning at the earliest, and a replacement killer would be unlikely to reach Punta Cana and El Mar Placida until the afternoon or evening at the earliest. *Unless there was a second killer already here.* The thought brought me up short.

"All right, ladies and gentleman," said Rita, using the singular for the lone male, "unless you wish to shop more, we'll return to our carts and we'll all head back to the lobby. Thank you one and all, for accepting the invitation to experience El Mar Placida. You have the rest of today and all day tomorrow to relax and enjoy your stay with us." Seeing no protests, Rita turned and led the way to the shop's entrance. I made a mental note to return for Holly's scarf later.

The other five agents and I followed behind Rita, our gifts clutched in our hands. The man announced that he couldn't wait to try a Cuban. "Cigar, that is," he added, which elicited a giggle from one of the women.

On the short drive back to the lobby entrance we passed the main pool. Rita pointed out the police tape that surrounded the area where the man's body had been found, and everyone craned their necks to see what was going on. "If I had to guess, I'd say the pool will be reopened soon," she said, sounding optimistic for everyone's benefit.

The only thing visible was the police tape and four uniformed officers standing at poolside, watching as a Dominican diver jumped in wearing a mask and snorkel. I guessed he'd make methodical passes across the pool bottom, searching for clues to the man's demise. I knew he'd find nothing. My lockback knife rested snugly in my Capri pants pocket. I wondered if the official cause of death would be drowning, or if the small wound to his left temple would raise alarms. An autopsy would clarify the cause, but that would take time. Twenty-four hours, maybe longer. That provided a little breathing room.

"I'm not sure I'd feel comfortable going for a swim in the pool any time soon," said one of the women, her nose wrinkling with distaste.

"Oh, my dear, the filtration system in the pools and canals screens and purifies every drop of water once every hour. It will be as if nothing happened," Rita hurried to reassure her.

As if nothing happened. I knew otherwise.

The carts stopped outside the main entrance, and after Rita added a final thanks and farewell, we disbursed into the lobby and back to our suites. Once in my suite, I used my cell phone to call Paul. He answered on the first ring.

"Miller," he announced.

"Hello, Miller. This is Kelly," I said, pitching my voice to sound husky, alluring. "I've got something for you."

"What a coincidence. I've got something for you, too. Been saving it for a long time now," he said, his voice sounding sexy.

"You're starting to be naughty. I'm talking about a surprise for you. A gift," I breathed.

"A gift? Who gave it to you?" Paul allowed a touch of jealousy to come through.

"El Mar Placida, for coming here."

"That sounds like a gift for you."

I grinned. "Technically, yes, but I think you'll like it, too."

"When can I see it?"

"Where are you?" I asked.

"In my room. Next door."

"Give me five minutes and knock on my door."

I set my phone down and stripped out of my clothes, standing naked in the bedroom. I opened the dress box and lifted out the beautiful green sheath dress I'd been given. Carefully, so as not to stress any of the seams, I pulled it over my head and worked it down over my nakedness. I eyed myself critically in the bathroom's full-length mirror. I was pleased to see that it fit perfectly, highlighting my every curve. I made no attempt to reach the zipper in the back.

One less thing to deal with, I thought, smiling. I stepped over to the bed and pulled the covers down.

The light knock on my door told me five minutes had passed. Paul loved precision. I stepped to the door, anticipating the moment when I swung it open and saw Paul standing there. Instinct took over, caution dominating.

"Who's there?" I asked, standing to the side in case an attacker shot through the door at me.

"It's Paul," came the welcome answer.

I swung the door wide and gazed lovingly at Paul, who stood before me dressed in a floral print bathing suit, a towel draped around his neck.

He gazed back at me, his expression changing to one of surprise. "I'm sorry, miss. I was expecting someone else. I must have the wrong room."

I reached out, grasped both ends of his towel, and pulled him towards me. "Get in here," I whispered, backing into the room.

Paul followed willingly, bumping the door closed behind him with his bare foot.

"Nice dress," he whispered. "Green. My favorite color." His arms encircled me.

"I got it for you. It's covering my second gift for you," I breathed, as I wrapped him in my arms.

"Oh, I love unwrapping presents," he said, his hands busy exploring. His right hand found the open back, the zipper down.

"Be careful. Wouldn't want you to tear the wrapping," I said, an impish smile brushing the corners of my mouth.

"I'll be careful. That way you can wrap my gift again. And again." He grasped the dress at the shoulders and lifted it slowly.

I raised my arms above my head to accommodate him. The dress slowly inched its way upwards, exposing my nakedness as it reached the halfway point.

Paul repositioned his grasp on the dress and lifted the last of it off me. He dropped it carefully to the floor.

With my arms freed, I grabbed Paul's bathing suit on each side and tugged it down, noting he'd made the task easier by not tying the drawstring. Paul complied by stepping out of the suit that now encircled his ankles.

We stood facing one another a moment, our hungry eyes enjoying the long-delayed feast. As if on cue, we stepped into one another, arms grasping, caressing, moving. Our mouths met in a passionate kiss that canceled all thoughts of time and place, leaving us alone in our moment.

I felt Paul's rising passion. Sighing, I whispered, "It's been too long."

"Way too long," he agreed, his voice husky with emotion. He bent down and lifted me in his arms, and I wrapped my legs around him. With strong, sure steps he carried me into the bedroom.

"Will you look at that?" he said. "The maid's already turned the bed down."

* * *

Paul and I lay side by side, our bodies touching. Toes touched toes, ankles linked to ankles, lower legs pressed against lower legs, knees rested against knees, hips lay against hips, a head contacted another head, and four arms encircled, rested upon each other as we luxuriated in the afterglow of our lovemaking. After so much time apart, neither of us could get enough contact with the other.

"Isn't skin great?" I whispered, my voice a contented purr as I moved my body, snakelike, to intensify the feeling.

"*You're* great," murmured Paul. "That makes your skin great," he added, as he brushed a strand of damp hair from my forehead and absorbed me with his eyes.

We lay that way for uncounted moments, not talking, not needing to talk.

Paul ended the silence. "You don't think the threat against General McKelvy's over, do you?"

Paul's question broke the spell. I pushed back and raised myself up on an elbow. "No, I don't. Since nothing's happened since last night, I think they sent that one assassin. When they get word he drowned, they'll send another assassin, maybe two, to finish the job."

"I still don't get why they want him dead," said Paul, hiking himself up on an elbow to face me.

"It's crazy, I know. As Walt explained it, the Washington elite, the gang that's been running politics in America for countless years, also known far and wide as the Swamp, are jealous guardians of the status quo. Every candidate for president has to get their stamp of approval before he or she can mount a campaign. Walt thinks it all started when that billionaire businessman got into politics and ended up being elected president by voters that the Swamp people called the ignorant masses, the forgotten ones. They tried everything possible to get him out of office, the special prosecutor starting, with impeachment following. When all that failed, they moved on to other, more subtle measures. With the media on their side, they covered up or made light of every success the man had made. He disrupted the old status quo to the point they vowed they'd never allow that to happen again."

"So they're willing to go to any length, even to killing any upstarts, to protect their hold on the political world?" asked Paul.

"That's the way Walt sees it. He thinks they fear Independents more than Republicans or Democrats, because they're considered true mavericks who don't give a damn about the old-time political parties. He's also concerned that enemies formed during his military career could reach out and eliminate him, too, out of spite. He believes there is jealousy, resentment for him because he could succeed where they have no hope of succeeding. So, he sees the threat to him coming from two directions at once."

"Do you think Walt will change his mind to run because of the threats to him and his team?"

"You know the man as well as I do, probably better. I don't see him as a quitter," I said with a toss of my head for emphasis.

"So the danger to him is at its greatest now. If he decides to back out, the Washington elite no longer have to worry about him. They'll call off the dogs. And if he declares his candidacy, he gets Secret Service protection. They'd be stupid to go against them, right?"

"Walt thinks so, but it wouldn't surprise me. It would have to be a well-orchestrated attack that couldn't be traced back to the elite. No easy feat, for sure, but desperation makes people do desperate things," I said.

"What's your guess? Will Walt run, or will he walk?" asked Paul, his hand resting lightly on my arm.

"My gut feeling says he'll run. He believes in the country, and he thinks he can make a difference if he's elected. I think the main reason for his delay in declaring is the money he'll need to raise to go up against both Democrats and Republicans with their huge coffers. His financial guy, Bob—you met him—is busy researching any and all options. A couple big commitments from wealthy independent donors could make all the difference."

"So until then, we're his army," Paul summarized.

"That's us," I said, brushing my fingers across his chest as I spoke.

"Which of us is in charge?" asked Paul as he duplicated my caress.

"You are," I said, and rolled against him.

With no hesitation, Paul took charge. It quickly metamorphosed into a mutual act of love. We were both winners.

* * *

My cell phone played "Reveille," put there as a no-nonsense attention grabber. I reached over to the bedside table and answered it. "Kelly here," I said, the huskiness in my voice surprising me.

"It's Walt. You had lunch yet?"

I thought of saying I had other things on my mind at the moment, but thought better of it. "No, not yet," I said, after clearing my throat.

"If you have nothing better to do, we'll meet you at La Placida, the buffet-style restaurant. You know where it is?"

"I do. My tour this morning included a swing through it. I'll get Paul and meet you there in, say, fifteen minutes?"

"Fifteen minutes it is," said Walt. The line went dead.

Paul, one eye open, had listened to my side of the conversation. "Where are we going?" he asked, raising himself up.

"Lunch at the buffet place. We got fifteen minutes," I added, smiling at him.

"Not enough time for an encore, sad to say," he quipped.

"Later, lover. Maybe Walt and his guys have made a decision."

"Let's get dressed and go find out."

* * *

The rush crowd at La Placida had come and gone by the time Paul and I arrived, which suited us fine. A crowded restaurant could easily hide one or more people set on ending Walt's existence. I wondered if Walt had delayed having his lunch for that reason.

I followed Paul inside, separated by three other diners so we didn't appear to be together. The change from bright sunshine to artificial lighting momentarily clouded my vision. My pupils dilated quickly enough, and I spotted Walt's group sitting at a table across the way with a clear view of the entrance. Paul spotted them as well, and we moved quickly in their direction. I scanned the people and tables to my right, Paul doing likewise to his left. Our Special Forces training took over seamlessly.

Walt stood to greet us, looking from Paul and then to me. "You've got a nice glow to your face, EZ. You get some sunshine?"

I blushed at the comment, guessing that the increased color to my face was put there by Paul's scratchy stubble. "Probably from my tour this morning," I said, guessing as I said it that Walt wasn't buying it.

"Well come, sit down you two. We just got here ourselves."

There were two places open at the table. One was between Walt and Kim Boucher, the other was between Jim Bennett and Tony Marino. Both seats allowed the occupant to keep an eye on the entrance, and each had an open view of half the restaurant. Walt had planned the seating like the old pro that he is.

I moved to take the seat between Jim and Tony, but Walt stopped me by saying, "Come, sit here, EZ. I had a good chat with Paul at breakfast." He indicated the chair next to him with a wave of his muscular hand.

Paul took the seat I'd been heading for while I sat by Walt. "Have any decisions been made?" I asked him, getting right to the point.

"Not yet. As you know, the big issue is going to be the financial end of things. Bob's been busy making phone calls and sending out emails, trying to get a handle on what kind of support we can count on. A couple big donors come on board and I'll step into the starting gate right away," he said, his face serious.

"Until that happens, Paul and I will earn our paychecks," I said, referring to our commitment to protect Walt's life.

"Speaking of that, the scuttlebutt is saying that the man in the pool died of drowning," he said.

"The autopsy will change that. They may have dismissed the small cut on the side of his head as something that happened to him before he drowned. You know, like he hit his head on the side of the canal. There wouldn't have been much blood coming from it by the time he was found, what with the time he spent bobbing about in the water, washing it off," I said.

"So, when do you expect to see round two?" Walt asked.

A waiter approached the table, a smile leading the way, and asked if anyone wanted something to drink. I watched as his eyes checked out the various wristbands, saw his eyebrows arch, seeing mine. His look said "VIP."

I smiled, thinking how far from the truth it was.

Everyone ordered. Three coffees, five iced teas. Ramon hurried off to get the drinks.

"To answer your question, round two could come at any time. We're guessing it'll take hours before the bad guys can send replacements for the man who did the dead man float to the main pool. Paul and I are hoping for an undisturbed lunch," I said with a wave at the food arrayed at the buffet line.

"Good. Let's eat," said Walt, standing to lead the way. Everyone joined him, with me walking next to him, conscious of the M9 pistol tucked behind my back. I knew Paul was on alert as he trailed behind, searching for any signs of a threat.

The buffet, I saw, had something for everyone, from the biggest appetite to the most finicky one, and everything in between. Although I considered myself an omnivore, the salad bar grabbed my attention. I saw fresh fruit and vegetables to heap on fresh spinach, kale, and several varieties of lettuce, plus tons of side additions that could turn the simplest salad into a gourmet banquet. I picked up a big bowl and started down the line, mindful that one excess could limit what I might want to add further along.

Meanwhile, Walt and the others made their choices and carried their mounded plates back to the table, Paul with them. I saw that Paul's plate bore meat and potatoes, an attractive array of each.

As I finished garnishing my salad with dressing, I spotted a man who appeared at the entrance and scanned the restaurant's interior, his eyes stopping on General McKelvy. I watched as he peered closely at him, and then he turned to stare at the other members of Walt's group. I set my salad bowl down and watched him intently, prepared to draw my pistol and defend Walt and his group if necessary.

I eyed the man for any signs of threat. I saw a lean, muscular build, standing a little over six feet tall. He looked to be in his thirties and dressed casually in light tan trousers and a dark green polo shirt, the buttons open at the collar. He held his hands at his side in a non-threatening manner, but his demeanor said otherwise. He hadn't glanced at me. His attention was directed solely at Walt and his entourage. That gave me an advantage. He wouldn't know where the shot came from in the instant before my bullet found its mark.

The man smiled and strolled towards Walt's table. I watched Paul's reaction. He shifted his position in his chair, clearly prepared to draw his pistol as the man approached. Between the two of us, the man was dead. He just didn't know it yet.

Walt saw the approaching man and his expression changed from relaxed calm to one of shock. Seeing Walt's face drop, I closed the gap between the intruder and me in a heartbeat, my right arm encircling his neck before he became aware of what was happening. I stepped close behind him and applied pressure, shutting off the blood flow to his brain. In ten seconds, he would be unconscious. If I continued the pressure, he would be brain dead in thirty seconds.

"No, EZ! I know Bill! I thought he was dead!" shouted Walt, getting his voice back and leaping to his feet.

I relaxed my stranglehold and stepped away from my would-be quarry, but not before I did a quick pat-down to assure myself that he was unarmed.

I wasn't entirely convinced I should release him, but Walt's shouted statement carried the day.

"Sorry, sir. I thought you meant to harm General McKelvy," I told the newcomer.

Occupied with catching his breath, he struggled to reply. "I understand. No offense taken," he said, offering up a weak smile as a peace sign.

I took the opportunity to examine him more closely. I stuck to my initial assessment of his age and height. He had close-cropped black hair and a scar just below his nose. I couldn't tell if it was a poorly sutured harelip or an old injury. He was clean-shaven, and he had a large wart on the side of his flat nose. I saw a single black hair growing out of it.

As a result of my close encounter with him I knew that he was strong and likely worked out to keep himself that way. Under other circumstances, he would be a worthy adversary.

"What the hell, Bill! I thought you were dead all these years," said Walt, his voice raised.

"It's hard to keep a good man down, General," he shot back, stepping up to the table.

"Come, sit. Join us. Tell me your story," commanded Walt.

A space was cleared and a chair drawn up beside Walt's. While this was taking place, I looked pointedly at Paul, who caught my expression. Without words, I conveyed the message I wasn't entirely convinced of the man's—Bill's—innocence. Paul got it. The subtle nod of his head told me so.

I stepped back to the salad bar and retrieved my salad bowl, returning to the table in time for the introductions. Walt was explaining to everyone that Bill had been a Special Forces soldier in Afghanistan. On his rookie deployment, he'd gone missing during a firefight with the Taliban, and it was assumed that he had been either captured or killed. A second scouting mission in search of him had turned up nothing. He was officially listed as missing in action as a result. "Now tell me, tell everyone, what happened to you, Bill?"

"As it turned out, I *was* captured by the Taliban," Bill explained. "I got separated from my team when the shooting started, and when the dust cleared, I was staring at the muzzle of an AK-47. I raised my hands in surrender and was bound and hauled off to a Taliban encampment. I figured I was a dead man and they were waiting for a chance to gain some publicity from my execution.

"During the second night of my capture, a boy, he was probably twelve or so, sneaked into the bare room that served as my jail cell. He held a knife in his hand, and I thought he planned to kill me. Instead, he cut my restraints and gave me Afghani clothes to put on. Once dressed, he led me out and to the edge of the village where he pointed out the direction I should follow. He returned to his village. I've since learned that it's an honor thing. The boy wasn't Taliban and he felt I deserved protection by his village."

"What happened next?" asked Walt, cutting to the chase.

"I used my training. I located a bright star in the direction the boy had shown me and used it to steer myself in a straight line. My first thought was, he'd given me directions to get back to my base, but after I'd been walking for two nights without coming to any American encampments, I realized that wasn't the case."

"How'd you get water, food?" asked Walt.

"My knowledge of Arabic was limited to a couple phrases everyone picks up, so I pretended to be mute. By using sign language, I was able to get the villagers to understand I was thirsty, hungry. They responded with food and water," Bill told Walt and his attentive team.

"I lost track of time. I gauged it as much by the length of my beard and hair as anything else. Funny, though. As my beard grew longer and longer, the people I met showed less suspicion towards me. They assumed I was a Muslim by my appearance, is what I thought. It didn't hurt any that my beard was black.

"My Arabic improved gradually over time, too. It's hard not to pick up a few phrases, hearing them repeated over and over, especially the initial greetings. I picked up 'salaam!' for 'hello,' and 'kaifa haloka' for 'how are you?' After wandering aimlessly for I don't know how long with the hopes of finding an American base or a team of American soldiers to join up with and never finding any, I figured I'd be better off finding my way to Pakistan. I knew that a lot of Pakistanis spoke English, and I figured I could get directions to the American embassy and get out of the mess I was in once I reached Pakistan.

"The next step was to figure out how to ask someone. I started by saying 'Pakistan' and the man I said it to got a funny look on his face and said, 'Bakistan?' So that got me going. I figured Pakistan was Bakistan to an Afghani. I turned in a circle, pointing, with a questioning expression on my face until the guy got it and pointed, and said 'bihadhih altariqa.' I figured Pakistan was that way, so I set off in that direction, doing my best to line my way using landmarks ahead that kept me moving in a straight line.

"As I made my way, if I met someone, I'd say 'Bakistan?' and they'd point out the direction. A couple times it was different than the way I'd been going. I began questioning if they really knew or hadn't a clue and were trying to be helpful anyway.

"I knew I'd been traveling in a generally southerly direction, which made sense since Pakistan lies south of Afghanistan, but it was easy to get turned off course, especially wandering through the mountains. Anyway, I kept at it, and one day I ran into a man and asked 'Bakistan?' and he eyed me oddly and said 'hadha Bakistan,' with a sweep of his arm in a circle. He was saying I was in Pakistan. I'd made it!" Bill grinned at the group.

"After I got over the shock, the surprise, I asked him if he spoke English. The funny expression came back on his face, and he said, 'You English?' as his eyes swept over me, my long beard and my Afghani clothes.

"'Yes, English,' I told him. I'm sure I sported a big smile on my face.

"'Where you come from?' he asked.

"'I got lost in Afghanistan,' I explained.

"'Easy to get lost in Afghanistan,' he agreed. Then he asked me where I was going. I asked him if he knew of an American embassy or consulate, and he said he didn't, but his cousin might. He led me to his cousin's house and it turned out that he knew of an American consulate in Peshawar, the closest one to where we were. Long story short, he gave me good directions to the consulate, and the rest is history. Turned out, the total time it took me to get there was thirteen months," Bill concluded.

"Ahsant! Laqad'ublit hasanana," *Well done! You did well,* I said, my knowledge of Arabic coming easy to me. The army had taught me well.

"Shukraan, ana aqdr dhlk," *Thanks, I appreciate it,* replied Bill without hesitation.

I tried to hide my surprise. Bill had not only understood what I said but had replied in complex Arabic. To my way of thinking, he'd minimized his knowledge of Arabic but blundered into showing he knew a lot more. My thoughts were interrupted by Walt's question.

"So, what happened to you after you got to the consulate, Bill?" he asked.

"Turned out, I picked up dysentery and cholera during my wanderings. I got shipped to Germany for treatment. And de-lousing," he added, scowling.

"How long were you there?" asked Walt.

"Nine weeks, total. They wouldn't let me go until all my tests came back negative," said Bill.

"Are you still active?" asked Walt.

"Yes. I got my back pay and unused leave. I booked into this resort for some R and R," he said.

"It's an amazing coincidence that you picked the same resort we all chose. What a small world we live in," said Walt.

"Yeah, it is. You can't imagine what a surprise it was to me when I saw you here," he added.

To me, he didn't sound all that surprised.

I glanced over at Paul, who subtly nodded his head at me. He got it, too. This man named Bill was guilty until proven innocent. He needed to be watched. Carefully.

I was sitting close enough to Walt to hear the conversation he was having with the soldier named Bill. It was all small talk, superficial chitchat. I gathered that the bond between the two men wasn't as strong as I was initially led to believe. I guessed that Walt recalled Soldier Bill because of the uniqueness of the situation. It wasn't every day a Special Forces soldier went missing in action. I knew from my own tours of duty in Afghanistan how rare it was. The intense training that every Special Forces candidate went through before earning his beret minimized the chances of that happening. Add to that Bill's story about wandering through Afghanistan for, what did he say? Thirteen months?

If it all turned out to be true, they should make a movie out of it. Not that I'd go see it.

I turned my attention to my neglected salad. After a couple bites, I realized how hungry I'd become. Paul had sharpened my appetite. For food, too.

I glanced over at him, saw Paul had done serious damage to his plate of food, shot him a sexy smile. Seeing my smile, he returned one of his own. I secretly prayed that Walt and Company could come to a decision soon so I could turn my undivided attention to Paul. A nibble here, a nibble there left me wanting for more. I craved a banquet, not a snack.

With his meal finished, Walt stood to leave, and his five team members rose as one. "Take your time, folks, and enjoy your meals. No doubt we'll all meet again," he said to Paul, Bill and me. I scooped one more bite into my mouth and got to my feet, joining the procession. Soldier Bill knew from personal experience that I was part of Walt's entourage after I came close to cutting off the blood supply to his brain, but he didn't know that Paul was a second bodyguard. Paul remained in his chair, understanding the situation.

Walt led us at a brisk pace back to his suite, and waved his wristband at the door lock to let us in. Once we were all inside, he swung the door closed.

"Sit. Everyone sit," he barked, taking charge.

We made ourselves comfortable, our attention on Walt.

Looking at me, his eyebrows raised, he said, "It looks like you've got something on your mind, EZ. Out with it." The man didn't waste any time.

"That whole situation with Soldier Bill seemed far-fetched to me, sir."

"Don't call me 'sir.' Name's Walt," he reminded me.

"Sorry, *Walt*. Old habits die hard," I said, trying to appear sheepish.

"Yeah, yeah. I know. What's your opinion of Soldier Bill?" he asked pointedly.

"I believe in coincidences, but that was a lot to swallow. First, he goes missing in Afghanistan without a trace. Second, he wanders around in Afghanistan for thirteen months without a single contact with American forces. And third, and to me the biggest, he books into this newly-opened resort in the Dominican Republic at the same time you and your advisors are staying here. Like you said, it's a small world, but to me it's a big pill to choke down," I said with a shake of my head.

"Your point is well taken. If he'd had a gun, he could have taken an easy shot at me when he first walked in. Surprise was clearly on his side," Walt conceded.

"He wasn't armed. I checked when I collared him. So, if he's one of the bad guys, I figure he plans to make his move later when your guard's down, in a way that allows him to escape afterwards," I concluded.

"I agree with you, EZ. He bears watching. He may have been hired by the army elements that don't want to see me running for president. I'll make a couple phone calls, see if I can confirm his story."

"Great idea, Walt. Keep me posted."

"Will do. I appreciate your frank appraisal." He turned his attention back to Bob and the others. "Now that's done, let's get back to the business at hand."

While they settled into their now-familiar routine, I got up and stepped to the outside patio door. I pressed my ear against it, listening for a sound that didn't belong there. Not hearing anything, I gripped the handgun that rested behind my back and brought it in front of me. In a fluid movement, I jerked the door open and rushed through the opening, my handgun moving right-left-right as I swept the patio for intruders. To my relief, nobody was there.

Expelling the breath I was unaware I held, I tucked the handgun in its place behind my back and pulled my blouse down over it. Satisfied, I made a complete search of the patio for signs of intrusion. A big sign would be unexplained drops of water. A small sign would be anything subtle, like moved furniture, any item out of place, anything indicating that an intruder had paid a visit. With nobody there when I raced out, my big concern was that someone may have intruded, placed a bomb and left undetected.

I weighed that possibility in my mind. With modern explosives like Semtex and C-4, a small amount could be devastating. Hide it inside an innocuous-looking outer container and detonate it remotely from a safe distance. The blast could easily pulverize the outer wall of a building and send the resulting rubble careering through the interior, killing anyone in its path with lethal debris. Not a pretty thought. I glanced at the substantial-looking stucco walls and knew chunks of flying concrete would add even more to the lethality.

With these gloomy thoughts in mind, I renewed my search for a bomb. I checked every nook and cranny and found nothing. Then, I stepped back and allowed my eyes to lose their focus as I considered a bomb hidden in plain sight. They were often the most difficult to detect because of that. Easy to overlook. After a careful search, I came up empty.

I paused, considering how a bomb might be planted, and a chilling thought struck me. Somebody could swim along the canal, bomb in hand, and simply lob it over the outer wall and into the patio area. Swim a safe distance away, hit the detonator switch, and BOOM! No more General Walter McKelvy. No more five aides. Mission accomplished, and nobody would ever know who had done the deed.

I realized full well that Paul and I had our hands full as the protectors of McKelvy and Company, and our lives were as much in danger as those we protected. It was a sobering thought. I took out my cell phone and sent Paul a text: *We need 2 talk ASAP.*

A short time later he replied: *Where R U?*

I answered: *6.*

After another search of the patio area, I used my purloined room passkey to open the door and go back inside. Walt looked up, saw me, and went back to the discussion with his team members. If he was able to read my mind, his powers of concentration would have been seriously affected.

I crossed to the hallway door in time to hear a single knock, our pre-arranged signal, and opened the door. Paul stepped inside and I quickly closed the door behind him.

Walt glanced over at us, interrupted by the intrusion. "What's going on, you two?"

"If you don't mind our joining your circle, we have security issues to discuss," I said as Paul and I moved towards them.

"By all means," said Walt, motioning us forward.

Since there were no more chairs available, Paul and I stood.

I spoke first. "I took some time to consider how many ways you might be attacked, Walt. You could be attacked while going from one place to another in the resort, or by one or more people using a passkey to open the hall door or the patio door. And you could be attacked by a remotely detonated bomb. The bomb could be lobbed over the wall from the canal by a swimmer and into the outside patio, or it could be hidden somewhere around the resort and detonated when you pass by."

"Shit, EZ. To hear you talk, we haven't left Afghanistan," said Walt, shaking his head.

"I know," I said. "But realistically, we need to think of all possibilities so Paul and I stand a chance to gain the upper hand."

"You're right. Guess you caught me off guard with your list of all the ways I could die. You're absolutely right to consider how the bad guys could come at me," said Walt, as he tried to regain his composure.

"If we can stay a step ahead of those bad guys, we'll be in a better position to stop them," I said. I turned to Paul and asked him what he'd learned about Soldier Bill after Walt and Company left the table.

"Not a lot, sad to say," Paul said. "I told him I thought it was cool that he and Walt knew each other from before. He nodded in agreement and then grilled me. He asked me how I knew Walt and I told him I'd just met him. I explained to him how I was eating breakfast alone and he invited me to join his group, so I did. Then Soldier Bill asked me if I was staying here alone, and I said I was. Made up a story about getting a divorce from my wife of twelve years and needing to get away, be by myself. I think he bought it.

"Anyway, I figured it was his turn to answer questions, so I asked him where he was from, back home. He said he grew up on a small ranch in Montana, loved hunting and fishing and roaming the mountains as a kid, and enlisted in the army to get away from a woman who hounded him about getting married. He wasn't ready to settle down, and nothing he said to her made any difference. So, he created his own irreversible separation by raising his hand and swearing his oath. She cried when he got on the bus, but that's the last he saw of her.

"He said he breezed through basic and caught the eye of several instructors who suggested he might fit in with Special Forces. He figured, what the hell, and signed on. He said he wanted to be a sniper, but he didn't make the grade. He didn't say why, and I didn't ask. I figured it might be a sensitive area for him. Anyway, he went on to tell me he was on his first tour in

Afghanistan, still a green horn when he got separated from his team. I asked him how it happened and he said, 'You know. Fog of war.' He asked me if I'd served, and I told him I'd enlisted but was turned down for medical reasons. Then I showed him the scars on the backs of my legs. He asked me how it happened, so I lied and told him I was working in a garage and a gas explosion behind me burned my backside. Guess it was a partial lie. Anyway, it seemed to satisfy him," said Paul.

"When we left the restaurant together, all buddy-buddy, I asked him if he wanted to meet up for dinner. His expression clouded over and he said he already had a commitment to meet someone, maybe we could meet some other time. I blew the clouds away by asking who the lucky girl was, and the clouds were replaced by a big shit-eating grin. He asked me how I knew. I tossed him a grin of my own and told him I was psychic, ha ha. Anyway, we parted company, and here I am," said Paul. He searched the faces around him for reactions to his summary.

Walt was first to react. "So, what do you think? Is he a threat to me and my team?" he asked Paul.

"I'd say he's guilty until proven innocent," said Paul, leveling his eyes on Walt. "His story of wandering for thirteen months in Afghanistan without contact with the Taliban or U.S. forces is a stretch, in my mind. I don't know what he was doing all that time, but I can't help thinking he left out a lot of important details. For some country boy from Montana who loved hunting, fishing, and roaming the mountains, wandering around Afghanistan would've been right up his alley."

"You make a reasonable argument, Paul. I agree with your assessment. So how do you two want to move forward?" asked Walt, his eyes bouncing from Paul to me and back again.

"We need to split up. I'll handle the front door and EZ will guard the back one," said Paul, with a glance at me for my concurrence. I nodded in agreement.

I took my turn at making suggestions. "The other thing we need to do is change suites for your meetings," I said. "We have four suites we can use, your three and mine. We'll leave Paul's out since Soldier Bill thinks Paul isn't connected to you, and we don't need to give him a reason to doubt that."

"I like it," said Walt, nodding thoughtfully. "And since I can assume I'm the number one target, I should sleep in a different suite every night. Makes me feel like a terrorist leader, moving around from place to place to avoid being the target of a drone attack."

"Let's hope they don't have drones at their disposal," said Paul, a grim smile flickering on his face. "That reminds me. I have some state-of-the-art technology in my bag, compliments of your general buddy at Bragg."

"What's it do?" asked Walt, curious.

"They call it a bug zapper. It senses the mini-transmission radio waves coming from hidden minicams and microphones, and homes in on them. Like a futuristic metal detector. I'll go get it and run a scan of the hallway and the suites, starting with this one," said Paul, getting to his feet and moving quickly for the door.

In the silence after Paul left, I thought how useful a bug zapper would have been to me, not only here at El Mar Placida but at that hotel suite in Cleveland.

"Think he'll find anything?" asked Walt, cutting into my thoughts.

"It wouldn't surprise me," I said, thinking of the bugs I'd already uncovered in my own suite.

Walt turned his attention back to business. "While we're waiting, let's move on with our evaluations, men," he said to his assembled team.

I took my cue and stepped outside to the patio area, my eyes sweeping the area for any changes, any additions since my last time out there. I saw nothing as I maintained a high level of alertness. After a thorough check, including the murky area behind the plunge pool, I stepped over and opened the door leading to the canal. Acting like a tourist checking out my new surroundings, I glanced casually at the canal in both directions. Nobody was in the water. Its surface was undisturbed.

I turned to have a look at the suites on the opposite side of the canal and a shocking possibility struck me. What if a sniper could position himself in such a way that he had a clear view of me and anyone else going through this door and into the water? BOOM! Target down for the count. With the thought raising the hackles on my neck, I turned away and closed the door, then went back inside.

Walt glanced at me, distracted by my expression. "Find anything, EZ?"

"Yes. Don't swim in the canal," I said without hesitation.

"Why? What do you mean?"

"A sniper positioned on the other side of the canal would have a clear, easy shot at you," I told him.

"Jesus, I'm starting to feel like a prisoner in my own room," he said, a gloomy expression clouding his face.

"I sympathize, but this will all be over once you reach a decision. Then you can swim to your heart's content," I said.

"We're working on it, believe me. Bob's running down a big list of potential donors, Jim's conducting his own polls to assess my favorability, Pete's setting up contacts with the media, Kim's doing his thing with publicity, and Tony's working on scheduling. The big thing is donors, as you know. Without them, I may as well back out. If I can't be competitive dollar-wise with the big names in the race, I'd be wasting a lot of good people's money," he explained, maintaining solid eye contact with me while he spoke.

"I hope things work out for you, Walt. For all of you," I said with a sweep of my arm to include the whole team. "I personally think you'd be one hellova fine president."

"Thanks, EZ. Now I only need another seventy-nine million, nine hundred and ninety-nine thousand votes," he said, his winning smile back where it belonged.

I returned his smile before going back out onto the patio, leaving Walt and his team to continue their work. I focused my attention on guarding the door to the canal and watching for bombs being tossed into the patio area. I prayed that, if a bomb got tossed, it wasn't already armed to explode. I knew I wouldn't survive if the fuse was already burning. A flash-bang grenade wouldn't be good, either. I recalled using them in Afghanistan in close quarters. It produced a blinding flash and a concussing explosion that paralyzed anyone within twenty, thirty feet of it. Charging in right after one of them detonated gave the guys who threw it a hell of an advantage, I knew that from personal experience.

I drew in a ragged breath, considering all the potential obstacles Paul and I faced. *Buck it up and climb off the pity pot, Kelly.*

My thoughts were interrupted when I heard a single knock on the main door to the room. Closing the patio door behind me, I hurried to the entry door. "Who's there?" I called out.

I heard Paul's voice in response, and I swung the door wide. Paul stepped into the room, the compact bug zapper held in his hand. I knew it was instinctual, how he held it. His right hand remained free to grab the handgun behind his back.

"I've got some good news and some bad news," he said, worry lines creasing his broad face.

"Give me the bad news first," I said.

"My little gizmo picked up four minicams in the hallway."

"Did you disable them?" I asked.

"I thought about it, and then realized that whoever planted them there would get an image of me as I approached them. Since they don't yet know I'm allied with Walt and Company, I figured that you should be the one to disable them. Once you're done, we'll put up four minicams of our own and catch whoever comes along to investigate," said Paul.

"I like it," I said. "Now, what's the good news?"

"I swept both of our suites and they're both clean."

"That *is* good news. Hey, I just thought of another place we can put our own minicams," I said, a sly grin tweaking the corners of my mouth.

"The canal, right?" asked Paul.

"How'd you know? Yes," I conceded.

"I thought of it on my way back here. It might give us the edge we need to be ahead of an attack from that direction," said Paul.

"There you go. Great minds think alike," I said, nodding in agreement.

"Check to make sure there's nobody out there," said Paul with a sweep of his arm at the canal.

I inched open the door leading to the canal and stuck my head out, looking left, then right along the waterway. "All clear," I whispered back to him.

"Good. Here, take the zapper and scan for bugs," he said quietly as he handed it to me.

I took it, glanced at the small screen, and moved it alongside the entry door as far as I could reach. The device remained silent, the line remained flat. I reversed my position and reached as far in the other direction as my arms would allow. "I get nothing, Paul," I told him.

"All right. Take this minicam and position it so it can scan to the left."

I found a small niche in the outer wall to plant it, making sure that the 'eye' was looking to the left along the canal. "Got it, Paul," I said when I'd finished planting it.

"Okay. Here's another one you can point in the opposite direction," he said, and passed me a second minicam.

Again, I located a crack in the outer wall and pressed the minicam in place. I scanned the canal once more to check for swimmers. Satisfied that no one was in sight and the water surface was undisturbed, I went back into the patio and closed the door. I handed the zapper back to Paul.

Taking it, he said, "Let's see how you did." He flipped a toggle to the 'view' position. The screen came to life. It showed a clear picture of the cam looking left along the canal. He turned a dial and the image changed to a scene that showed the canal to the right. I smiled, seeing the effectiveness of the miniature cameras.

"You done right good, girl," he said, smiling down at me.

"Don't call me 'girl'," I said, punching him in the ribs to emphasize my point.

"Ooof! I forgot you don't like to be called that. We've been apart too long," he said. He leaned in and snuck a kiss.

"Mmm, that's better," I murmured, but forced myself to break away.

"I know. We have work to do," he said softly and handed me the bug zapper. "Get out there and de-bug the hallway."

We turned and went back into the suite. Paul gave Walt a thumbs-up sign as we walked to the hallway door. Once there, Paul explained where he'd located the bugs.

"Got it," I said, as I eased the door open and scanned the hallway. A young couple, totally preoccupied with each other, passed by and headed for the lobby, oblivious to their surroundings. *I hope that's Paul and me when this is over.*

With the hallway empty, I held the zapper in my left hand and set off down the hallway, doing my best to appear casual. When I neared the first location Paul had indicated, the screen displayed a line climbing skyward. When it reached the highest point, I searched the area indicated and spotted the camera. I plucked it from its hiding spot and dropped it into my right front capri pants pocket.

Maintaining the same casual stroll, I moved to the next location, found the minicam and dropped it in with the first one I'd found. I continued along, finding and capturing the other two. I continued down the hallway to the lobby, checking to make sure Paul hadn't missed any. I was relieved to find that he hadn't. I stood in front of one of the fine paintings in the lobby long enough to satisfy myself that nobody was watching me, and then I retraced my steps to Walt's suite. Paul opened the door when I knocked once.

"How'd it go?" he asked, worry lines crinkling his eyes.

In answer, I pulled the minicams from my pocket, careful to cover their 'eyes' so they didn't 'see' Paul and placed them carefully into Paul's outstretched hand.

"Sweet," he whispered, grasping them tightly. "I'll go commit them to a watery grave." He marched into the bathroom.

I got a momentary image in my head of an army of minicams floating along in the sewer line. I shook off my brief smile.

When Paul came back out, he handed me four minicams from his own stash. "Go back out there and do your thing, g—, I mean good lady," he amended, catching himself before 'girl' popped out.

I smiled at him, my eyebrows arching. "That was a close one, Paul," I whispered. "I guess I won't thump you this time."

"I'm a slow learner, but once I do—"

I didn't wait for him to finish. I opened the door, saw the hallway was empty, and stepped out. In less than five minutes I was back.

"How'd I do?" I asked Paul.

Paul fiddled with the controls on the zapper and brought up the four new camera images. "Couldn't have done any better myself," he whispered, nodding his approval.

Together we viewed the six camera images, four in the hallway and two watching the canal. Nobody showed up on any of them. I silently hoped it remained that way.

"Sorry to interrupt," Paul said to Walt and his crew, quickly getting their attention. He filled them in on what he and I had done. Walt and the others smiled and nodded their approval before returning to business.

Afterwards, Paul and I sat together, our eyes on the zapper screen. Paul set it to highlight each camera image for fifteen seconds. Every ninety seconds an image was highlighted for fifteen seconds. Paul realized that a minute and thirty seconds went by with no feedback from the cameras, but he told me he saw no way around it.

I thought a moment. "Why don't you cut the time of each highlight back to five seconds? That way we'll only have a thirty second gap between them? In five seconds, we can see if anything's coming our way," I reasoned.

"Why didn't I think of that?" said Paul, a teasing grin playing upon his mouth.

I crinkled my eyes, smiling back. I wondered if I'd been set up. *Did Paul intentionally set a long view time for each camera in order to get my two cents' worth?* I knew I'd never know for sure.

Paul tweaked the controls and restarted the scan, with each camera image playing for five seconds, repeating every thirty seconds. We agreed it was much better.

"What would be even better is if we could get a big screen and show all six images at once, each in their own outlined space. Our eyes could scan them continuously, and spot a problem right away," I said.

"Now you're talking," whispered Paul, trying not to distract Walt and his team. "I'll go get the manual for this gizmo from my room and see if that's a possibility." He stood and moved to the door, leaving me to watch the monitor.

At the door, he turned to me, his eyebrows raised as I checked each camera image. "All clear. Go," I told him, the camera images confirming the hallway was empty.

Paul opened the door and ducked out, closing the door quietly behind him. I kept my eyes glued to the monitor as he moved purposely along the hallway to his suite. The farthest camera showed his backside as he reached and entered his room.

I glanced at my phone clock and saw it was almost three. I turned my attention back to my monitor vigil. One of the canal cameras showed a swimmer moving slowly towards the suite. He was maybe fifteen seconds from reaching it when the image switched to the second canal camera pointed in the opposite direction. It showed a second swimmer dog-paddling along. I realized that one swimmer, the first, was a man, and the second was a woman. Innocuous enough. Or were they?

The camera image switched to the hallway, five seconds each, leaving me to wonder if the swimmers were a danger during the blackout period. I didn't hesitate. I moved swiftly to the patio door, opened it and stepped out without a sound, then pulled the door closed behind me. With my attention riveted on the canal door, my ears alert to sounds of stealth, I closed the gap. I heard muted splashing sounds coming from the canal and turned my eyes back to the images. I suppressed a giggle at the display.

The two swimmers, clearly a man and a woman, had become intertwined in the canal. The man had his swimsuit draped over his head and the woman had her bikini bottom similarly displayed. Their attention was divided between keeping their heads above the surface while they struggled to have sex. I wondered why they didn't retire to their room for a much less stressful go at it. I considered two possibilities. One, they loved adventure, putting a little spice into it. Two, it was a clandestine meeting, their spouses unaware of their romantic goings-on.

I watched the two lovers drift past the entry door in the direction of the main pool. I wondered idly if they'd stop at the swim-up bar for a celebratory drink. I chuckled at the thought. *I'll tell Paul about them. Maybe he'd be up to duplicating their efforts if we get through this.*

The hallway cameras showed a male figure striding purposely towards the suite. It was Paul. I let myself back inside and strode over to the hallway door. I got there as he knocked once, and I swung the door open for him. He stepped inside wearing a smile.

"Good news?" I asked.

"Good news," he confirmed while brandishing a laptop. "We merge this with the zapper, flip a couple toggles, and presto! All the feeds will be displayed on the laptop monitor at the same time. Here, help me hook it up," he said as he held out two USB cables.

I took the cables and, following Paul's directions, plugged them into the laptop and the zapper. Done, Paul powered up the laptop. We both stared expectantly as the monitor came to life and we smiled as one when all six camera images were displayed on the laptop's screen.

"That's so much better," I whispered. "Now we can spot any movement on any camera feed immediately. We just gained a huge advantage."

I saw that the two swimmer-lovers had drifted out of camera range. The water of the canal was calm, undisturbed. I told Paul in hushed tones what I'd seen. He chuckled.

"If we get through this in one piece, do you want to try that?" he whispered to me.

"Mind reader! You have an uncanny way of echoing my thoughts," I whispered back as I nested my hand on his forearm. Together, we directed our attention to the monitor. To business.

Sometime later, our concentration was broken by Walt. "Hey, you two. It's after six and we voted to go have dinner. What do you say?"

Six pairs of eyes were leveled at Paul and me.

"One of us needs to stay and watch the monitor. Since Soldier Bill and maybe others know I'm allied with you, Paul should stay here and watch the camera images. Maybe he'll catch someone replacing the cameras we found in the hallway," I said.

"Point well taken, EZ. I agree, we need to keep Paul off the radar. He's much more valuable to me that way. We can bring a doggie bag back to the room for you, Paul. How do you like your steak?" asked Walt as he locked eyes with Paul.

"As rare as they allow," said Paul, a warm smile breaking out on his rugged face.

"Consider it done. We're going to that El Gaucho restaurant and Argentine beef is all over their menu," said Walt.

"Have you made a reservation?" I asked.

"Nope. I didn't think we needed to telegraph our movements to interested parties. At this hour, I think we should be able to walk right in and be seated," he said.

"You're right," I said. "A lot of the guests think of dinner as seven or later."

My mind was already turning over the best way to guard the party of six. The restaurant was a five-minute walk from the lobby entrance. We'd be outside, along a tree and bush-lined walk, with plenty of places for an ambush to take place. I hoped whoever wanted Walt dead had a less public, less attention-getting plan, but I knew I needed to be ready for all possibilities. My right hand went to the small of my back and the loaded pistol tucked there. I slipped my hand around its grip and felt a comforting wave of confidence. *I can do this.*

"Let's go," said Walt, his words sounding more like an order than a mutual agreement as he rose to his feet.

His five advisors followed suit and stood, waiting for Walt to lead the way. Each of them reacted to having been sitting inactive for hours. Bob slowly pinwheeled his arms, working out the kinks and the numbness. Jim bent over and waved his fingers at his feet in a stretch. Tony rotated his body at the waist, his arms held upright and close to his chest. Kim shrugged his shoulders and rotated his head to and fro. Peter glanced about at the others, an amused smile on his face, and made no effort to join in the action.

"Bob, you lead the way. I want to have a few words with EZ," Walt said.

Another order. No question about it. The man knew how to direct people. The military had given him years of practice.

Taking his cue, Bob opened the hallway door and stepped out, with the other four advisors following on his heels. They went two by two, with Peter the odd man out, walking behind the other four. I glanced over at Paul who was watching the scene on his laptop screen. He sensed my eyes on him and rewarded me with a warm smile before going back to his scrutiny. Walt and I took up the rear, and I pulled the door closed behind me, leaving Paul alone in the suite with the monitor.

As we all moved down the hallway, I cranked my five senses to their maximum settings. First in importance was my eyesight. I keyed in on anyone I saw as we made our way towards the lobby door. Were they suspicious in any way? Did they show more interest in the group, in Walt, than casual glances? Were their hands where I could see them? More important, were they empty?

My concentration was interrupted by Walt speaking to me, and I turned some of my attention to hearing what he was saying. I quickly realized I had no idea what he'd said. "I'm sorry, Walt. I didn't catch what you were saying," I whispered to him while trying to sound contrite. I continued to keep my eyes everywhere but on Walt.

"No matter, EZ. You've got your job to do. We'll talk when we get seated in the restaurant," he said in a low voice that carried well beyond me.

I glanced his way, bobbed my head to confirm I'd heard, then turned my focus back to his protection.

Bob pushed open the lobby door and stepped outside, and we all followed along on the wide path that led to El Gaucho. My senses cranked into high gear, I searched everywhere as I probed our surroundings for points of vulnerability, potential ambush sites.

It was eerily similar to being back in Afghanistan, creeping through Taliban territory with my team, everyone, not just me, keenly watchful for anything out of place, anything not quite right. It included not only sight but sound, and yes, smells. Unbathed Taliban—and most of them were unbathed—gave off a strong smell that included body odor mixed with hash, maybe opium. Or maybe it had something to do with what they ate? Whatever it was, once it hit your nose you remembered it, and then never forgot it. Sometimes, getting a faint whiff of that strong odor was all you needed to save your life, the lives of your team, and prepare for the onslaught.

The odors that greeted my nose as we strolled down the path to El Gaucho were nothing like what was so indelibly etched into my memory of Afghanistan. These were fragrances, not smells. These were the aromas of many different tropical flowers, interspersed with the pungent odor of the damp earth they sprang out of. The combination was intoxicating. I concentrated on being watchful for danger and pushed the alluring fragrances into my periphery.

Ahead of Walt and me, Peter strolled alone. While the other four team members moved along with their eyes directed ahead, Peter showed much more interest in what lay to either side of him. He seemed absorbed by the incredible variety of tropical flowers and flowering shrubs and seemed he couldn't get enough of them. His short, stocky body shuffled along, seemingly enthralled by all the beauty surrounding him. *The big-city media man has never experienced such pleasure before,* I thought.

Walt, watching me watch Peter, leaned in and whispered, "City boy in the country."

I smiled at his observation. Walt had picked up on it, too.

The path took us past thick vegetation and out into a cleared area just before El Gaucho. Opposite it sat the exercise center with its rows of treadmills, stationary bikes, and other instruments of torture displayed in the large plate glass windows that spanned the entire front of the building. A few committed workout enthusiasts trotted or spun their way, their bodies glistening with sweat. *Do twenty minutes of exercise, and then go have a huge dinner. Justification,* I thought idly.

Bob held the door open while the other four team members filed in.

When it was Walt's turn, he smiled at Bob and said, "After you," as he took over door duty.

I scanned the restaurant entrance for any signs of danger. The few customers I saw took no interest in Walt or his crew. I glanced behind, saw no threats, and pushed through ahead of Walt, my eyes racing everywhere, unencumbered now.

Bob had assumed control and approached the maître' d to ask for a table for seven. No, he didn't have a reservation, was that a problem?

"No problem, sir. I will arrange a table for seven right away." He turned away from Bob and corralled a waiter, who trotted off to 'set up a table with seven place settings, and don't forget the flower arrangement, Ramon.'

I drew a breath and exhaled it silently, relieved the biggest opportunity for ambush was behind us. I had a closer look at the other patrons. I saw a table with four family members, mother, father and two children under the age of six. I knew better than to guess at the children's sexes.

The other occupied table had a young man and woman. They sat next to each other instead of across from one another, allowing the man to overtop both the woman's hands with his. Their attention was directed at each other. Newlyweds? Lovers? I put them in the 'low threat' category.

The waiter returned, smiling broadly, and gestured for our 'party of seven, no reservation' to follow him. Bob led the way and we followed as before, with Walt ahead of me, making me the caboose, or as we called it in the army, the six, or six o'clock position. Walt claimed the seat that looked back at the entrance, and I staked my claim on the seat next to his. It offered me the same vantage point. I noted with satisfaction that nobody at the other two occupied tables had taken the time or effort to look up at us as we shuffled along and claimed our seats at the table.

After the waiter confirmed to all that his name was Ramon, he moved deftly around the table, setting large tan menus with gold braid down their spines in front of each of us with a precision rarely seen amongst waiters. He bustled about taking drink orders and reciting a list of the specials. After asking if there were any questions, and nobody had any, he disappeared to fill the drink orders.

Like Walt, I ordered iced tea. I noted scattered orders for beer, but nothing stronger.

The El Gaucho restaurant consisted of one large, open room with two doors on the right side leading to the kitchen, one marked Enter, the other marked Exit so waiters wouldn't collide going and coming. I counted twenty-one tables, arranged with enough space between them so conversations at one table wouldn't drift over to neighboring ones. The walls were hung with tapestries that depicted scenes from Argentina. I particularly liked the ones featuring gauchos, the Argentine version of cowboys. I identified the bolos held loosely in their hands. Instead of tossing lassos to secure unruly cattle, the gauchos slung their bolos at the critter's legs. The weighted balls, attached to leather thongs, were flung with precision and encircled both front or rear legs, stopping them from further movement. Very efficient when held in the hands of an experienced gaucho.

The waiter returned with a tray of drinks and circled the table, setting them down in front of each person with unerring accuracy. When the last glass found its mark, five hands reached forward to pick them up and sip a sample. I smiled, watching the unorchestrated precision of my tablemates, and then joined the party, sampling my tea. It was strong. Perfect. *Just the way I like it.*

When the waiter asked, "Are you ready to order?" Walt answered for everyone. "You bet, Ramon," he said, grinning. He remembered my comment that all the male staff were called by one easy-to-remember name.

"Ramon" busied himself with another circumnavigation of the table, writing down each person's dinner order. Not surprisingly, I heard 'steak' six times. When my turn came, I made it seven. When in Rome. I remembered to ask the waiter to duplicate my order in a to-go box when the meal was over. I planned to take over for Paul while he enjoyed his steak.

Idle chatter dominated the table while our meals were being prepared. I turned to Walt and asked him what he wanted to talk about with me.

"As you know, fundraising is the most important part of my running for office. Without the generous support of donors, my campaign will go nowhere, fast. Bob's been busy sending out letters to a list of well-heeled donors in the hopes of getting some of them to commit assets to my campaign fund. He keeps telling me not to worry, the money will come in, but I want to be sure. He also tells me that most high-roller donors take their time making the decision to donate. Hell, I'd take my time, too. Those donors didn't get wealthy by throwing their money around without careful thought," he said, brushing his hand through his close-cropped grey hair.

"So the decision process might take longer than you thought, am I right?" I asked.

"You got it. So, my question to you is, do you need more help? You and Paul are spread damned thin as it is," he said, his eyes on mine, his voice pitched low.

"I'll talk to Paul, see what he thinks. I don't think we need an army, but another able body might be helpful. We have to sleep sometime, and whoever wants you silenced is aware of that," I said as I watched Walt for a reaction.

"You think I'm most vulnerable when I'm sleeping? You're probably right," he added, answering his own question.

"Yes, but we can't rule out an attack happening at *any* time," I said. I glanced at the doors to see Soldier Bill making an entrance. I watched him intently as he spoke to the maître' d and then as a waiter escorted him to a table for two. As he followed the waiter, he glanced our way and spotted Walt and our group. He smiled and waved a greeting at us. Once he'd been seated and his waiter went off to get his drink order, he got up and strolled casually over to Walt's side.

"Looks like we choose a common chow time," he said brightly. "Must be we're all used to eating on a military timetable." He reached his hand out to Walt who shook it firmly.

"Why don't you join us?" said Walt, ever the gracious host, or maybe the budding politician.

"No, no," Soldier Bill promptly replied. "Enjoy your meals. I'm sure we'll meet again."

As I watched the scene play out, I saw Soldier Bill pass his clenched left hand over Walt's iced tea glass and casually open it as it hovered there. His words flowed easily from his mouth, offering a distraction. It happened in an instant, and if I hadn't been watching Soldier Bill closely, I could have missed what he did.

Soldier Bill turned away from our table with a smile and a wave, then sauntered back to his own table.

I leaned over to Walt and whispered, "Don't drink your tea." I told him what I'd seen.

"Jesus H. Christ! The nerve of that asshole," he breathed.

"We don't know what he did, but I'll see that your tea is tested for poison," I whispered back.

Soon after, two waiters bore down on our table, trays heavy with steaks and side dishes. The waiter who took our orders joined them, and he bustled about, setting the orders in front of each of us with unerring precision. *Three Ramons working together,* I thought, smiling inwardly as I watched their effortless teamwork.

After the last dish had been set down on the table, Ramon asked if everything was satisfactory, and could he bring anything else? He was met with shaking heads and muttered *no's* until Walt spoke up. "I put too much sugar in my iced tea. Could you bring me a fresh one?"

"Certainly, sir!" he replied as he reached to remove the sugary one.

Walt placed his hand over the glass and said, "It's okay, Ramon. Leave it. I'll mix the two."

"Very good, sir," he replied, then turned and hurried to the kitchen for a replacement glass of iced tea.

I leaned in to whisper, "When he brings Paul's dinner, I'll have him bring a to-go cup. We'll carry your tea out in it."

"That'll work." To the assembled table he intoned, "Good food, good meat. Good God, let's eat!"

No further prompting was needed. Silence surrounded the table as everyone, armed with knives and forks, tore enthusiastically into the steaks. The waiter returned with a fresh glass of iced tea and set it on the table to Walt's right, then retreated.

In between bites, I glanced at Soldier Bill. He'd seated himself with his back to our table so eye contact with him was out of the question. He lounged casually in his chair, patiently waiting for his meal, seemingly content to pass the time without distractions. He looked like the poster child for Alfred E. Neumann: *What, me worry?*

The remainder of our meals were polished off without incident. With every team member committed to making all the food disappear, conversation was scattered. I took the longest to finish because I interrupted every bite with a search of the restaurant. Whenever new arrivals came into the restaurant, I took longer chewing and swallowing, making a thorough inspection of them to reassure myself that they posed no threat.

Seeing that all cutlery had been set down at our table, the waiter reappeared. He recited a tempting list of desserts, but he got no takers. "Coffee for anyone? No? Then I will bring the to-go order."

I waved him over and asked for a to-go cup. "Certainly, Miss," he answered, his eyes dancing over my 'top priority' bracelet. He hurried back to the kitchen.

Walt rolled his head toward me and whispered, "What could Bill have put into my tea?"

"It would have to be a lethal substance that takes a while to kill," I whispered back. "Cyanide would be too quick, killing you fast, leaving Bill exposed as the most likely assassin. But both strychnine and arsenic take longer to kill. He'd be well on his way out of here before you die," I said.

"You know a lot about poison. Where'd you learn it?"

"I took a course in college on toxic plants. It's surprising how many deadly ones are out there. Hemlock, oleander, rhododendron and azaleas, plus amanitas mushrooms, to name a few. That led to my checking out the other popular poisons, including thallium," I said with a slight nod of my head.

"I'm impressed. But where will you go to get my tea analyzed quickly?" asked Walt.

"I made an impression on a waiter at the pool yesterday," I said, holding back the details of his misinterpretation of my intentions. "I'm thinking that he'll know where we can get it checked out locally."

"I'll leave it in your capable hands. Let me know what you find out. Maybe there's nothing in there," said Walt.

"Maybe not. Better to be safe than sorry, though."

The waiter's return stifled further comment. He had a large Styrofoam container with silverware wrapped up in a cloth napkin resting on top, plus a large paper cup and plastic lid. He set it down next to me. "Here is your requested dinner and cup, Miss."

"Thank you so much, Ramon," I said, careful to make eye contact with him.

"Not at all, Miss. It is my pleasure," he fairly gushed, his eyes going once again to my wristband.

"I will be sure to leave praise with Miss Haversham for your excellent service," I said, smiling at him.

"That is not necessary, Miss," he replied, though I could tell he still hoped I would. A well-placed compliment could go a long way towards advancing his career, I suspected.

With the waiter's departure, Walt asked Bob to leave a generous tip. Bob drew out his wallet to comply while I poured the suspicious iced tea into the paper cup and secured the lid.

Seeing I'd finished, Walt said, "Shall we?" as he stood.

Everyone took his cue and rose to their feet.

I gathered up Paul's dinner and the suspect tea and whispered to Walt. "Do you mind carrying these? It'll free up my gun hand."

Walt, getting it, took the two containers while offering me an understanding smile. We filed out as we'd come in, Bob leading, the rest of us following behind. As we passed Soldier Bill's table, I said to him, "Hope you're enjoying your dinner." *It may be your last,* I thought.

"Thanks. I am," Soldier Bill replied, a chameleon smile working its way across his face.

Once outside, I concentrated on getting Walt and his team safely back to their suite. It turned out to be an uneventful journey. *My favorite kind,* I thought with satisfaction.

As we reached the suite entrance door, Paul swung it open. He'd watched our return on his monitor, timing it perfectly.

"You remembered my dinner," he said, seeing the Styrofoam box and utensils in Walt's hand. "And a drink, too," he added, reaching for it.

"Dinner, yes. Drink, no," I said, pulling the cup back from Paul's reach. I explained to him what I'd seen Soldier Bill do.

"Guess I'll take a rain check on the drink," said Paul.

"I'm going to take it to the friendly waiter at the swim-up bar and see if he knows someone who can test it for poisons," I explained. I'd told Paul about my misadventure with Antonio the night before. He'd listened with a touch of concern.

"Sounds like a plan. I'll hold down the fort while you go."

I thanked him and exited the suite, cup in hand. I followed the overland route to the main pool. Faster. And drier. As I walked up to the little restaurant above the swim-up bar, I could see Antonio tending bar below. He was alone, no customers at that hour. I took the steps down to poolside and hailed him.

"Hey, Antonio. How are you?" I said, keeping my voice neutral, not wanting to give him another wrong impression.

Antonio turned and smiled, somewhat sheepishly, seeing me. "Why hello, Miss EZ. What brings you here?"

I explained what I needed him to do for me, holding the cup aloft for emphasis.

"Who could possibly want to see you dead?" he asked, concern in his voice.

"A possessive man who believes that I belong to him, and him alone. If you can find out if there's poison in my drink, I'll be able to get rid of him and move on with my life."

Antonio took the bait. "I have a cousin in the police crime lab. I will take it to him and ask him to check it for poison. He's very good. If there's poison, he'll find it and tell me what it is."

"That's perfect, Antonio. I can't begin to tell you what this means to me," I said, adding a smidgen of seduction to my smile as I passed the cup of iced tea to him.

"My shift is over in fifteen minutes," he said after a glance at his watch. "I will take it to my cousin directly after. How shall I notify you of the results?"

I considered giving Antonio my cell phone number but thought better of it. "Call me at my suite. It's suite 16," I said, knowing full well he already knew that.

"Very well, Miss EZ. You'll know as soon as I know. Stay safe now."

"And you as well. Don't drink it by mistake," I said. I tossed him a wave before retracing my steps.

Paul saw my approach on his monitoring screen and opened the door for me. "How'd it go?" he asked, seeing me without the cup.

I told him in a few words.

"Now we hurry up and wait," I said. Paul nodded. We'd both had plenty of that while in the army. Paul used the time to eat his cold dinner while I manned the monitors.

We discussed how best to handle security for the next twelve hours and decided that Walt and Bob should take Paul's room for the night. With me in the room next door to them, we'd have a good chance of seeing them alive the next morning. We also discussed Walt's suggestion of adding another security person, but neither of us could come up with the right person right off. We agreed to think about possibilities and talk it over later.

I asked Paul if there had been any hall activity while he watched the monitors. He told me no, that nobody had attempted to plant new cameras, but he didn't think whoever planted the ones we found would wait much longer.

"Maybe it'll be done during the night when the likelihood of being caught in the act is at a low point," he said.

"I'll bet you're right," I said.

Paul glanced over at Walt and his five team members. When he saw they were fully engrossed in their work, he turned his attention back to me. "What are you willing to bet?" he asked, a follow-up to my statement, his eyebrows doing the dirty mambo as he waited for my answer.

"Sounds like a case of 'Heads you win, tails I lose,'" I whispered, my eyebrows mimicking Paul's. "And you know I don't like to lose."

"Think of it as coming in second, not losing," whispered Paul.

"Well, since you put it that way, I'll bet the whole enchilada," I said, adding a sexy smile to the mix.

"Now you're talking!" Paul whispered with enthusiasm.

"Keep in mind, now. Win or lose, collecting on the bet may be delayed by circumstances beyond our control," I said. I rested a hand on Paul's arm.

"That's okay. A delay will only serve to sharpen our appetites," said Paul.

"What's that?" I asked, pointing at Paul's laptop screen. He turned his attention to the image of a man swimming slowly toward the suite's patio.

"Soldier Bill," we whispered in unison, identifying the man in the canal.

I rushed to the patio door, opened it silently, and stepped out, my hand already gripping the pistol behind my back. Paul stayed inside, his eyes alternating their focus between the screen and me through the open door.

My ears picked up the sound of a subtle splash beyond the door to the canal entry. I drew the M9 pistol and leveled it at the closed door, expecting Soldier Bill to come through at any moment. Time passed. Then Paul whispered to me, beckoned me back inside.

"What did I miss?" I asked when I rejoined him.

"I watched Soldier Bill swimming along the canal. When he reached the steps outside Walt's suite, he hitched himself out of the water and sat on the bottom one, seemingly using the place for a rest. I could see both his hands were empty, which took away much of my concern. After a short pause, Soldier Bill pushed off and slipped back into the water, resuming his slow swim away from the suite and in the direction of the main pool. I watched the camera image until he was out of sight, then waved you back inside."

"I'll go out and check, make sure he didn't leave something behind," I whispered. I ducked back outside, moved quietly to the outer door, and opened it by a few degrees. I inched my head out so I could look both ways along the canal. Seeing no one, I eased my way down the steps towards the water. I saw the impression left by Soldier Bill and his wet bathing suit and searched the area below and on either side of the step for signs of a bomb or other device. When I was satisfied that there was nothing left by him, I retraced my steps and rejoined Paul.

"Anything?" he asked me in a whisper.

"Nothing I could see. I'm guessing he was reconnoitering," I whispered back.

"Either that, or we're giving him more credit than he deserves," said Paul.

"If Walt's tea comes back clean, I agree," I said.

While we talked, I became aware that Walt was watching us, a puzzled expression on his broad face. Paul saw it, too. "This looks like a good time to discuss Walt and Bob's room change," I whispered.

Paul nodded in agreement and the two of us approached Walt's circle.

"What's happening, you two?" asked Walt as he followed our approach.

I spoke first. "We talked it over and we think it would be best if you and Bob stay in Paul's room tonight. If someone thinks you're in this room, they'll move against you here," I said, watching for a reaction.

"I don't have a problem with that," said Walt, answering for Bob as well.

"Good. We'll escort you down there once activity in the hall dies down. If you'll pack up overnight kits and a change of clothes for tomorrow, you'll be ready for the transfer when Paul sees that the hall is clear," I said.

"I'll do that now. Come on, Bob," said Walt in his commanding voice. The two moved together to the bedroom to gather their necessities for the transfer.

"Where will you spend the night, Paul?" I asked him when Walt and Bob were out of earshot.

"I know where I'd like to spend the night, but from a security standpoint I should shelve that thought," he whispered, his voice full of inuendo.

"I'll shelve it, too," I whispered back.

"Which leaves the question: where do *I* spend the night?" asked Paul. "I'm thinking I should stay right here. You can cover Walt and Bob from your suite, and I can watch for an attack here. That way our slim resources will be spread out appropriately.

"That makes sense. Do you have any more of those mini-cameras? A couple outside our digs isn't a bad idea," I said.

"I do. Good thought. I'll get a couple after you escort Walt and Bob to my suite," said Paul.

"Tap once on my door and I'll stick my hand out for them. I'll go for an after-dinner swim and plant them," I said as I brushed an errant strand of unruly hair behind my ear.

"Something to look forward to," said Paul, smiling.

By eight-thirty, Paul saw the hallway traffic had dropped to a few stragglers. It appeared to be as good a time as any for the move to his suite, and he alerted Walt and Bob. Taking their cues, Jim, Tony, Peter and Kim ducked out and hurried to their own suites. Once they were safely into their rooms, I stood in the open doorway and checked in both directions. Seeing no one out there, I motioned for Walt and Bob to follow me. With the two of them trailing behind me, I hurried along the empty hallway to Paul's suite. Using my purloined passkey, I quickly opened the door and escorted them inside, then closed the door behind us.

"There you go, gentlemen. My room is right next door, and I'll be watching out for you," I said, awarding the two men with a warm smile.

"Tell Paul we appreciate this," said Walt. "Staying safe is good."

"I will. If you need anything, or something comes up, call Paul or me on our cell phones. You've got our numbers, right?"

"Got 'em filed away," said Walt, holding up his cell phone.

"Perfect. Have a good night," I said.

"A good night will be a quiet night," said Walt.

"There you go. With our help, have a good, quiet night," I said, amending my statement. I opened the door, saw the hallway was clear, and hurried to my room next door after pulling their door closed behind me.

The message light on my phone was flashing when I got inside. I did a quick visual search of the room to assure myself that everything was as I'd left it. Satisfied, I moved to the phone, lifted the receiver and punched in the two-digit message code. I smiled, hearing Antonio's voice.

"Hello, Miss EZ, it is Antonio. I took the cup of tea to my cousin at the police station and explained to him what you feared had happened. He immediately ran his tests, and I am happy to inform you that he found no poison in it. I continue to be concerned for your safety. Please let me know what I can do to protect you from the horrible man who is a threat to you. I will return to work at nine tomorrow morning, and you know where to find me. Until then, I will worry about you. Good-bye." There was a short pause, and then he added, "For now."

You're a good man, Antonio. Maybe a little impulsive, but a good man, I thought as I replaced the receiver in its cradle. I stood there, considering options for a moment, and finally knew what I needed to do. Soldier Bill was going to have an unexpected visitor. Poison or no poison, I saw what he did with his hand over Walt's glass.

I called Paul to give him the news. After hearing me out, he said, "He's still way up there on my list of suspects, especially after hearing his cockamamie story about wandering about in Afghanistan for what, a year?"

"Uh huh. I think it's time I paid him a visit."

"Where's his room? Do we even know?" asked Paul.

"Not yet. I'll do some sleuthing and find out."

"Okay. Keep me posted. All's quiet at this end."

"Quiet here, too. Bob and Walt are settled into your room for the night. Hey, how was your steak?"

"Other than being a little cold, it was fantastic. We'll have to go to that restaurant together when this is all behind us," said Paul.

"It's a date," I said while all the things that could prevent that date from happening flashed through my mind. Shaking it off, I turned my attention back to the business at hand.

Where are *you, Soldier Bill?* I had no last name, so a call to the front desk wouldn't work. I had a maid's passkey, so I could open every door until I found him. No. Too risky. I could sit in the lobby until he showed up. No. That could take too long. Then, an idea came to me.

Worth a shot.

I checked how I looked in the bath mirror, dabbed on some make-up, grabbed my purse, and set out to find Soldier Bill.

The maître d' looked up as I entered El Gaucho and offered me his stock smile. "Good evening, Miss. Did you perhaps leave something behind?"

Good. He remembered me.

"No, but I'm hoping you can help me. The young man who sat by himself and came over to our table invited me to join him after dinner for a drink. The problem is, he didn't tell me where we could meet. I'm wondering if there's some way you could look up his room number for me," I asked sweetly, my eyelashes fluttering.

"We usually don't do that sort of thing," said the maître d', his face taking on a neutral expression.

"Oh, I completely understand. The problem I have, and I feel so stupid, is that I'm sure he told me where we could meet and then I was distracted and I can't remember what he said…" I let my voice trail off, trying my best to sound like an embarrassed young woman with a short attention span.

A pregnant silence developed, during which the maître d' eyed me critically as he weighed his options. His gaze took in my color-coded bracelet. At length he said, "Although I could get in a lot of trouble for disclosing such personal information, I am a romantic at heart. Give me a moment, please, Miss."

"Oh, thank you! Thank you! I can't begin to tell you what this means to me," I gushed. *If he only knew.*

The maître d' thumbed backwards in his reservation book and found the page he wanted. He set it open before me and pointed to a table. "Is this the table he sat at?" he asked.

I studied the drawing of the dining area, found the table Walt's team had sat at, and saw with satisfaction that the maître d' had chosen the correct table where Soldier Bill had dined. "Yes, yes! That's it!" I exclaimed, clapping my hands together.

"The young man's name is William Wardak, and he is staying in suite number 24," the maître d' disclosed.

"You're a life saver, Señor," I gushed. "How can I ever repay you?"

"Please, young lady. Do not disclose to anyone that you got this information from me. It would surely cost me my job here," he said while his hands made a vigorous wringing action in front of him.

"It will be our little secret, forever," I promised. "Thank you again." I turned and hurried off in search of suite 24 while I turned over the name Wardak in my eidetic memory. I remembered an Afghan province: Maidan Wardak, in the central/eastern region. When I was stationed in Afghanistan it was a Taliban stronghold. I couldn't wait to get an explanation from good old Soldier Bill on how he ended up with the last name Wardak. Getting it from his parents seemed unlikely.

I knew from my escorted tour of the resort that suite 24 was in the 20 to 40 block of suites, located to the left of the 1 to 20 block where Walt's team and I resided. Instead of swimming to the right towards the main pool, I could swim to the left and reach suite 24 a lot faster.

As I considered my options and whether to approach suite 24 from the pathway or the water, a large muffled explosion shook the ground.

What the hell was that? It had come from the direction of the lobby.

I raced from the restaurant and ran headlong back to the lobby, dashing through the confusion and mayhem there, and into the hallway leading to Walt's suite. Smoke and dust filled the hallway, stinging my eyes and making me choke. I drew in a lungful of sooty air and ran to the suite. It was easy to identify. The entry door had been dislodged by the blast and hung uncertainly on one hinge. Suite 6. Walt and Bob's room, recently vacated. By everyone but Paul.

Paul! Oh my God, Paul! I raced into the suite.

An eerie light enveloped me. I realized it came from outside the room, the light filtering through a huge hole in the canal side of the suite. Furniture was overturned, scattered haphazardly throughout the main room.

"Paul! Where are you, Paul?" I cried out, my vivid imagination picturing his broken, bleeding body lying somewhere nearby.

"EZ?"

I heard his faint voice coming to me from somewhere near the hallway wall.

I peered through the smoke and dust that hung in the air, obscuring my vision, struggling to find him. I shuffled slowly towards the direction his voice had come from, not wanting to add to his injuries by stepping on him. I bumped into an overturned chair. As I moved around it, I found Paul. He was stretched out on the floor, face down. I could make out dark stains on his shirt. *Blood.*

I knelt beside him, set my purse down, my hands touching, exploring his injuries. They came away wet with his blood, but I was relieved to find that he had no life-threatening injuries. My hands moved to his head, neck, fearful of finding bone or tissue injuries. Relief flooded through me when I found everything I explored was intact.

"Can you hear me, Paul?" I practically shouted at his unmoving body.

"What?" came his weak response.

"I asked if you can *hear* me," I said, my voice even louder now.

"Barely. My ears are ringing," said Paul, his voice stronger.

The blast. Affected his hearing, I thought. "Do you think you can sit up?" I asked him.

"Oh. Yeah, sure," he said. He began by exploring the range of motion in his arms. Once satisfied that he sustained no breaks, he moved his legs, flexing and extending them. A small smile lit up his soot-covered face and he said, "Looks like I dodged a bullet."

He rolled over and winced in pain when his pockmarked back and legs contacted the carpet. He had managed to be faced away when the blast came. The front side of his body remained intact. He drew himself up into a sitting position, moving slowly, gingerly. He reached to retrieve the pistol from the small of his back and passed it to me. I tucked it away under my blouse. His grimacing face told me his pain was significant, despite his casual attitude. Words weren't needed.

"Anyone in here?" came a loud voice from the shattered doorway.

I turned to see three men dimly through the smoke. The speaker was dressed in the uniform of security. The other two men were dressed in white. One carried a supply case. Both had stethoscopes draped around their necks. The emergency medical team had arrived, accompanied by security.

"Over here!" I called out to them, waving to attract their attention.

They peered through the haze. Spotting me, they hurried over.

"Are you all right?" asked one of the medics, his eyes searching me for injuries.

"I'm fine. I wasn't in here when the explosion happened. He has injuries, though," I said, my hand gesturing at Paul who remained sitting, his head drooping against his knees.

The medic who'd spoken to me knelt beside Paul, his eyes sweeping over him, on the lookout for obvious injuries as he did so. He put his stethoscope earpieces into his ears and placed the diaphragm on Paul's chest while his other hand searched for a pulse at his wrist. He listened, then moved his stethoscope to a different spot, nodding as he did so. Then, he let it drop to his chest. "You are a lucky man to survive that explosion of gas," he said while his hands did a search of Paul's head, neck, body and extremities for fractures. He carefully taped a large trauma bandage to Paul's back to protect it from further damage. Finished, the medic sat back on his haunches, contemplating Paul through the slowly clearing haze.

"Do you know your name, Señor?"

Paul sat silent a moment, and then said, "My name is Walter McKelvy."

"Walter McKelvy," repeated the medic as he wrote the name on his clipboard. "And do you know where you are?"

"Yes. I'm in my room that just got blasted. With a gas explosion, you say?" He lifted his head to make eye contact with the medic.

I saw where Paul was taking this and silently praised him for his quick thinking, which I found extraordinary under the circumstances.

"Yes. We were told that a gas line ruptured, causing the explosion. We will be taking you to the hospital for a more complete examination of your injuries," said the medic. While he spoke, the second medic left to secure a stretcher for the transport.

"What's the hospital's name?" I asked.

"It is called Hospital IMG of Punta Cana. Mister McKelvy will receive excellent care there," the security person added.

"Do you have your cell phone, P-Walt?" I asked. I prayed that neither the medic nor the security guy had picked up on my near slipup. Turned out, they hadn't.

"It's somewhere. When I sensed something was wrong, I leaped over the chairs so there would be something between me and the outer wall," he explained, shedding light on how he'd managed to survive the blast.

I stood and searched the area between the gaping hole and Paul. The clouds of smoke and dust had dissipated, making my search easier. I spotted Paul's laptop. One glance told me it had been trashed beyond repair. His cell phone lay close to it. I picked it up and checked the display. Everything seemed to be working. *Another minor miracle.* I carried it over to Paul, who took it from me, a sly smile on his soot-covered face. "Call me when you know what's going on," I said.

The second medic arrived with a stretcher in tow, and the first medic and security guard went to help.

"Consider that the attacker will learn that you're being taken to the hospital, and could plan an attack on you there, *Mister McKelvy*," I whispered.

Paul nodded at me, understanding the possibilities. "If my ears would only stop ringing, I'd be a lot better off." He shook his head from side to side.

We were interrupted when the two medics wheeled the stretcher alongside Paul. They gently scooped him up and positioned him on his side to protect his rubble-peppered backside, then secured the straps across him.

"Wait a second," I said. "Do you have something to cover his face? He's very shy in public, doesn't want people to stare at him."

"Of course," said the medic in charge as he nodded towards his partner. A white terry towel was produced and Paul's head was surrounded by it. His face was obscured from any curious onlookers.

That done, the medics wheeled the stretcher out into the hallway and raced to the lobby. A large crowd of curiosity seekers had gathered. They stared at the stretcher as it rolled along, a path opening for its passage. I'd grabbed my purse and followed behind them, busy searching the crowd for any suspicious-looking bystanders. I half-expected to see Soldier Bill, aka William Wardak, but he was nowhere to be seen.

An ambulance with its lights flashing sat waiting under the entrance overhang. The two medics opened the rear doors and swiftly loaded the stretcher inside, then hurriedly climbed in behind it. Doors closed and the ambulance driver accelerated away, the siren wailing a warning to drivers ahead of them.

I shook my head at the unnecessary display. I turned and went back into the lobby. A portly woman dressed in a skimpy bathing suit that was mercifully covered with a diaphanous pink shift approached me. "Miss! Miss! Who was that unfortunate man?" she asked in a loud voice.

"His name is Walter McKelvy," I replied in a voice loud enough to be heard over the general din.

"Oh. Never heard of him," she replied, turning away.

You will, I thought, pleased at how my announcement to the crowd had gone. If one of the bad guys had heard me, they'd be redirecting their attention to the hospital, not at suite 6. *And to Paul!* I thought, conscious of his handgun in my waistband. Unarmed, defenseless. What chance did he have? The goons trying to kill Walt probably didn't even know what he looked like. An unpleasant picture formed in my mind. But what could I do?

The first order of business, I decided, was to check on Jim and Tony. Their suite was right next to suite 6 where the blast occurred could have sustained damage as well. Moving slowly, seemingly without purpose so I wouldn't attract attention, I made my way to the hallway and turned back towards the blast area, stopping at suite 8. With all the commotion in the lobby, I had the hallway to myself. I stopped at the door and knocked once.

After a brief pause, a male voice asked, "Who's there?"

"It's EZ, Jim," I replied, recognizing his voice. The door swung open and I stepped inside. Jim closed the door quietly behind me. I was relieved to see that neither man bore any injuries. The blast had spared their room. Tony and Jim stared at me, their faces brimming with questions. I spoke slowly, my voice calm, telling them what had happened, finishing with Paul identifying himself as Walt to the medics. I told them to phone Peter and Kim to explain what had happened. I would go brief Walt.

The smoke and dust had cleared away by the time I stepped back into the hallway. Two teams of housekeepers were already busy waving their magic cloths to make all traces of the calamity disappear. They didn't look up when I passed them. The dangling door to suite 6 would take more than a magic wave. A third team, I guessed, with more sophisticated wands, would address that.

I reached the door to suite 14 and knocked once.

It swung inward and Walt filled the doorway. "What the hell happened?" he asked, anxiety etched into his voice.

"Your room took a direct hit," I said quietly as I stepped inside and shut the door behind me. Bob stood off to the side, taking it all in.

Walt was quick to react. "Sons of bitches are serious," he spat out. "Is Paul okay?" His expression said he hoped so.

"Paul reacted quickly. He got a scattering of flesh wounds from flying debris, and his hearing took a beating. His ears were still ringing when they hauled him off to the hospital," I explained.

"Thank God that's all. If I'd been sitting in there, I doubt if I would've been lucky enough to hit the floor before the blast hit me," said Walt, shaking his head with the thought.

"No doubt we ducked a possible disaster by having you change rooms. Oh, and Paul told the paramedics his name was Walter McKelvy, and it got spread around as they wheeled him out to the meat wagon. If any of the bad guys heard, they'll be planning a visit to the hospital to finish what they started," I said.

Walt's eyes showed his alarm. "What can we do to protect Paul? He'll be a sitting duck if they arrive at the hospital with guns blazing. If he gets killed over this, I don't think I could forgive myself," said Walt, concern written all over his face.

I couldn't, either.

"I have a plan, but it means leaving you and your team without my protection while I'm gone," I told Walt.

"Hell, girl, I've been looking out for myself for a long time. Guess I can do it while you're gone."

I bristled momentarily when Walt called me 'girl,' one of my pet peeves.

Walt saw the glint of anger flash in my eyes. "Hey, what did I say?" he asked, clearly puzzled.

My dad had drilled into me the importance of owning my feelings. *Making light of them never helps,* he said over and over until I got it. I locked eyes with Walt and, in a voice devoid of emotion, told him how I felt about being called 'girl.'

Walt nodded, understanding. "I'll remember that. My bad."

"Apology accepted. Do you have any guns to protect yourself?" I asked, changing the subject back to the business at hand.

"No, but Paul's duffles might have something," he said, gesturing at the two olive drab bags lying in a corner.

"Let's check," I said, stepping quickly to them. I unzipped the nearest bag and plunged a hand inside, probing for weapons. It came out clutching an M4 carbine, a broad smile lighting up my face.

Walt's face brightened, seeing it. "Now there's an old friend," he said as he reached for it.

I handed it off to him. Knowing Paul wouldn't keep magazines for it in the same bag for obvious safety reasons, I turned to the second duffle. I worked the zipper and reached inside, searching for I knew what. I pulled out a thirty-round magazine, fully loaded, and passed it to Walt. By the time I finished my search, I'd taken out a total of four magazines, all full. One hundred and twenty rounds. Walt beamed at me, seeing them.

"Guess that should help to discourage any attacks while I'm gone," I said with a nod towards the armament Walt held.

"I hope the bastards come for me. I'll give them what-for," he said.

Bob winced at Walt's language, but he held his tongue.

"Remember to keep a low profile," I cautioned him. "They don't know you changed suites, so let's keep it that way."

"Point taken, EZ. Now go protect Paul," said Walt with a sweep of his hand at the door.

A picture of Paul, his shirt and shorts bloodied from the 'gas' explosion, came to mind. I returned to Paul's duffles. "I think he'll appreciate a change of clothes. The ones he was wearing are kind of messed up," I told Walt, leaving it at that.

I dug back into the duffles and came up with a clean pale blue polo shirt and dark blue shorts. *Just what the doctor ordered.* I waved the clothes at Walt, picked up my purse, and hurried from the suite with the clothes hiding Paul's Beretta M9 handgun at my waist. It was identical to the one I hid in the small of my back.

I took my time, not wanting to attract undue attention from the scattered lobby loiterers. Nobody paid me any mind as I pushed the entrance door open and stepped outside into the gathering dusk. Two taxis sat waiting for customers. I opened the rear door of the one first in line and climbed in, startling the driver who had been 'resting his eyes.' He turned around in his seat to have a look at me. I saw a broad-faced Dominican male with an unruly mop of black hair and a thin goatee. When he smiled at me, I noticed that his two upper front teeth were absent. "Good evening, Missy. My name is Ramon. Where can I take you?" he asked.

Ramon. Of course it is, I thought. "To Hospital IMG of Punta Cana," I recited from memory.

"Oh my goodness! I trust that you are not ill." It was more a question than a statement.

"I'm fine, thanks. I'm going to visit a friend who is not so fortunate," I said. I guessed he feared I might blow dinner in his tidy cab. The thought had a smile flickering across my face.

"Very well. I will have you there in no time," he said, pulling away from the curb.

Otherwise unoccupied, I considered his statement, one I'd heard many times before. Having me there *in no time* suggested some form of instant time travel, didn't it? Had I finally found someone who could make good on his promise, or was he making a claim he couldn't possibly deliver? I glanced at my watch. When we got to the hospital and the hands on my watch hadn't moved, I'd know he'd delivered on his promise. I realized that the answer was available right away. If *any* time went by, even before we got to the hospital, he'd joined the ranks of the countless hordes who were all bluster.

A second glance at my watch showed that the hands had moved before we cleared the resort drive. I decided to let the driver off the hook. "It's okay, Ramon. You don't have to get me there in no time. I'm not in that much of a rush," I said to the back of his head.

"Oh, okay, Missy. I will obey the speed limits, but I will still get you there in no time," he said, turning slightly in my direction as he spoke.

I decided to let it go. Clearly, Ramon had a different concept of 'in no time' than I did. I turned my thoughts to the hospital and to Paul instead. I wondered how bad his injuries were. Could they be dealt with in the emergency room, or would he need surgery to remove the numerous missiles that had hit him? I glanced through the windshield and knew I'd find out soon enough. I saw the illuminated sign on an impressive two-story building. We were nearing the entrance to Hospital IMG of Punta Cana.

As Ramon turned in the driveway, he announced, "You see, Missy? I have taken you here in no time, no time at all." He beamed at me.

"Well done, Ramon," I said as I opened my purse to pay him.

"Do you want me to wait for you?" he asked.

"That won't be necessary. I don't know how long I'll be in here. How much do I owe you?" I asked.

He told me, I paid him, including an appropriate tip, and climbed out.

As he drove off, I couldn't help thinking about the movie *Back to the Future.* I'd streamed it recently during one of my slower weekends. Ramon's taxi was a far cry from Marty McFly's DeLorean. I pushed the idle thoughts away as I hurried toward the hospital entrance door. As I neared the doors, my eyes searched for cameras that would record my approach. I saw one, off to the side of the entrance, its 'eyes' on the path to the door.

The pistols tucked in my waistband felt huge. I worried that an alert security officer might spot their contours through my shirt. I made every effort to obscure their lines by clutching Paul's change of clothes against my waist. *Would there be a metal detector set up inside?*

With my mind awash with these thoughts, I reached the automatic glass doors, which opened with a soft *whoosh*. Stepping into the air-conditioned reception area I was relieved to see there was no metal detector. I spotted the PATIENT INFORMATION counter and hurried to it.

A middle-aged Dominican woman dressed in white, her greying hair contained in a white cotton cap, looked up from her computer screen as I approached. "Hello, Missy. How may I help you?" she asked, a serious expression on her round face. Since most visitors came to see the injured, sick or dying, I understood the appropriateness of her non-committal facial expression.

"I'm here to see Mister Walter McKelvy. He was brought here a short while ago by ambulance," I said.

The woman tapped her computer keyboard, then looked up at me. "Is McKelvy with or without an 'e' at the end?"

"It's M-C-K-E-L-V-Y," I spelled for her.

"Thank you." She finished typing and examined her screen. "He's not entered into the system yet. He is likely still in the emergency department. I'll call them and see what I can find out."

Nodding at me, the woman picked up her phone and tapped in a three-digit number. In the relative silence of the hospital lobby, I could hear the tinny sound of ringing coming from the phone. It wasn't answered. After a time, the woman replaced the phone in its cradle and said, "When they get busy in there with patients they don't answer the phone. I'll try again in a few moments."

"All right. Thanks," I said. I stepped away from the counter, debating whether to wait there or go to the emergency area, my eyes searching for signs pointing that way. I saw none and concluded that the path there began outside. I knew most emergency departments had their own entrance separate from the main hospital one. I considered the wisdom of going outside to find the emergency department. Doing so meant I could miss the Patient Information lady's successful call.

The decision was made for me when the lady waved me back over. I approached her now-smiling face. "Mister McKelvy is having his injuries treated by the emergency doctor, and he will be kept overnight for observation because of injuries to his head that have caused partial hearing loss to him," she recited.

"Do you know what room he will be going to?" I asked. I felt a surge of relief, learning that Paul wouldn't need surgery.

"Not yet. That is the doctor's decision. As soon as I know, I'll pass it on to you," she said.

"Thanks. I'll go sit over there," I said, pointing at the waiting area.

"I'll send someone to get you as soon as I know," she said, offering me an encouraging smile.

"Thank you." I strolled over to the clusters of chairs and tables that made up the waiting area. A young couple sat together, heads nearly touching, their hands held between them. The young woman silently mouthed the words of her rosary as her fingers moved along the circle of beads. The man stared in silence at the woman's moving lips.

I chose a seat apart from them, not wanting to disturb them, Paul's clothes resting snugly in my lap. As I sat down, the entry doors opened with an air-assisted *whoosh*. My eyes opened wide in surprise as I saw Soldier Bill, better known as William Wardak step inside, his eyes searching, then seeing me. He moved quickly in my direction, a beguiling smile curling the corners of his mouth.

What the hell is he up to, I pondered, seeing him. I watched his approach, my eyes moving over his body in search of bulges that could be weapons. He appeared to be unarmed. He stopped in front of me and said, "I remember Walt calling you Easy. Am I right?"

"Yes. Capital E capital Z," I spelled out. "They're the first initials of my first and middle names."

"That's different," he said.

I was thankful he didn't get into the whole *easy* thing that I'd endured so much in my adolescent years. I had little patience for guys who thought they were being cute asking me just how easy I was. Many bore the scars of their stupidity to this day.

"I'm guessing you came here to see Walt," I said, deflecting his attention from me.

"I did. When I heard what happened at the resort, I came to find out how he's doing."

"He's being treated in the emergency department. It looks like they're going to keep him overnight. Something about a possible concussion and hearing loss from the explosion. They're going to let me know when he gets a room assignment," I said.

"So until then, we wait. By the way, my name's Bill Wardak," he said as he extended his hand to me.

I took it, giving it a strong squeeze. "I'm EZ Kelly, as I think you already know."

"Your handshake reminded me of the strong neck-hold you put on me when I walked towards Walt. Where'd you learn that shit?" he asked, his eyebrows raised with the question.

"Same place you did. Army Special Forces," I said, my eyes holding his.

"You're Special Forces? No wonder you did it so smoothly. I'll have to watch my ass in the future," he said, nodding at me while he tried to work a smile onto his face.

"I'm curious. You said you picked up your Arabic while you wandered around the Stan," I said, using the slang expression for Afghanistan. "But when I spoke to you in Arabic, you used words, expressions far more complicated than you'd have picked up on a casual basis."

"You're sharp, EZ. I'll give you that. Yeah, I knew Arabic before I got separated from my unit and wandered around the Stan for nearly a year. Special Forces taught me."

"Special Forces taught me, too. They also taught me how *not* to get separated from my unit," I said.

"You want the whole story, right? Okay. When I finished my Arabic training, I got approached by the CIA. They wanted me to wander around the Stan and gather information on how the Taliban was moving back and forth from Pakistan. You probably already know that Wardak is an Arabic name, so that helped me," said Bill.

"Yeah. Wardak Province is a tough area in the Stan. There's been a lot of pitched battles between the Taliban and our troops there over the years," I said.

"You know your shit, EZ," said Bill, clearly impressed.

"You pick up a lot of shit after two tours in the Stan," I said.

"Yeah, right. Anyway, as you've no doubt already guessed, my going missing wasn't an accident. When I went out that morning, I had a bag of Afghani clothes, and my beard was already growing. I hid out, and when my unit couldn't find me and headed back to base, I changed clothes and blended into the countryside. One more solo Afghan man wandering the mountains and valleys," said Bill.

"Why'd you do it? You risked life and limb, for what?" I asked.

"A hundred thousand dollars, deposited in an account in my name," said Bill, grinning.

"What would've happened to it if you got yourself killed?"

"It would've gone to my mother."

For the past several moments I had been thinking that Bill Wardak, talkative Bill Wardak, was less of a threat than I originally thought. The money changed my mind. If he was willing to snoop for the CIA in the Stan for a year, and get paid a hundred thousand dollars, how much would someone need to offer him to kill Walt McKelvy? And then, there was the issue of his pretending to put something in Walt's iced tea. I decided to confront him about it.

"So tell me, why'd you move your hand over Walt's glass like you were dropping something into it?" I asked, holding his eyes with mine.

"Ah… I made sure you saw me do that. What, did you get it tested for poison?" he asked, maintaining eye contact.

"Matter-of-fact, I did," I said.

I saw Bill's expression change for a nanosecond, and then he was smiling again. "So, what did you find?"

"Nothing. No poison, anyway. So, answer my question. Why'd you do it?" I pressed.

"Simple, really. I was testing you and your loyalty. If you saw me do that and didn't stop him from drinking it, I'd know you weren't a hundred percent on his side," said Bill.

"What side is that?" I asked, watching his face for a reaction.

"You know. Candidate McKelvy's side," said Bill, his head cocked to the right.

My reply was cut off by the approach of a Dominican man dressed in scrubs. "Excuse me, Missy. I am Doctor Munez. Are you the lady waiting to see Mister McKelvy?" he asked, his eyes meeting mine.

"Yes, I am," I said.

"We have dealt with his injuries and he has been moved to the intensive care unit, room number 22," he informed me.

Bill, sitting off to the side, listened intently.

"Will he be all right?" I asked, concern for Paul uppermost in my thoughts.

"It is a precaution. In addition to his numerous puncture wounds, he received a head injury. We want to make certain there are no developing issues." He didn't elaborate, but I knew some of the possibilities. Intracranial bleeding, with death resulting, came to mind.

"Thanks for taking the time to come tell me, Doctor," I said, the worry clearing from my voice.

"It is my pleasure. Now if you'll excuse me, I will get back to my duties," said Doctor Munez. He headed back the way he had come.

I sat silently a moment. Something Bill had said to me was off, but I couldn't put my finger on it. Not yet. I turned to him. "You heard everything, right?" I asked.

"I did," he said.

"I'm going up to see him by myself. When I'm done, I'll come back and tell you what I've learned, and whether or not he's in the mood to see you. You okay with that?" I watched him closely while I spoke, looking for *what* I didn't know. Not yet, anyway.

"Sure, that's fine with me. I'll stay here and wait for you to come back," said Bill, gesturing to the waiting area for emphasis.

I nodded at him, then got to my feet and moved to the elevators across the way. It was an unmanned 'punch and go' type. I stepped inside and pushed the button for two. I was alone as it rose. I continued to puzzle over what Bill had said that didn't ring true.

The elevator dinged and the door opened on the second floor. I stepped out and spotted the nurses' station for the intensive care unit and strode quickly to the counter.

A nurse saw me and asked, "May I help you?" She wore a neutral expression on her dark, broad face. A classic hospital-issue expression.

"I'm here to see Mister McKelvy," I said, matching the nurse's neutral expression.

"May I have your name?" she asked.

"It's EZ Kelly."

The nurse consulted a clipboard, then smiled. "Your name is on the list of people he has authorized. Because of his condition, I must ask you to limit your visit to ten minutes so he can rest. Okay?"

"Yes, of course," I said.

The nurse led the way to room 22. I followed closely behind her. When she opened the door for me, I saw Paul lying in bed, a monitor beeping regularly by his head. There was a strong smell of antiseptic in the air.

He looked at me, a broad smile twitching the nasal canula in his nostrils. I hurried to his bedside as the nurse let the door close behind me. I leaned down and brushed his lips with mine, careful of the oxygen canula.

"Is that the best you got?" he asked, his smile metamorphosing into a sly grin.

"I didn't want to dislodge your oxygen tube," I said, dropping his fresh clothes on the bedside table.

"I can fix that. Let's try it again," he said as he pulled the canula off his face.

I bent close to him, and he held my face in his hands. The results were much more satisfactory for both of us.

"How's your backside?" I asked after my breathing returned to normal.

"Feels like a swarm of yellow jackets used me as a target. The doc said he took out all the deep pieces, and the shallow stuff will work out over time. I remember an old vet on my team saying he still had pieces surfacing after two, three years. Something to look forward to," said Paul with a grim smile.

"I'm just grateful you're still with us." I took his hands in mine.

"Yeah. Dodged a big one, no question."

"I hate to change the subject, but my visit's limited to ten minutes, doctor's orders, and there's lots to tell," I said, struggling to regain control of my emotions.

"I'm all ears," said Paul, offering a squeeze to my hands.

I recounted the events following the explosion and what happened after. I finished by explaining that Soldier Bill was downstairs, waiting to see Walt McKelvy. I told Paul what Bill had said about working for the CIA, that the whole MIA, missing in action thing was staged so he could cut loose and get data on Taliban movement between Pakistan and Afghanistan. As I spoke, it came to me what I'd found odd in Bill's comment. "Paul, did you ever hear Walt or anyone on his team tell Bill he was considering running for president?"

Paul thought a moment. "Nope. It was all small talk about Afghanistan and Bill's going missing. Why?"

"Downstairs, Bill spoke of being on 'candidate McKelvy's side,' I believe were his words. If Walt and his team didn't speak of it, how'd he know?" I asked.

"We have to assume he's on the 'kill Walt Mckelvy' bandwagon until he proves otherwise," said Paul.

"I agree." I reached behind my back and withdrew the M9 Beretta. I handed it to Paul and moved the second pistol to the vacant place behind my back.

"How thoughtful of you," he said, taking it. He withdrew the slide far enough to confirm a round was in the chamber, then let it close again. He tucked it under the bedcovers, within easy reach.

"Bill is likely to come up for a visit when I go down and report your status to him, so you may need that," I said.

"He's not on my authorized list of visitors," said Paul.

"If he wants to see you, kill you, a little detail like that won't stop him."

"If he manages to get in my room, the surprise of finding me, not Walt, should stop him in his tracks long enough for me to neutralize him," Paul said, his right hand patting the covers over the pistol that lay beneath.

"Let's hope you're right. I want to spend a lot of time with you when this situation is all behind us. One close call is more than enough." My hand caressed his cheek.

Paul reached for me but was interrupted by the door swinging open. His hand dove under the covers, but stopped, seeing the nurse.

"I'm sorry to interrupt, but ten minutes has passed. The doctor is very strict about it. I must ask you to complete your visit, Miss Kelly," she said, her smile blunting the abruptness of her arrival.

"It's okay. We were just finishing." I spotted a telephone on the bedside table and looked at the dial, committing the number to memory.

The nurse, watching, said, "Oh, you should feel free to call Mister McKelvy at any time. If he wants to talk, he can pick up his phone."

"I'll do that," I said. Then I looked at Paul, "You take care. I'll call you with any news, okay?"

"Perfect. Thanks for coming in to see me," he said.

I followed the nurse out of Paul's room and took the elevator down to the first floor. When the door opened on the reception area, I saw Bill sitting where I'd left him. I hurried over to him.

"How is he?" were the first words out of his mouth.

I described Paul's injuries, following with the news that Bill wasn't on his visitors' list and the nurses wouldn't allow him in to see him.

"Oh, shit. I never thought of that," said Bill as he slowly shook his head from side to side. "You want to share a cab back to the resort?"

"Works for me," I said. *Allows me to keep track of you.*

As we walked side by side to the entrance door, I caught a glimpse of Bill's hand moving towards the small of my back and rotated my body away before he could make contact. He dropped his hand to his side as I twisted away. *Nice try, crumb bum,* I thought as we left the air conditioning for the humid night air. A short line of cabs stood waiting at the roadway.

Bill waved his arm and the first cab in line peeled off and took the circular drive to the hospital entrance, stopping by us. When Bill opened the cab's rear door, expecting me to climb inside, I stepped around to the opposite side and got in. I figured I'd dodged another attempt by him to check me for a weapon. He climbed in on his side and we faced each other, both acting as if my actions were no big deal.

"Good evening, lovely couple. Where can I take you?" asked the driver, smiling back at us by way of the rearview mirror.

I sat, silent, letting Bill get the impression that he was in charge. "To the El Mar Placida," he said after a slight pause.

"Ah, a beautiful new resort. Sit back and relax. I will have you there in no time," he said as he flipped the flag that started the meter.

I wondered if all cab drivers here in the Dominican Republic spoke that way. I didn't bother checking my watch. I knew full well that time was passing and the cab hadn't even started moving.

Bill broke the silence first. "So tell me, how is he, really?" He rested his arm casually on the seatback between us.

"Considering the damage the gas explosion caused to the room, he got away with minor injuries. He had pieces of flying debris embedded in him, but none penetrated very far. The big concern is for his head injuries, as the doctor told us," I said, turning sideways to face Bill.

"I'd say he's one lucky guy. Could've been a whole lot worse," said Bill.

"Yeah. He could've ended up dead," I said, watching his face for any reaction to my bluntness. I saw none, leaving me unsure as to his true intentions. Recalling he worked for the CIA when he went missing in Afghanistan, I figured he'd likely mastered the art of hiding his reactions from those around him.

"That would've been awful. The guy's barely started to enjoy civilian life after a great military career," said Bill. He shook his head from side to side for emphasis.

"You're right there," I said. "Let's hope he's out of the hospital tomorrow after an uneventful overnight stay."

The cab slowed, and I looked out the side window to see we were turning under the portico of El Mar Placida. "And here we are, lovely couple. Am I not right? We are here in no time," said the upbeat driver.

I bit my tongue and agreed. I wondered what his reaction would be if I said, "Since you got us here in no time, there's no charge, right?" I felt the smile working my mouth as I pictured his expression if I'd actually spoken the words.

"I'll get this," said Bill, bringing my thoughts back to the here and now. He took out his wallet as he checked the meter.

"Thanks," I said with a glance his way. I opened my door and stepped out. The fare paid, Bill emerged on the opposite side. He looked over the cab's roof at me, and smiling, asked me if I wanted to join him for a nightcap.

I glanced at my watch, saw it was nearly ten. I looked back at him, formed a non-committal smile on my face before I said, "Thanks for the invite, Bill, but I think I'll pass tonight. It's been a long day and I wouldn't be very good company."

"Okay, I get it. Have a good night. I'll see you tomorrow," he said as he stepped back from the cab.

"Thanks for understanding." I circled the cab and joined him.

We walked together to the lobby entrance. Bill held the door open for me and I stepped inside. Bill remained outside. "Aren't you coming in?" I asked him, a puzzled look playing across my face.

"Not right away. I'm going to go for a walk, clear my mind," he said, smiling.

"I guess old habits die hard. You did a lot of walking back in Afghanistan," I chided.

"You got me there," said Bill, the smile still draped over his mouth.

"Enjoy your walk. See you tomorrow." I tossed him a wave before I turned towards the reception desk.

What are you up to, Soldier Bill? I walked to a lobby chair that afforded an unobstructed view through the entrance doors and out to the cab line and sat down. I scrunched down to make it harder to see me from the outside, and waited, my eyes on the cab first in line.

I counted off ten minutes in my mind and was about to abandon the wait and head for my suite when I saw movement in the relative gloom. A male figure approached the first cab from the opposite side and opened the rear door. As he ducked to get in, the spotlight from the entry portal illuminated his face.

Got you, Soldier Bill!

I watched the cab pull away into the night. I got out of the chair and hurried to my suite.

I paused at the door, listening. Hearing nothing, I used my wristband to unlock the door, and crouching, holding my handgun ready in front of me, I stepped inside. I groped the wall for the light switch and flipped it on. The room was instantly bathed in bright light. Nothing. No one. I moved cautiously through the suite, checking the other rooms, and finished with a sweep of the outer courtyard. Everything was as I'd left it. No visitors. *Good.*

I went back inside, closing the door behind me, and used the phone to call the hospital. After a brief delay, I got through to 'Walter McKelvy'. Paul answered on the second ring. I told him about Bill getting into a cab and driving off.

"Be prepared for a surprise visit," I said.

"The nurses won't let me sleep anyway," he said. "They tell me that sleep may mean I've got swelling in my brain, so the response is to keep me awake. That tells them that I don't have swelling. Go figure."

"What'll you do if Soldier Bill shows up? A dead body in your room will take some serious explaining," I said.

"I'll kill him only if there's no other way. I'd really like to ask him a few questions, find out who's behind all this," said Paul.

"You want me to come back, give you a hand?"

"No. You stay there and look out for the main man. I've got this covered. Forewarned is forearmed. I'll be ready for Soldier Bill."

"Stay safe, my love."

"You, too, my love. I'll call you with news."

"You better."

* * *

My phone trilled, breaking the silence in my room. I had barely finished my exercise routine and my brow was still moist with perspiration, my breathing still elevated. The phone I.D. said it was Paul. Nearly two hours had passed since I last spoke with him. Two hours with Soldier Bill to deal with.

"Hey, Paul. Everything okay?" I asked, my voice sounding shaky even to me. I knew the exercises I'd just finished weren't to blame.

"Everything's A-O-K," he said.

I felt the pent-up tension in me drain away. "Tell me what happened," I urged.

"Sure. So, after we spoke, I got out of bed and arranged pillows to look like I was lying there, snug as a bug, as they say, and I moved over to the door, pistol in hand. I figured if Soldier Bill came in, I'd be behind him out of sight and he'd think it was me, or rather General McKelvy, lying there in the bed. If anyone other than Bill caught me standing there, they'd have had a good laugh at the sight of me. There I stood in my gaping blue cotton johnny with a pistol in my hand, hunched over a little from the leftover pain caused by the flying debris."

A low chuckle escaped me, picturing the scene he'd painted.

"It was a funny scene. Anyway, as I stood there listening for sounds of Bill approaching my room, I realized I could hear better. Sounds from down the hall by the nursing station were reaching me. I couldn't necessarily understand what was said, but hearing the voices told me my hearing was slowly coming back."

"Thank God for that," I breathed.

"You know it. It seemed like I'd been standing there forever. When I checked my watch, I saw it was a quarter to eleven. Visiting hours were long over and I figured the nurses were likely busy putting their notes in charts and checking for any new medical orders. If it was like any other hospital in the world, the nurses' shift change would be at eleven. The new nurses would arrive, the departing nurses would give them a review of each patient on the unit, any questions would be answered, and the departing nurses would exit stage left. That would be at around eleven-fifteen, give or take a few minutes either side."

"So you figured you had a half hour to catch Bill as he came to pay you a visit, right?"

"You got it. About then, I heard a male voice coming toward my room from the vicinity of the nurses' station. I couldn't hear exactly what he said, but a nurse answered him. Then silence took over. I recognized the man's voice. It was Bill. No doubt about it. I tensed, waiting, not knowing what to expect. I heard light footsteps approaching my door, then pausing there. I moved my arms about, loosening them up, getting ready. I figured it was nearing showtime.

"The door opened slowly, revealing Bill's head in the gap. His entire focus was directed to the bed and its human-shaped mound. He wore a white doctor's coat, which clearly fooled the nurses. He had nothing in either hand. I wondered for a second if I'd made a mistake about his intentions, but in the next instant he removed any doubt I may have had. He stepped into the room and moved swiftly to the bedside while he drew an ugly-looking dagger from a sheath hidden under his white coat. I stepped behind him, moving silently on bare feet, staying in Bill's blind spot as he advanced to the bed."

"That inescapable moment of truth," I whispered into the phone.

"You've been there. When he raised his arm to deliver a fatal knife blow to the pillows, I cocked my arm and struck the back of his head with the point of my elbow. The force of the blow drove Soldier Bill forward and across the bed. He collapsed across the pillows without a sound, and I plucked the dagger from his limp right hand. Then I shoved my pistol under the mattress, well out of sight.

"Though stunned by the blow, Soldier Bill wasn't unconscious. He began moving his head from side to side in obvious confusion. I dashed to the opposite side of the bed, pressed his head into the pillows with my left hand and put the point of his dagger against his right eyelid. Bill flinched, feeling the prick of the blade. He stared up at me, clearly confused. He'd expected to find General McKelvy, not me. That took him a moment to digest."

"Added to his confusion and your advantage."

"It did. I whispered to him that I had some questions for him, and I told him that if he answered satisfactorily, he'd get to keep his right eye. I asked him if he understood, increasing the pressure of the knife point for emphasis, and he whispered a weak but clear yes. When I saw that I'd drawn a pinprick of blood from his eyelid I backed off the pressure a hair.

"Seeing I had his full attention, I told him that I'd cut out his right eye if I thought for a moment he was lying to me, and then I'd go to work on his left one. The expression of abject terror on his face told me that he believed me. I asked him who set him up to kill General McKelvy, and he said he didn't know, he never got a name. His voice was overflowing with panic. I think he figured he was close to losing his right eye. I asked him how come he didn't know who was ordering the kill, and he said he got a text message telling him that if he killed McKelvy he'd be paid a hundred thousand dollars, same as he got paid for spying on the Taliban in Afghanistan."

"That's a convenient amount," I said.

"Isn't it? It gets even weirder. I asked him what proof he had that he'd get paid, and they texted back and told him to check his bank account. When he did so, there was a hundred thousand extra bucks in there, and then moments later it was gone. They told him the money would be back for good when McKelvy was dead. He said whoever they are, they have the power to access and manipulate his bank account any time they want to. In other words, he believed them."

"We're up against some powerful people in high places," I said.

"There's more. I followed up by asking how many other people were competing with him, and he said there were two others out to kill McKelvy and collect the hundred grand. They told Bill that they'd know which one of them was responsible for McKelvy's death, and that man, and that man alone, would get the money.

"My curiosity prompted the next question. How did he know that General McKelvy would be here in the Dominican Republic? He floored me when he said they gave him all the information, from the name of the resort, right down to McKelvy's room number."

"That makes it even more important that we have Walt play musical suites. Keep the bad guys guessing as to his whereabouts," I said.

"Yeah, our job is simple. Keep them guessing until Walt makes his decision to run or not. That works for me," said Paul.

"What happened next with Soldier Bill?" I prompted, getting Paul back on track.

"I surprised him by asking him how he got his little explosive device into General McKelvy's courtyard. He acted dumb a moment, but the pressure of the dagger on his eye caused him to reconsider. He told me that when he found out the minicams he planted in the hallway had been taken out, he figured you had cams of your own, maybe planted them in the hallway, maybe even set them up to watch the canal. To avoid being picked up on a camera, he swam underwater to McKelvy's suite, surfaced and lobbed the C-4 into the courtyard, then submerged again before he hit the detonator switch. He said he felt the explosion through the water, but it all happened well above him, didn't harm him."

"Clever. It almost worked," I said, thinking back on how close Paul had come to dying in Walt's place.

Paul seemed to sense the subtle shift in my voice. "*Almost* doesn't get you the brass ring, though."

"No. You're right. It doesn't," I said, feeling relief as I spoke.

"So, I figured I'd gotten all I could from Bill. I told him if he spoke to anyone about our conversation, or made another attempt on McKelvy's life, that he could start looking over his shoulder for me because I'd hunt him down and kill him and he'd never know where or when it would happen. He got the point loud and clear. He said he hoped I believed him. I countered by saying I hoped he believed *me*. He said he did.

"I changed the subject by asking Bill why he was wearing a white doctor's coat, and he explained he'd found it in the staff locker room and put it on so he could con the nurses into letting him into my room. He said he told the nurses he was a neurologist and my doctor had asked him to check me out. Clever. Might have worked, if it hadn't been for your warning, EZ."

"Tell me this long story has a happy ending, Paul." I drew in a long breath and blew it out.

"I'm happy to report, it does. I took the dagger point away from Bill's eye and let go of my grip on his head, and he stood up, still shaky. The clock on the hospital room wall told me it was eleven-fifteen. I told Bill that a nurse would be showing up any moment, and it was time for him to act like a neurologist. I rearranged the pillows and slipped back into bed, the dagger held in my right hand in case Bill changed his mind and tried to attack me. He took his cue and straightened his white coat, then stared at me with vacant eyes. The door swung open and a nurse appeared. She saw Soldier Bill in his white coat and apologized for interrupting, said she'd come back when he finished. Bill turned to her and said he'd finished his exam and told her to stay and carry out her duties. As he turned to go, I whispered that I hoped he'd remember what I said. He said he'd never forget. He left the side of my bed and stepped out of the room.

"When the door closed behind him, the nurse clucked over the disconnected monitor leads and busied herself with reattaching them to my chest. I don't think she bought my explanation that the doctor removed them to do his tests. Anyway, she checked my vitals and scribbled the results in the chart at the end of my bed, said it looked like I was coming along just fine and then she was gone. That's when I called you," said Paul.

"The bottom line is, we still don't know who's behind this whole thing. If Bill's telling the truth about how many are trying to kill McKelvy, we're down to one unknown if we count the guy I dropped into the canal."

"Yeah, and he could be anyone and anywhere. Is everyone tucked safely in their beds back there?" asked Paul.

"All's quiet here. Walt and Bob are settled into your room, Walt has your M4 locked and loaded at his side, and the other four are in their suites next to Walt's destroyed one. I'm guessing they'll be sleep-deprived, come morning. Jim and Tony are getting the worst of it since they're right next door to Walt's wrecked room. There's a work crew scrambling to make all the damage go away, and they're making a sleep-wrecking racket doing it," I said.

"Good one, EZ," said Paul.

I reminded him of what the nurses had told him, that they wouldn't be letting him get any sleep, that drowsiness could be a sign of a bleed in his brain.

I knew I'd made my point when he said, "Get some sleep, EZ. One of us should be alert tomorrow."

"That's first on my list of projects," I said, feigning a yawn.

"Sweet dreams, my love," whispered Paul.

I heard the click as he set his phone in its cradle.

You, too, my love.

Chapter Four

Thursday, January 26th

My phone's shout-out brought me back, sending whatever dream I was having into a million unrecognizable shards. I glanced at the bedside clock. Six-fifteen. I'd overslept by fifteen minutes. I made a mental note to set the alarm next time while I grappled for my phone, my eyes still fighting me. I grasped it and brought it to my ear. "Hello?" I said. I knew I'd failed miserably at keeping the sleep from my voice.

"Morning, EZ. You up and at 'em?" It was Walt with his ever-cheerful voice.

"That's me. Up and at 'em EZ," I said, while swinging my legs over the side of the bed and shaking off the cobwebs in my head.

"Good. Let's do breakfast."

Nothing fazes Walt. "Sure. Oceania or La Placida?" I asked. La Placida was buffet, all you can eat style, go back as often as you like. Oceania, I remembered, was menu-driven.

"Hey, why don't we try La Placida? A little variety can't hurt, right?" said Walt.

I considered saying I'd had enough variety in the last two days to put some serious hurt on me, but I held my tongue. "Is the rest of your team up and running?" I asked, hoping for a little extra time to put on my morning face.

"Yeah, well, they didn't get much sleep. Turns out, maintenance thumped and banged all night, trying to make my room look like nothing ever happened to it," said Walt. I heard the amusement in his voice.

"Ouch! They should get a refund. Come to think of it, you should, too. They think it's you in the hospital, but Bob's homeless, too," I said.

"Suggest that to them when you see them. Fifteen minutes work for you?"

"Sure, no problem," I said, thinking about the hurry that put me in.

"Knock once, and then we'll go collect the sleep-deprived team," said Walt.

"Got it," I said, then disconnected before I bolted from bed and padded to the bathroom.

* * *

I rapped once on McKelvy's door with a minute to spare. I mentally thanked the army for teaching me all about scrambling and double-time. Walt swung open the door and offered up a smile. Bob joined us in the hallway, and we made our way together to pick up the other four team members. On the way, I gave Walt a shortened version of Soldier Bill's visit to the hospital and how it had ended.

"I'll never understand how some people will do anything for money," he commented.

"Yeah. A hundred grand for another man's life. We both know there's assassins out there who are willing to kill for a lot less than that," I said.

"True. Despite Bill's promise, I still don't trust him. He could still try to kill me."

"I agree. We'll be watching his every move," I said, holding Walt's eyes with mine for a moment as I tried to reassure him.

We collected Jim and Tony from suite 8 and Peter and Kim from suite 10. Their lack of sleep showed in their haggard faces and their slow, shuffling gaits. Four monosyllabic greetings and dull expressions further gave them away. It bore a strong similarity to taking a stroll with four cast members from *The Walking Dead*.

As we made our way to the buffet breakfast at La Placida, we passed a young couple dressed in shorts and tees hustling to the health club. Other than them, we had the place to ourselves. Made sense. Vacationers like to sleep in. Despite what appeared to be a world of peace and contentment, I maintained my acute level of awareness, the M9 tucked comfortingly behind my back, ready in case the atmosphere around us changed quickly.

We made it to La Placida without a hitch. Silence dominated our sleep-deprived stragglers while Walt and I spoke with enthusiasm of his approaching decision. There were ten other breakfast clubbers munching away when we got there, in a room that could accommodate well over a hundred. None of them paid us any mind. Their attention was directed at the heaping plates in front of them. I turned my attention to the source. The buffet line offered pre-made choices like bacon or sausage, pancakes, waffles, French toast, scrambled eggs, muffins, bagels, biscuits, and every topping anyone could ever hope for.

A second line formed at a specialty egg-cooking station. Two chefs dressed in white and wearing their unique head toppers were surrounded by eggs as they waited for breakfasters to make their requests, which I saw ran from simple fried eggs to complex omelets.

A waiter, his name tag said RAMON, showed us to a table for seven and took our beverage orders. This morning, not surprisingly, coffee was the unanimous winner. Jim, Tony, Paul and Kim sat quietly waiting for their caffeine fixes while Walt, Bob and I headed for the buffet line.

Walt and Bob took bacon and sausage plus bagels and an English muffin while I scooped up a lemon poppy seed muffin. Then it was off to the egg station where Bob and Walt ordered well-dressed omelets and I got two eggs over easy. Ordering them always tickled me. I couldn't help smiling at the image it brought to my mind: me standing there with two eggs draped over me. It was something Paul had brought up years ago and still made me laugh.

Seeing my smile, Walt asked me what was so funny. I told him. He grinned at me, catching it at once. A sharp mind, no question.

Armed with our egg choices, we returned to our table. The Sleepless Four didn't appear any better after their caffeine infusions. Walt suggested food might help, and they dragged themselves to their feet and shuffled off to the buffet line while we started on our choices before they cooled off. Silence ensued. I ate and scanned, then scanned and ate. Nobody paid us the least bit of their attention. I finished my eggs and dipped muffin chunks into the remnants while Walt and Bob did justice to their own breakfast platters with boyish enthusiasm.

After Ramon refilled our coffee cups, we sat back and enjoyed the after-glow of our breakfasts. Walt was first to break the silence.

"You want to tell her, Bob, or should I?" he said with a glance in Bob's way.

"You tell her, Walt. It's your party," said Bob, a sunny smile taking charge of his face.

"How can you not like this guy," said Walt as he reached out and draped an arm on Bob's shoulder. "He hates to take credit for anything."

As he spoke, the Sleepless Four ambled back to the table, their heaping plates held in front of them.

"Hey, guys!" said Walt. "Grab your chairs. We got news," he said with a grin big enough for all of us. They set down their plates and turned their faces towards Walt and Bob.

Seeing that he had everyone's attention, Walt broke the news. "Bob got a hit on one of the letters he sent out. A big donor from Texas agreed to spon-sor my campaign to the tune of: drum roll, please! A hundred grand," said Walt, his face unable to contain his excitement.

I watched the other faces as he gave the news. Everyone looked pleased. I know I was.

"Bob made it clear to me that it's only a start, and we need much more than that to make a difference in the race. But hell, it's one fine start if you ask me. Let's give Bob a round of applause for his fine work."

Everyone at the table joined Walt in clapping their hands for Bob's accomplishment, with several "Way to go, Bob" comments offered up. The applause drew a few curious stares from the scattered diners, but I watched as they turned their attention back to their plates in short order, the fuss of no concern to them.

"What's your goal?" I asked Bob when silence returned to our table.

"I'd like to get commitments totaling a million before Walt tosses his hat in the ring. The cost of running a decent presidential campaign is crazy high, and a million will get us off to a good start. Then, it'll be up to the other donors who like what they see in Walt and send him their contributions. Ten dollars times a half a million supporters adds up to five million bucks," he said with emphasis.

"So, you're a tenth of the way there," I said, summarizing. "How many more letters have you sent out, Bob?"

"If I remember correctly, there are just under a thousand I'm waiting to hear from," he said with a nod of his round head.

"And all you need is nine more at a hundred thou each? How can you miss?" I asked.

"True. Nine more, or eighteen more at fifty thou each, or even thirty-six more at twenty-five thou each. I'll take it anyway it comes in. Raising money is a curious business. The more commitments we get, the more likely it is for the more cautious donors to jump on the bandwagon," he said, a cocky smile spreading across his florid face.

"I like your positive attitude," I said.

"Hell, I like this job. If I don't reach my goal, I'll send out another thousand commitment letters, keep on sending them until we get what we need," he said emphatically.

I turned to Walt. "No doubt about it, Walt. You've got yourself one fine fund-raising treasurer," I said.

"Yeah, I think I'll stick with him. He seems to know what he's doing," said Walt, smiling broadly.

"Thanks for the vote of confidence, Walt. I appreciate it," said Bob.

I watched as the two men made solid eye contact.

Walt, seeing that everyone had finished eating, said, "Let's get this dog and pony show back to my—" then seemed to remember his suite was in disarray, "correct that, Pete and Kim's suite." The sound of friendly chuckles ran through the revitalized group as we stood and made our way to the restaurant entrance, my attention once again focused on the group, and specifically Walt's safety.

Once we were all outside, I became aware of a much larger flood of guests making their way to La Placida. An hour later made a difference in the number of guests out and about. I positioned myself slightly ahead and to the side of Walt, prepared to step in front of him and take a bullet, or maybe fire a bullet of my own. That's what the Secret Service was trained to do, and what I was getting the big bucks to do. It felt a lot like being point man for my team in Afghanistan. Back then, nothing stood between me and a potential ambush or sniper fire than the training I'd gone through, plus my own wits. I figured a lot of it had to do with having a strong desire to return to base unscathed. For me, luck had nothing to do with it.

We made it to the suite without incident. I had a sense Bob and the four other advisors took their safety for granted, that what we did together was a walk in the park. They never showed any signs of concern for their safety. Walt was just the opposite. I sensed his focus on a possible attack kept him wired, alert, and his attention devoted to identifying the problem and getting past it. He portrayed a military mind in action.

Pete and Kim's suite mirrored mine. Seeing its eerie similarity, I guessed every other suite mirrored the one next to it. Pete and Kim rushed about, picking up articles of clothing scattered about the living area and tossing them into their shared bedroom while they mumbled apologies for their sloppiness.

"Hey, don't sweat it," said Walt, doing his part to put them at ease.

I grabbed a chair from the bedroom and added it to the four already in the living area. Then, I excused myself and went out onto the outer courtyard, my right hand resting behind my back on my M9, ready to respond to any trouble.

Having the choice of four suites to hold the team's planning sessions eased my mind a notch. Anyone looking to end Walt's political career before it got started would be hard-pressed to figure out where he was at any given time. His analogy of a terrorist chieftain moving from safe house to safe house to avoid detection fit the scenario perfectly. Still, I knew one slip could mean the difference between a campaign and a funeral service. I hoped the bad guys weren't endowed with drones. That could level the playing field in a jiffy, and I was a big part of the playing field. Not a nice thought.

It took me no time to see the outer courtyard was clear. Thinking that, I recalled the taxi driver's promise. He'd put a crazy notion into my head.

As I searched the patio, I could see no signs that Kim or Pete had ever ventured out there. Everything was undisturbed, waiting for their first foray outside. The plunge pool was immaculate. The neat stack of towels was untouched. I eased open the door to the canal and cautiously stuck my head out. The waterway was clear of swimmers in both directions. I wondered whether queasy guests were still opting out of a swim because of the body found floating in it a little over twenty-four hours ago. Management's guarantee that all the water was run through filters every hour, thus removing any traces left behind by the drowned man, may not have been enough to persuade squeamish guests who now chose to use the ocean instead. A soft chuckle welled up inside me as I thought of all the nasty stuff nature, including mankind, deposited in the sea on a regular basis.

My inspection complete, I closed the canal door and turned to face the enclosed courtyard. Knowing Walt and his team were busy with their planning, I dropped into one of the padded chairs to rest. I closed my eyes and cranked my ears to full-listen mode. I heard a lone bird chirping somewhere off in the distance, but that was it. No human sounds reached me. The canal was silent. I didn't like it. Too quiet. I remembered silences before ambushes in Afghanistan. One moment all was quiet, and the next moment all hell was breaking loose.

I reminded myself this wasn't Afghanistan, but the worry wouldn't go away. I strained to hear something other than the bird, but it might as well have been the last bird on Earth for all the response it got for its efforts. It kept right on pumping out chirps, unfazed by the silence around it. It could've been a poster bird for a lesson in determination.

The trilling of my phone pulled me back. Caller I.D. showed it was Paul. "This is EZ," I said, getting up.

"Good. I didn't call the wrong number." Paul sounded bright-eyed and bushytailed despite his night of forced sleep deprivation.

"Hey, what's the news?" I asked him, happy to hear his cheery voice.

"My doctor, not the imitation Doctor Bill but the genuine article, stopped by my room and waved his stethoscope at me. After he finished, he declared I was ready for discharge. No signs of brain hemorrhages or concussion, so no need to keep me here any longer. He's writing up my discharge summary and getting me antibiotics to keep the holes in me from getting infected. Then, I can be on my way."

"That's great, Paul. Want me to come and help you with your first few steps, share a cab ride back?"

"Much as I'd like to see you, it makes more sense for you to stay put and protect the future president of the United States. Where are you?"

I told him that Walt and his team were hard at work in suite 10, AKA Pete and Kim's suite, and I was standing guard in the suite's outer courtyard.

"Stay right where you are. I should make it back within the hour," said Paul.

"I'm not going anywhere. By the way, Paul, keep in mind there may be someone out there who doesn't know what Walt McKelvy looks like, but has heard he got shipped to the hospital."

"I get it. Maybe I'll get the opportunity to use the M9 you dropped off for me," said Paul.

"If I were you, I'd try like hell not to create a ruckus. The Dominican police may not appreciate an interruption in their tranquil island life," I said.

"Only as a last resort. See you soon, EZ." He disconnected.

I sat for a moment listening for sounds around me. I heard nothing but the steady chirp from the lonely bird. It wasn't a quitter, that was clear. No other sounds reached me.

Reassured, I used my passkey to open the door and go back inside. Though I did my best to be quiet, unobtrusive, Walt looked up as I eased the door closed, a quizzical expression on his rugged face.

I stepped to his side. "I just heard from Paul. He's going to be discharged this morning. His head passed all the tests, and his puncture wounds have been treated. He's on an antibiotic in case of infection, but he refused pain meds," I told him, noting the other five men were listening in.

"Hey, that's great news," said Walt with enthusiasm.

"It looks like he dodged a bullet," said Bob.

"Whoa, Bob! You're starting to sound like EZ and me. 'Dodged a bullet', huh?" said Walt.

Bob's face flushed red. Walt's other four advisors grinned broadly at Bob, triggering a deeper shade of red in his cheeks. "Hey, I'm glad he's going to be all right, is what I meant," clarified Bob.

I jumped in to rescue him. "Your heart's in the right place. I share your sentiment," I said to Bob.

"Hell's bells, we *all* do," said Walt while he rested his hand on Bob's shoulder as a signal the kidding was over. Smiles disappeared and the team got back to business.

* * *

When I heard the single knock on the hallway door, I guessed it had to be Paul. Despite my certainty, I approached with my M9 ready in my hand on the off chance it turned out I was wrong.

I wasn't. Paul identified himself, then stepped inside and I closed the door.

Walt was first to speak. "Hey, Mister McKelvy, welcome back. You done good," he said, grinning broadly.

I watched Bob's expression cloud over with Walt's use of poor grammar, then clear once more. I thought maybe he was starting to get used to Walt's vocabulary.

"It's good to be back, out of that hospital where I wasn't allowed to close my eyes," said Paul.

"Why not?" asked Kim, a puzzled expression on his narrow face.

"They said that one of the signs of serious head injury was sleepiness, with increasing difficulty waking up. Every time I drifted off, a nurse rushed in and shook me back awake. After the third time, I lay there and forced myself to stay awake," explained Paul.

"You should take a nap," said Walt. "You won't be much good to us if you can't stay awake."

"Oh, I can stay awake. I've been in some situations where sleep meant death. Don't worry about me, but thanks for the offer," said Paul.

"You change your mind, just let me know. Let EZ know, too, come to think of it," said Walt with a smile directed my way.

"Will do," said Paul.

The team went back to their work, and Paul and I huddled in a corner away from them. I filled him in on the first big donation to Walt's war chest and Bob's hopes of more to come.

"Hey, that's great! Now all we need to do is keep him safe until the donations flood in," said Paul in a whisper.

"From your, ah, discussion with Soldier Bill, it looks like we need to worry about one other threat. The guy who floated down the canal is one, and Soldier Bill is two, though I still think Bill could make another try despite the warnings you gave him," I said in hushed tones.

"I agree. Though I think Soldier Bill is smarter than the average assassin, I don't think he's all that bright. The prospect of a hundred grand could seriously cloud his judgment."

"So, who's the mysterious number three and when will he come at Walt?" I asked.

"If I knew, we could end this," said Paul.

We sat in silence a moment, each of us thinking about what we needed to do to keep the next president of the United States safe until the Secret Service stepped in and took our jobs away. Paul was first to break the silence.

"What do we know about Walt's team?" he asked with a sweep of his hand in their direction.

"That's a really good question. I knew I included you for a reason."

He ignored my subtle compliment. "Let's run through them one by one and see what we come up with. You know the most about them, so you start," he suggested.

I realized I knew damned little about them and had assumed Walt had vetted the men to his satisfaction. Maybe he had, but Paul's exercise couldn't hurt. I glanced over at the team, hard at work and ignoring us, to refresh my memory.

"Okay, first one on the list is Bob Hixon, the man Walt picked to be his treasurer and fundraiser. Everything I've seen of him suggests a hard-working but out of shape accountant type. I'd put him low on the list of threats to Walt, but of course you never know. Looks can be deceiving."

Paul shrugged, a non-committal confirmation of my assessment.

"The next team member is Jim Bennett, Walt's pollster. I'm guessing his real work begins once Walt declares his candidacy, so right now he sits and listens. He's tall and lean, so he's more likely to be a threat, but he's no youngster. I'd guess he's in his sixties."

"Who's next?" Paul asked.

"Tony Marino. He's in charge of scheduling, so his real work lies ahead of him. He's big, but my sense is he's also out of shape. I'd guess him to be in his forties, so he's of an age where he could pose a threat if he chose to do so."

I glanced at the group, then back at Paul. "There's Peter Spaulding, in charge of all things to do with the media. Just looking at him says he's unlikely to be an assailant. His short, stocky build and full, round face suggests a man unaccustomed to exercise, so I'd rank him low for an assailant, too."

"And last on the list is Kim Boucher, the man in charge of publicity. I'm sure he's had some work to do, but it won't come into play until Walt throws his hat in the ring. He's my height, has a wiry frame, and I'm guessing he's in his fifties. He could end up being a threat."

"Listening to your summary, I didn't hear you rule out any of them completely. I'd say our next step is to get Walt alone and ask him if he has any suspicions about any of them," said Paul.

"Agreed." I was secretly glad Paul had brought up the dedication of Walt's team. It was an oversight on my part. How could I have overlooked the possibility of betrayal coming from within?

* * *

A little over an hour later Walt called for a break. "Coffee all around?" he asked everyone.

"I'll have tea," said Jim, looking apologetic.

"No problem, Jim," said Walt, with a cheerful wave in his direction. He picked up the phone and called room service to order the drinks, plus a dozen pastries.

While a line formed outside the bathroom, I approached Walt and asked him for a moment alone.

"Sure. Where?"

"Let's step outside to the patio," I suggested.

"Lead the way, EZ," he said, with a hand toward the outer door.

I went through my usual sweep of the area to assure myself that no threats were lurking. Paul followed behind with Walt, and I secured the door once we were outside.

"What's this all about?" asked Walt, clearly puzzled.

"Paul and I had a discussion over who Bill's third would-be assassin might be. What do you know about those five men inside?" I asked, cutting to the chase.

"Now that's getting right to the point," said Walt, a grim expression on his ruddy face.

I kept my silence, waiting for him to collect his thoughts.

"Okay, here's the deal," he explained. "I knew that a fundraiser, a treasurer, was key to any success I might have, so I spent a lot of time screening, and ultimately, I picked Bob. Once he was on board, I asked him what other resources I needed, since he's done this many times before and I'm quite clearly a greenhorn. He told me I needed a pollster, a good man to handle scheduling, someone to interface with the media, and a capable guy to work on publicity. Bob saw the blank expression on my face and volunteered to do a search for those positions. I thanked him profusely, and he found Jim, Tony, Pete and Kim. To a man, they vowed to do everything in their power to get me elected." He made a sweeping gesture with his hands at the door and his team members beyond it.

"Since they came on board, have you had any reason to doubt anyone's loyalty or commitment?" I asked.

"I like your style, EZ. You don't mince words. Maybe I can find a position for you on my team." Walt said it in such a neutral manner that I was left wondering if he was pulling my leg or not.

"I'm a travel agent now, Walt. I appreciate your offer, but I think I can do better by you by scheduling your travel plans than I could be working in your campaign. Now, getting back to my question, do you have any doubts about any of your team members?"

"Yeah, okay. I used that break I created to give your question some thought, and to be honest, I don't have any misgivings about any of the team members," he said, confidence in his voice.

"That's good enough for me. Paul and I will be watching everyone equally. If anyone gives you a bad feeling, whatever it is, let us know, okay?"

"I will. Now that I know one of them might be a threat, I'll be more watchful of them."

"That's all I ask."

"If we're done here, I've got to get back to it," he said, moving to the door.

"We are. Thanks for your time," I said.

"Thank *you* for your thoroughness."

Walt went inside while Paul and I huddled over what Walt had said. We weren't any closer to identifying who the third assassin might be, but at least we'd alerted Walt to the possibility that one of his own might be working against him.

"Are you really okay, Paul? I mean, not getting any sleep can have its effects," I said, watching his face for a reaction.

"Please, don't worry about me. I'll be fine. This isn't the first time I've had to stay sharp when I've been sleep-deprived," he said, a grim smile playing across his mouth.

"I know, but a short nap can make a big difference. Since the team's here in suite 10, it'd be, let's say, more difficult to figure out where Walt is. That gives us an edge. I'll stand watch while you grab a quick one."

"A quick one? And you're going to stand watch during it? Sounds kind of kinky to me," said Paul, an impish smile spreading across his face.

"I guess you're more alert than I thought," I said, ignoring his not-so-subtle flirt.

"Yeah, I'll be fine. I'll hold off for a full-length feature instead of a quick one," he said, his grin holding.

"Okay, then. You stand guard out here and I'll go inside to watch over the team. If you find yourself falling asleep, give me a shout-out." I whacked his upper arm with my fist for emphasis.

"Works for me," said Paul.

I passkey-carded the door lock and stepped back inside, leaving Paul to watch for an assault coming from the canal. Eyes glanced briefly my way. Seeing nothing of concern, they turned their attention back to their coffees and tea, their choices of pastries held in their hands. I knew they would soon resume their ongoing planning, strategizing, investigating, and whatever else occupied their minds. A glance at the room service tray showed me two unclaimed coffees. Walt hadn't forgotten Paul and me.

Not for the first time, I wished we still had eyes in the hallway. Sadly, the laptop Paul had set up to monitor the cameras in the hallway and along the canal took a direct hit when Soldier Bill's explosive device blew the wall out in Walt's suite. If the monitoring software was destroyed, too, then there'd be no way to get the cameras back up and running using a different laptop. Paul would know.

With our coffees in my hands, I ducked back out on the patio.

Paul turned to face me, his eyebrows arching with a questioning look which metamorphosed into a happy face when he saw the coffee. I held his cup out to him and took a sip of my own. We both took it black, no sugar. Nothing but coffee.

"I had a thought," I said. "Any way we can get the camera images up and running again, maybe with another laptop?"

"Damn, why didn't I think of that?" he said with a slow shake of his head.

"Because you had other things on your mind." I summarized all the things he'd gone through, from the explosion that peppered his backside with shards of masonry and reduced his hearing to a minimum, to his painful time in the emergency room where the doctors dug out the bigger pieces, to the confrontation in his hospital room with Soldier Bill, who came to kill Walt but who got pinned down by Paul instead. Yeah, I guess he had a few distractions.

"Still," said Paul, making light of everything he'd been through, "I've got the CD with the software back in my room, so all we need is a laptop. Once the software's installed, we can monitor the cameras again."

"Beautiful! I'll ask Walt if he or his team have a spare laptop. Be right back." I hurried back inside. I felt six pairs of eyes on me once again, so I spoke up before they returned to their work.

"By any chance, do any of you have a laptop you're not using?"

Six pairs of eyes turned from me and bounced from one to another as they considered my request. Walt was first to respond. "What do you need it for, EZ?"

"The one Paul set up to monitor the cameras got trashed when the wall of your room got blasted," I said.

"Oh, hey! I've got a laptop I'm not using right now. I'll need it when I start the polling process, but for now it's all yours," said Jim. In response, he picked up his laptop and held it out to me.

I stepped over and took it from him. "Thanks a million, Jim. I'll take good care of it."

"I'm sure you will. Glad to help," Jim said, a faint smile washing over his normally placid face.

I turned back to the patio door and the team returned to their labors.

"Look what I got," I said to Paul as I held the laptop aloft.

"Way to go, g—" He caught himself in the nick of time, finishing lamely with "great work!"

His near-miss didn't escape me. "That was a close one, Paul," I said, my eyebrows raised.

"I may be a slow learner, babe, but I *am* learning," he countered.

"Babe, huh? Where'd that come from?"

"C'mon, EZ. You're my sweet babboo."

"Enough! Go get the software," I said, trying to sound in charge.

"Aye, babe." He hurried inside before I could respond. I stood there alone, sipping my coffee. *Sweet babboo.* Really?

* * *

Paul was back in less than five minutes, software disc in hand. I handed him the loaner computer and he slipped the disc into it before he tapped the keys.

The computer whirred in response, and soon Paul had the camera images displayed on the computer screen.

"Ta dah!" he said, while he held it out for me to see.

I could see the four hallway camera feeds and one of the two canal feeds, the one that showed the canal in the direction of the main pool.

"What happened to the other canal feed?" I asked, already guessing the answer.

"Who knows? Maybe the explosion dislodged it. Anyway, the canal camera that's working is aimed along the canal from Walt's suite and in this direction, so we'll have warning from anyone coming at us from the direction of the main pool. Oh, and if someone comes from the other way, the camera will pick them up when they swim past Walt's suite and in this direction. It's not perfect, but it's a whole hell of a lot better than nothing," he said, sweeping his hand for emphasis.

"I agree wholeheartedly. Since most of our cameras cover the hallway, I'll take the laptop and monitor things from inside the suite. If I see anything suspicious happening on the canal side, you'll be the first to know."

"Works for me. I feel better already, having eyes on the hall and the canal again. Glad you thought of getting another laptop," said Paul.

"Me, too. Now I can look forward to having you thank me in private when this is all over," I said, tossing Paul one of my patented impish grins.

"It's a date."

I slipped back inside, leaving him on patio sentry duty.

I hunkered down in the lone chair set well away from the hard-working team, the laptop set in my lap, and stared at the five displayed camera images. To say it was a boring task would be an understatement. Ninety-nine percent of the time there was nothing. It was the other one percent that kept me sharp, watchful.

A glance at my phone clock told me that Walt and his team would be breaking for lunch soon. It was past eleven-thirty and Walt was regimented to his mealtimes from his long time in the military. I considered how Paul and I should handle it. One or both of us go with the team? My vote was for both of us. Safety in numbers.

* * *

Fifteen minutes later, Walt declared in a loud voice it was time to break for lunch. I love it when I'm right. The team members stood as one. They'd learned when the boss man said, "Let's eat," they ate.

"Where are we going?" I asked.

"We haven't tried La Trattoria yet. How does a light Italian lunch sound?" asked Walt.

"*Molto buona*," I said, putting on my best Italian smile.

"*Andiamo!*" said Walt, not to be outdone.

I opened the patio door to tell Paul we were all heading off for some Italian food.

"You don't have to ask me twice," he said. He followed me inside, joining the party.

I led the way, with Paul taking up the rear. Between the two of us, we covered Walt and his team members as best we could. To a bystander it would have seemed like an unusual formation, with me walking in front, then Walt's team strolling two by two, and Paul taking up the rear. As it happened, we attracted zero attention from any of the guests, and we made it to La Trattoria without any surprises. Success is always welcome.

Walt, ever the leader, stepped forward to arrange a table, and learned that informality was the rule at La Trattoria. No maître d' was present. A waiter, his name tag said Ramon, assessed the size of our group and led us unerringly to a table for eight.

While we shuffled along towards our assigned table, I searched everywhere for any signs of threat. I made a rough guess there were some forty tables in the large dining area, and half of them were already occupied. No question about it. La Trattoria was a popular choice for lunch.

I skimmed over tables with parents and young children seated at them, which had to be a good half of those present. The other ten tables accommodated couples for the most part. One table stood out. A single occupant sat at it, positioned well away from our table. No question who it was. Soldier Bill. I watched him closely for any indication that he posed a threat. Although he was seated so he could look our way, his attention was focused on the meal set in front of him. He had to have seen us when we all filed in, so it was obvious to me that he was purposely avoiding any eye contact.

Paul, seated across from me, gave me a nod to say he'd spotted him, too. Alternatingly, we checked on him to see whether he showed any interest in us. He didn't. He devoted his entire attention to his pizza. I watched him as he finished, placed a tip on the table and got to his feet. He headed for the door, his eyes everywhere but on our table. At one point, he passed within fifteen feet of our group, all the while avoiding eye contact. It had to take a lot of effort on his part.

Walt watched Soldier Bill's exit. He turned to me and said in a soft whisper, "Looks like Paul's little talk with Bill made a big impression on him."

"It does look that way," I said as I watched Soldier Bill exit the restaurant.

One thing troubled me about him. If he no longer planned on taking out Walt, why hadn't he left, checked out, put El Mar Placida in his rearview mirror? Maybe that's what he was off to do now. Have lunch and then head to the airport. Maybe. Then again, maybe not.

Our meals came and everyone turned into magicians, waving their knives and forks to make the food set before them disappear. In between bites, I continued to monitor the other diners for any sign of recognition or interest in Walt and our party. I knew Paul was doing the same. I managed to do justice to my antipasto salad, finishing in last place because of my determination to spear the last piece of marinated artichoke heart.

Nobody wanted dessert, so we were up and out of La Trattoria a little before one o'clock. We formed up the same as we had for the walk there, and with me taking point, we headed back to Pete and Kim's suite. I searched ahead and to the sides on the walk back but saw nothing unusual. That included no sign of Soldier Bill.

Once we had made it safely back in the room, Paul resumed his watch outside on the patio while I focused on the laptop images showing the hallway and canal. All five images were still there. Nobody had messed with the minicams during our lunch break. Walt and his team sat with their pens, pads and laptops, and settled into the work that lay ahead of them.

Standing watch is my least favorite occupation, no matter where it takes place. From my time in the army I learned how important it was, but that didn't make it any easier. You sit or stand, depending on the situation, your eyes and ears kicked into high gear, and wait for something to happen. I've heard it said it's like sitting up in a deer stand, waiting for the big buck to saunter by. Hours can go by while you wait. When the day ends with nothing to show for it, you climb down, all those hours a waste of time. What makes it all worthwhile is the moment when that big buck shows up and you're ready for him. In the army, you sure as hell better be awake, alert, and ready to react when the bad guys show up. I kept that in mind as I continued to stare at the images on the laptop screen. An occasional couple or single person moving along the hallway raised my level of readiness. Once he or they had passed beyond suite 10 and were no longer a possible threat, I settled back into my 'watchful waiting' status, my eyes flitting from camera image to camera image in my constant search for trouble.

I was on autopilot, with no hallway activity to hold my attention and the drone of voices from Walt and his team to further lull me, when I felt the floor shudder under my feet. The sound of a huge splash of water followed. After, silence settled over the room.

"What the hell was that?" It was Walt, leaping to his feet, reacting to whatever had happened.

"Stay here!" *Paul!* I leaped from my chair, dropped the laptop onto it and bolted for the patio door, not knowing what I'd find but fearing the worst. I swung the door wide and stepped out, instinctively drawing the pistol from behind my back and holding it in front of me, ready for trouble.

Paul stood at the open outer canal door, staring out at the canal, his back to me. He was drenched to the bone. The patio was awash. Water rippled and ran everywhere under my feet.

"Paul! You okay?" I called out to him.

He turned to face me, a grim expression on his face.

I saw no blood, no evidence he'd been injured. Relief flooded through me. "What happened?" I asked as I waded towards him.

"That was one *fucking* close call," he said, his voice unsteady. He closed the door and turned towards me, his arms outstretched. We came together and hugged, my hands, arms mindful of the injuries to his back.

He leaned away and spoke in a shaky whisper. "I was sitting there," he pointed at the chair by the wall, "and out of nowhere something came flying over the outer wall and landed against the inner one. I knew at once what it was: another explosive device. I had no time to think. I leaped out of the chair, grabbed the device and lobbed it over the outer wall and into the canal, the whole while thinking it was going to go off and blow my sorry ass into an unrecognizable pink mist."

"But it didn't," I said, my arms encircling him, reassured by his solid frame.

"It didn't," echoed Paul. "Until it was back in the canal and under the water. I got a hellova bath when it went off," he said, his dripping arm sweeping over the water-soaked patio.

"We all felt the shock wave through the floor inside," I said.

"If you think it was bad inside, you should have been out here," he said, a faint smile pushing away his grim expression.

"Who do you think threw it?" I asked, while the name Soldier Bill filled my thoughts.

"I *know* who it was. His mangled body's floating out there." He gestured at the canal. "It was our old pal, Soldier Bill."

"He must have figured out which suite we were in, maybe watched us from a distance when we came back from lunch," I said, piecing it all together.

"I guess a hundred thousand dollars was too much for him to pass up. Well, he got the big payoff, but not the one he expected," said Paul.

"So, he swam up to the outer wall of suite 10 and lobbed the explosive charge over the wall, same as he did to Walt's suite yesterday. Then, he dove down and hit the detonator he had in his hand," I said.

"Uh huh. Only I was quick enough to pick up the explosive charge and hurl it into the canal. When Bill hit the detonator switch, it sent a huge shock wave that drove all the air out of his lungs and scrambled his brains, along with everything else. If he was still alive after the initial blast, taking in a breath of pure water wouldn't have done him any good. My guess is, he was dead before that happened. The blast blew him to hell and sent a geyser of water up and over everything. Unpleasant way to exit stage left, ask me," said Paul, with a shake of his head.

"What the fuck happened out there?" came Walt's voice from the doorway.

I turned to see him staring out at the saturated patio, his muscular body framed by the door. "Soldier Bill's final try to get you," I said, keeping my voice low. I didn't want to broadcast that information to anyone within earshot who might be curious about what had happened.

"Tell me," he said, his eyes on Paul as he waded out to us.

Paul stepped over to him, and in muted tones, recounted to Walt what had happened.

"Shit, Paul, you could've been killed," was his first reaction to Paul's summary.

"I didn't think about it. I just reacted when I saw the bomb," said Paul.

"Spoken like a true Special Forces soldier," said Walt, offering a smile and an arm around his shoulder. That said it all.

We all heard a loud knock on the hallway door and Walt went back inside.

"Let me get it, Sir," I said, as I squeezed past him and the other four team members who had clustered around the doorway.

"Good idea, EZ," he said.

I approached the hallway door, my right hand on the pistol behind my back. "Who is it?" I asked in a loud voice, as I stood off to the side in case someone fired through the door.

"Security," announced a male voice.

I swung the door inward, my right hand still occupied behind my back, and saw a young Dominican in an official-looking pale green uniform, complete with shoulder epaulets, looking up and past me.

"Have you come to tell us what happened?" I asked, taking the offensive.

"I have come to find out what you know about what has happened," he said, doing his best to sound authoritative. His eyes continued to search the room beyond.

"Come in. Let me show you what happened," I said, beckoning him inside and closing the door after a glance down the hallway confirmed he was alone.

Mister Security stepped inside, looking everywhere, seeing Walt and his team, all of whom wore expressions of confusion. Perfect, I thought.

"As near as we can tell, there was an explosion in the canal outside. Maybe it was another gas leak," I suggested, planting a seed. I walked with him to the patio door and pointed at the water-soaked patio. "The explosion, or whatever it was, threw a sheet of water over everything, as you can see. Mister Miller there," I said, pointing at Paul, "got drenched by all the water."

"He certainly did," said Mister Security. "Do you mind if I have a look at the canal from the door there?"

"Not at all," said Paul. He went over and opened the canal door for him, then stepped back.

Mister Security splashed through. Paul followed him, with me right behind. He glanced to the left and to the right along the canal.

I could see the water still rippling against the sides of the canal. It looked like a tsunami had passed by. The water had a pale pink hue to it, thanks to the leaks in Soldier Bill's body.

Paul and I watched Mister Security search the agitated water, could tell that he wasn't looking far enough down the canal, so Paul decided to offer some assistance.

"What's that?" he asked Mister Security, pointing along the canal towards the main pool.

Mister Security followed Paul's pointed finger. His eyebrows raised in surprise, seeing the remains of Soldier Bill bobbing along in the slight current, a pink sheen of blood surrounding him. The salty sea water in the canal helped to buoy up the body.

"Son of a fucking bitch!" spat Mister Security as realization of what he was looking at struck home. It sounded like he said *Sone uf a fockin beech.* "Oh, por favor, please excuse my Spanish," he said, realizing what he'd shouted out in English. He did an abrupt about-face and raced for the suite door without further comment. In a flash, he was through the suite and into the hallway. I hurried to close the door behind him and to secure us all inside.

Paul, soaked to the skin, closed the door on the now-vacant patio. "If I don't hear any objections, I'm going down to my suite to get into some dry clothes. I might jump in the shower a moment, wash off any traces Bill left behind," he added.

"Do it," said Walt. "You deserve a long hot shower after what you've just been through."

"I'll stand watch until you get back, Paul. Take your time," I said, knowing how he was feeling. I remembered being in a firefight in Afghanistan when I shot a Taliban fighter about to throw a grenade at us. It dropped at his feet, and when it exploded, bloody chunks of him flew in a wide circle. I personally felt several pieces impact me. When the fighting was over and the surviving Taliban fighters had withdrawn, my only thought was to get back to our base and take a long, hot shower. I remembered vividly how wonderful it felt, and knew Paul looked forward to the same pleasure.

"Thanks, Walt. I'll be back here before you know it," said Paul, moving to the door.

"You take your time, son," said Walt. He knew as well as we did what a cleansing shower meant in a situation like this.

"Hold on a sec," I said, holding up my right hand. "If I had to guess, this suite isn't going to be a suitable place to work, concentrate, in no time at all. The police will be here to do their thing and load up Soldier Bill's remains, plus they'll be doing a search of the canal to determine what happened. I suggest we take this party to my suite," I said.

"I second the motion," said Walt. "Meet us there when you're cleaned up, Paul."

"Roger that," said Paul. He finger-saluted Walt and then turned and ducked out the door.

I watched him go, closing the door after him.

Meanwhile, Walt took charge. "Everybody grab what you'll need to carry on our meeting and let's get out of here. We don't need any more distractions," he said to his team members.

They hurried to do his bidding, scooping up their pens, notepads, laptop computers—everything they needed to proceed. Once everyone was ready, everything they needed clutched in their hands, I opened the door and checked the hall.

All clear. No one in sight.

I stepped out, the laptop held at my side in my left hand, my right hand available if I needed to draw my pistol. I led the way to my suite, Walt and his team following closely behind. At my door, I beckoned for everyone to wait outside as I swept my wristband across the lock and shoved the door wide open. Remembering previous 'visitors' who had been inside lying in wait for me, I stepped through the doorway, all my senses tuned for trouble, my M9 held in front of me.

To my relief, the suite was empty. The only sign of visitors was from the maid service. The bed was made, and fresh towels had been placed. I turned back to the doorway and swept my arm to signal all was clear. Walt and his team filed in, clutching all their gear and quickly took over my living area. Chairs were moved, and in a matter of moments my suite looked like a carbon copy of every space the team had occupied. Chairs were quickly grouped in a circle, lights turned on. It was obvious that campaign work was uppermost in everyone's mind.

As before, I moved to the opposite side of the living area and took up a position that covered both doors. I opened my laptop and resumed the tedious task of scanning the different camera images.

I considered where we stood. With Soldier Bill out of the equation, it looked like we were down to one threat if Bill's statement to Paul was to be believed. He'd told Paul that he knew of two other people looking to collect the hundred grand for eliminating Walt. The first one had floated down the canal after I interrupted his brain functions, and Bill joined him when he got his Semtex, or whatever it was, tossed back at him by Paul. So, I had to assume that at least one more threat stood in our way. I also considered that Bill's count might have been off by an assassin or two. In other words, Walt was still in at least one more assassin's crosshairs, and possibly even more. The time to whoop and high-five hadn't come yet.

My thoughts were interrupted by a single knock on the hall door. Paul. Gun in hand, I moved to the door and stood to the side before I called out, "Who's there?"

"It's Paul," came the terse reply, his voice unmistakable.

I opened the door and seeing Paul alone, tucked the M9 in the small of my back. He ducked inside and closed the door behind him while his eyes swept over the team and their positions in the circle they'd formed.

He looked both clean and comfortable in a pale blue polo shirt and dark blue shorts. "You look good, Paul," I whispered.

"I *feel* good. I couldn't wait to wash the remains of that man out of my hair and send him on his way," he said, doing his best to remember the words to an old show tune.

"I know what you mean," I said simply. We'd had the discussion before. Each of us had been exposed to blood and body parts during our time in Afghanistan and we shared the common experience of ridding ourselves of it under a blasting shower head.

"Everyone looks like they're getting used to these distractions," he said, eyeing the team. They all appeared to be concentrating fully on the business at hand, the attack and death of the attacker a fast-fading memory.

"That, and the fact that they're getting closer to making the big decision," I offered.

"How close do you think they are?" asked Paul, his eyes playing over the team members.

"I'm not sure. We'll ask Walt when they take their next break."

"In the meantime, I'll go out on the patio and watch for trouble while you cover the computer screen and the hall door from here, okay?"

"Do you want to switch off, have me do patio duty and you monitor the laptop images? You must be close to exhaustion."

"I thought of that, but I think it's more tiring to stare at a computer screen. Outside, I get to lounge in a deck chair and smell the flowers," said Paul, his quirky smile taking charge.

"Works for me," I said. I watched Paul move quietly to the patio door and step outside, pulling the door closed quietly behind him. None of the team looked up. Paul's and my movements no longer caught their attention.

Here we go again. Hurry up and wait. I set my chair so I could keep an eye on both the hallway door and the members of the team as they worked while I focused once again on the camera images on my borrowed laptop.

A half an hour or so later I spotted a familiar looking uniformed officer saunter down the hallway and approach my suite, his image sharp on my laptop screen. He stopped outside and rapped hard on the door. I closed the laptop and approached the door. I called out, asking who was there, my voice casual, neutral.

"Security," came the Dominican voice from the hallway.

I made sure that my shirt covered the M9 tucked behind my back before I opened the door. There stood Mister Security, the same officer who'd come to Pete and Kim's suite after the explosion in the canal. I made a quick visual search of his body for weapons and came up empty. Guess he didn't want to alarm the guests by carrying a pistol. If he was an assassin, he came unprepared. To be sure he was unarmed, I held the door wide and when he stepped inside, I pretended to stumble and brought my hand to his chest, then closed the door. I felt nothing but chest. My move aroused no suspicion. I turned to see every team member look his way. He had everyone's attention.

"What did you find out?" I asked him.

"More to the point, why did you all leave?" he asked, his tone accusatory.

"These men have a lot of work to do, and we thought it would be quieter to come here, away from any disturbance that you and the police might cause during your search," I said.

"How many suites do you have access to?" he asked.

"Five in all. Suites 6, 8 and 10 are the six men here, and this is my suite. As you know, suite 6 was rendered unusable by the gas-line explosion, so two men from there are using suite 14, another man's suite, until repairs are made," I said.

"Where did the other man spend the night?" he was quick to ask.

"He was the one injured in the gas-line explosion. He spent the night in the hospital," I said.

"And what about you?" he pursued.

"I was here, in my own suite," I said.

"How do you all know each other?" At last, the big question.

"I'm a travel agent, here courtesy of the resort, and I met Walter McKelvy and his team when I came here. In case you didn't know, Walter McKelvy is here with his team of five men to evaluate whether he should run for the presidency," I said.

"The presidency? Of the Dominican Republic?"

"No. The Presidency of the United States," I said. I watched him closely for a reaction. When his eyes grew large and his mouth sagged open, I knew he hadn't a clue who Walt was and he was duly impressed.

"Yes, and you must promise me not to tell anyone." I kept my reply short and to the point while I took him off my list of possible assassins. His surprise when he learned that Walt was a possible presidential candidate was far too genuine.

Wait. Maybe he's a superb actor. Back he goes to the suspect list. Nah! He doesn't fit the profile.

"I promise, Miss. Do you know how long he will be here?" asked Mister Security.

"I guess as long as it takes to make the big decision. What have you found out about the second gas-line explosion?" I asked, changing the subject.

"The Dominican police are on their way. There will be a complete investigation because one of the resort's guests was killed in the explosion," said Mister Security.

"Oh, how terrible," I said, loading my voice with sincerity. Then I thought of another diversion. "Should I, we be worried about another explosion? Perhaps we should all go somewhere else if it isn't safe."

"Please, no. I hurry to reassure you that you are all perfectly safe," said Mister Security, his hands steepling between us, a gesture of reassurance.

"I don't know. Two gas explosions in less than twenty-four hours. It has me worried," I said, adding a tremor to my voice for effect.

"You force me to reveal something that I was told not to reveal to our guests, Miss. These explosions. They were not gas explosions. You are perfectly safe here in the resort," said Mister Security, his contorted face bearing witness to the agony of revealing the truth to me.

"If it wasn't a gas explosion, then what was it?" I asked, offering him an expression of concern, worry.

"I am not at liberty to say right now. When the police have completed their investigation, they will tell the management and management will tell you, tell all of the guests. The canal will be closed off for their investigation, but you are free to use the rest of the resort amenities at any time," said Mister Security, now secure in his role once more.

"Very well, sir. I trust you, and I will keep our secret, just as you have promised to keep the secret of Mister McKelvy. I will inform the others of the situation," I said, walking Mister Security to the door.

"Thank you, Miss. If management finds out that I told you, it would most likely cost me my job," he said, urgency in his voice.

"It will be our little secret, Sir," I reassured him.

"Thank you, Miss. And please, call me by my name. It is—"

"Ramon, right?" I interrupted him.

His smile broke through. "That is correct, Miss. You are very, ah, perceptive, I think the English term is."

I smiled back at him. "Just a lucky guess."

He stepped backward and out the door. I closed it after him.

"What the hell was that all about?" Walt hadn't missed a beat.

"That was the same security guy who came by after Soldier Bill's blast. He wondered why we'd left suite 10. I told him you and your team were hard at work and needed a quiet place, away from the gas explosion scene."

"Did he figure out what happened?"

"Not yet, other than there was a dead guest floating in the canal. The Dominican police are on their way to check out the scene. He confided in me that there were no gas leaks, yesterday or today, and we shouldn't worry about any future blasts. If he only knew," I said with a shake of my head that set my blonde ponytail dancing.

While Walt was speaking to me, his team members stood and stretched, shaking off the tightness in their arms and shoulders after sitting for a long time. They took turns using the bathroom as well.

A cell phone rang, and I watched Bob pick it up, put it to his ear. He listened for a bit. A broad grin swept over his face. He set his phone back on the table and looked over at Walt, the smile still there.

"Looks like Bob got some good news, Walt," I said with a gesture in Bob's direction.

Walt turned to look at him, his eyebrows raised in question.

Seeing Walt's expression, Bob hurried over to him. "I just had a call from my Texas contact, Walt. He said he might be getting a serious commitment from one of the names on his list."

"When will he know? Did he name a figure?" asked Walt. He kept his voice neutral, not giving away the anxiety or anticipation he may've felt. True professional. The kind of leader the country needed.

"He said he'd be back in touch with me as soon as he knew more," said Bob.

"Well, that's something," said Walt.

"I think it's more than something," said Bob, his grin spreading across his face once again.

"If you're right, we have a lot of ground to cover, stuff to discuss. Let's get on with it," said Walt and made his way back to the circle the team had created. All six men resumed their seats and picked up where they'd left off.

I opened my laptop and checked the five images for any threats. Seeing none, I hurried over to the patio door. When I opened it, I spotted Paul hunkered down in one of the chairs, positioned so he could watch everywhere from the one vantage point. He looked at me when I opened the door. I held up my thumb, and he returned the gesture. All was well, inside and out, spoken without a word.

I stepped over to him and told him about Ramon's AKA Mister Security's visit, what he knew, and that the Dominican police were on their way to the resort. Then, I told him about Bob's encouraging phone call.

"That's great," he said, in a low voice. "Maybe we can look forward to some quiet time together when all this is behind us."

"That's the plan and I'm stickin' with it," I said. I gave his shoulder a squeeze and ducked back inside to resume my watch.

* * *

Walt interrupted the silence that had settled over the room with an announcement he was hungry and needed dinner, though not in so many words. He simply said, "Mess call."

I knew what it meant, and his team had figured it out, too. *Time to eat.* There was no bugle call, but the message was loud and clear. I checked the time on my phone. Not surprisingly, it was six o'clock. Traditional suppertime in the military.

I wondered idly which of his five team members would get the task of 'adjusting' Walt's mealtimes. Whoever it fell upon, I knew he'd have an uphill battle on his hands.

I reflected back on my own military experience. It had taken me a couple of months to get past six without feeling the urge to eat, and Walt was career military. His adjustment would be harder, longer.

"Where are we going, Walt?" It was Bob, asking the big question.

"I don't much care, as long as it's hot and plentiful," said Walt.

"That sounds like La Placida, the buffet place," said Bob. "All in favor, say aye."

'Ayes' filled the air.

"Opposed, say nay."

Silence.

"The ayes have it," said Bob, getting to his feet. The others quickly joined him, and Walt took the lead.

"Forward, *harch!*" said Walt, with a beckoning gesture towards the door.

"Excuse me, sir. As general, you should walk behind your troops. We need a sergeant to lead the way," I said.

"And who might you have in mind?"

"Sergeant Miller, sir! I will fetch him straightaway." I stepped briskly to the patio door, opened it and beckoned Paul inside. I explained his role. He hurried to take the lead. We set off, Paul setting a comfortable pace while I trailed behind, covering our six.

We reached La Placida without incident. As expected, at that hour of the early evening, few people were out and about, which made Paul's and my job easier. We made our way inside and a waiter who looked a lot like Ramon led us to a table for eight set close to the far wall. Three other tables were occupied, each accommodating parents with children. No one even glanced up as we filed past. All was well.

Paul, in the lead, took a seat facing the entrance and Walt sat to his right. I commandeered the seat on the end of our table, affording a view of all the other tables. The other team members sat around us in their usual haphazard manner.

Ramon circled our table taking drink orders, then told us we were free to go to the buffet line whenever we were ready. Walt and Paul rose from their seats and made tracks for the chow line. Two military men responding to entrenched impulses, appetites triggered by the clock. I stayed with the group, my eyes dancing everywhere around the large dining room.

The waiter returned with his trayful of beverages and set them one by one in front of each of us, his memory batting a thousand. Four beers, two iced teas, two coffees. Not surprisingly the coffees were for Walt and Paul. One of the iced teas was mine. Six glasses were lifted and sampled, then set back down as Walt and Paul returned, plates heaped high with food, most of which appeared to be meat.

"Hey, you guys, wait'll you see the fantastic selection! There's definitely something for everyone," Walt said as he set down his plate and eased himself back in his chair. Six pairs of eyes scanned his choices and interest in food suddenly skyrocketed. Walt's five team members and I pushed back our chairs and bustled across the room to the cafeteria line.

I scanned the line as we approached, choosing what I'd take before picking up my plate. It saved me from taking more than I wanted, needed, or so I hoped. I ended up taking more than I'd planned on, but that's what buffet lines do to you, right? I headed back to our table, taking up the rear, wondering what possessed me. Mom and Dad had raised me to eat what was set before me, so I knew I had an uphill battle on my hands.

Back at the table, Paul and I took turns scanning the room and the other diners for any threat. I'd take a mouthful and glance his way, our signal that I watched. Then we'd reverse roles when he took a bite. That way, our eyes always watched for trouble.

In our discussions about where trouble would come at us, at Walt, we agreed that a frontal attack was the least likely and that stealth and surprise made more sense. We figured an assassin would want to kill Walt and escape to enjoy the fruits of his labors. To attack in a public place with a roomful of witnesses seemed foolish. Despite all our rationalizing, we stayed watchful. Who knew? Maybe we were up against a fanatic who didn't care what happened to him, or maybe he'd made arrangements for the reward money to be paid to someone else. A wife. A family member. It was all within the limits of possibility, so we maintained our watchfulness.

The meal concluded without incident. Light conversation resumed. Walt and Paul got more coffee while Tony and Peter went off to explore the dessert table. They came back with chocolate delights piled on their plates.

Kim, seated to my right, had been mostly silent during the meal. I asked him if he was interested in checking out the desserts.

"No. I gave up desserts a while back. You probably wouldn't guess looking at me, but I allowed myself to gain a bunch of weight. Skipping desserts was one of the things I did to shed the weight," he said.

"You're right. I never would have guessed. How much did you lose?" I asked.

"Thirty pounds. I went from two-twenty down to one-ninety."

I knew from standing next to him that Kim and I were close to the same height, so thirty extra pounds would have been a burden to him. "Congratulations. You look good."

"Yeah, and I feel a whole lot better, too," he said, smiling at me.

"So tell me, Kim," I said, changing the subject, "how did you get into publicity work?"

"I started in college. I joined a lot of different clubs, and two of them arranged to have guest speakers come to the campus and give lectures. Somehow I fell into the role of promoting them, getting publicity out on them so we'd pull in decent crowds to hear what they had to say. Turned out I got pretty good at it, and as an added bonus, I enjoyed doing it. After college, I set up a public relations firm and promoted a wide range of personalities and businesses. Next thing I knew, I was promoting local politicians. Got so I could see them through successful campaigns. One thing led to another, and Bob got wind of me and my successes. He asked me if I wanted to work with a presidential candidate, and here I am," said Kim, his hands making a sweeping gesture for emphasis.

"What do you think of Walt? Do you think he has a chance to win if he throws his hat in the ring?"

Kim paused a heartbeat before responding, and I was beginning to think he had his doubts. He surprised me. "I think he could go down as one of the most successful presidents in modern history. He has it all. He has great leadership skills, he listens, and he has a love of the country that goes well beyond the usual. I like that he's running as an independent. If we can overcome the barriers that running as an independent present, and we can show the American people how committed he is to working with both balky democrats and resistant republicans to get the job done, I think Walt has a great chance to win. Meanwhile, we all have plenty to do to help secure his victory," said Kim with a wry smile.

"I've known Walt, or I should say General Walter McKelvy for over five years now. I served under him in Afghanistan for two years. Sometimes you get a feeling about a person that goes beyond personal exchanges and brief contacts. Walt, for me, is such a man. His personality is bigger than life, and his ability to connect with people, with me, in a way that made me feel special, is a unique gift. I agree with you. I think he's got what it takes to be an outstanding president."

"Now if we can only get him to clean up his language, we'll be good to go," said Kim as he nudged his glasses upward on his nose.

"That may be true," I said, "but think back on our past presidents and what they got away with. Harry Truman never minced words, and neither did Franklin Roosevelt. Americans shrugged their shoulders and accepted them the way they were. They rolled with the punches, so to speak. Old ladies winced and old men applauded."

"Is everyone finished eating?" It was Walt, taking charge once again. Everyone nodded in the affirmative.

"That being the case, I move that we get back to the business at hand," he said, his big grin at work on his face after executing his play on words.

We all stood and made our way to the entrance doors, with me leading the way, taking point, and Paul taking up the rear, covering our six. The late afternoon heat and humidity hit us when we stepped out of the air-conditioned restaurant. Reality sometimes takes your breath away.

The casual stroll back to my suite was uneventful. A few passing couples eyed us askance, I'm guessing because we looked organized, purposeful in the midst of an otherwise relaxed, laid-back atmosphere. I guessed their thoughts: vacations weren't meant for business.

Once in the lobby, the return to air conditioning drained the excess heat from us and evaporated the accumulated moisture from our skin, our clothing. We passed four people, two couples by their mannerisms, speaking low amongst themselves. They didn't look our way when we strode purposely by them. I caught an occasional word they said. "Terrible." "Another explosion." "Should we leave?" "Is it safe?"

They had to be whispering about Soldier Bill's demise. I wondered what the police had found, what conclusion they had reached. The resort bigwigs would want it all to go away. Bad for business. Would the police comply, maybe say Soldier Bill was a suicide? Truth to tell, in some ways it was. Better Bill than Paul.

Our purposeful team reached my suite without anything slowing our progress, and Walt and his team settled right back into their routine. Seven-fifteen. How late would they work?

I picked up the house phone and called the front desk, asked if the police were done with their investigation.

"We are not yet able to reply, Miss," said the operator in a well-rehearsed manner.

"Reason I ask, the two men in the suite involved are wondering if they can return, or whether other arrangements will have to be made," I said.

"I understand. Let me make inquiries and I shall call you back, Miss," said the cooperative operator.

"Thank you." I replaced the phone in its cradle and told Paul what I'd learned. He nodded, understanding, and then let himself out onto the patio. The evening watch had begun.

I heard Bob's cell phone chirp. A text message was coming in. He picked it up, swept the screen and read the message. I watched his face light up, a huge smile overtaking him.

He jumped to his feet. "Here ye, here ye," he practically shouted, getting everyone's attention.

All eyes turned to him.

"What's happened, Bob? You a father again?" asked Walt.

"Better than that. I just got a message from my financial contact in Texas. You ready for this? He says he has seven new confirmed pledges to your campaign. The smallest pledge is for a hundred grand. Drum roll, please! The largest is for two hundred grand. Gentlemen; and lady," he added with his eyes on me, "we are over the top. We have commitments totaling one million, one hundred and fifty thousand dollars. Retired General Walter McKelvy is, as of this moment, an official candidate for the presidency of the United States! *And* I should add, we're still waiting for responses to close to a thousand more inquiries!"

Everyone stood, huge grins dominating faces, and rushed to congratulate both Walt and Bob. Both men smiled back. Walt's smile was looking more presidential by the moment.

"This calls for a celebratory drink!" said Walt, his strong voice breaking through the general hubbub. "Let's adjourn to that little bistro we've passed by so many times."

I remembered seeing it. The Tipsy Frog, if I recalled right, but I already knew I did. I hurried over to the patio door, opened it and beckoned Paul inside. He was close by, probably having heard the commotion Bob's announcement caused. I quickly filled him in.

Hearing the news, he stepped over to Walt and extended his hand to congratulate him. Walt ignored his hand and enveloped Paul in a huge bear hug. Paul returned the hug. Soldier to soldier. De hombre a hombre. The gesture said it all. Fellowship. Equality. Brotherhood. Walt the man, Paul the man.

They stepped back from one another, and Walt assumed command. "Follow me, my fantastic team!"

He headed for the hallway door but I beat him to it, all business again, ready to take the lead to protect our prized asset. Walt and Bob lined up behind me, followed by Tony and Peter, then Jim and Kim. Paul trailed behind, guarding us from the rear.

The stroll to the Tipsy Frog was uneventful, but the bar was crowded with patrons, so we were instantly immersed in a cacophony of voices. A young waitress led us to a large round table in the rear. It overlooked a sizeable pond, a three-foot high block wall separating us from it. I guessed it was where the tipsy frog made his home when he wasn't enjoying a drink or two.

As we were occupied with seating ourselves, Jim stepped up to Walt, a big smile leading the way. "I want to congratulate you, Walt, for reaching your financial goal in such a short time." He emphasized his words with a quick pat on Walt's back, and then he turned away.

I assumed he was going to take a seat at the table, but he didn't. He stepped briskly into the bar's interior. Perhaps he needed to find the men's room.

Something about the whole bizarre scene puzzled me and I turned to look at Walt, his back to me as he pulled out his chair to sit down. The glimmer of an object caught my attention. In the dim light of the bar, I saw what looked like a fat brown button on the back of Walt's shirt. No button belonged there.

I acted on impulse. I darted to Walt's side, snatched the button from his shirt and flung it over the wall and into the frog pond. It landed with an insignificant splash, tiny ripples moving out from it in enlarging circles.

"What the hell was that all about?" Walt asked me, a puzzled expression flooding his broad face, his eyebrows knitted.

I was at a loss for words to explain my impulsive action. I opened my mouth to speak when a blast erupted from the spot where the button had disappeared into the pond. A geyser of water gouted upwards in a spreading column, and then collapsed back into the pond. Major waves fanned out from its center. Some of the bar's patrons glanced briefly at the spot, and then went back to their drinks and their companions. I guessed that they dismissed it as a special effects show by the management. I wondered how the frog population had taken it, if there even were frogs in the pond.

Paul figured it out as quickly as I had, and he hustled off to find Jim before he could get away. An image of what the explosive device would have done to Walt flooded my mind. I shook it off when Walt seized me by my forearm, his grip telling me he was clearly shaken.

"Holy crap, EZ, what was that?"

"When Jim walked up to you and slapped you on the back, supposedly congratulating you, he stuck an explosive device on your shirt. I saw it and, well, I reacted," I told him. I put a calming hand on his shoulder as I spoke.

"And you saved my life! Again! My God, EZ, how can I ever repay you?" he asked, his voice charged with emotion.

"You know, I've always fancied being one of your cabinet members. How do you think I'd do as Secretary of Defense?" I said, joking.

Walt caught my attempt at humor. "Hell, yeah! Now you're talking. I'll put you down for it."

I glanced behind Walt to see Paul coming towards us. He had Jim secured in a hammerlock, his right arm twisted painfully behind his back. Jim's total compliance said it all.

As Paul moved Jim along, a big young man spotted them and said, "Hey, man! What the hell are you doin'? Let that guy go!"

Paul paused and turned to face the man. Their eyes locked and Paul glared daggers at him. Seeing Paul's intensity, the man turned away from him, making a dismissive gesture at Paul and his captor as he dropped his threatening behavior.

Paul continued to our group, his left hand holding up a small triggering device for us to see. He stopped in front of Walt.

"I guess you've already figured out, he tried to kill you, Walt. He had this triggering device in his hand when I caught up with him, and I grabbed it from him. When I searched him, I found two more explosive devices. If I had to guess, he was going to detonate them, take his own life, having failed to take yours."

"Where are the other devices?" asked Walt.

"I left them in his pocket. Since I had the detonator switch, I figured they were safe enough there," said Paul. He continued to maintain his grip on Jim's arm.

"Give me the detonator, Paul," said Walt in a commanding voice. "It seems only fair that I'm the one to flick the switch and blow Jim's ass off." He held out his hand.

Paul dropped the detonator switch into Walt's hand and stepped back, positioning himself away from the devices.

"Any last words, Jim? Maybe shed some light on why someone in your position would stoop so low as to kill the man you're working for?" asked Walt.

Jim stared straight ahead, avoiding eye contact with Walt, his lips taut, tight. No words came from him.

"The money is all I can think of. A hundred grand in cash, up front. Funny thing is, if you'd stayed on board with me you'd have made way more than that over the next year and a half alone. So, what else could it be?" said Walt, his steely gaze leveled on Jim.

"Blackmail," whispered Jim, his face expressionless, fixed, his grey eyes vacant, staring at nothing.

"Blackmail? Who's blackmailing you?" asked Walt in a voice ordering, not requesting, the truth. He waited for Jim's response. It didn't come. He continued his blank, staring silence.

Frustrated, Walt turned and hurled the detonator switch into the black waters of the Tipsy Frog pond. It landed with an inconsequential splash and disappeared into the water's depths. Nobody, none of the bar's patrons witnessed the splash or the tiny ripples that followed.

"Get him out of here, Paul. Put him somewhere until we can deal with him," said Walt, his frustration coming through in his strong voice.

Paul nodded, his right arm maintaining a steely grip on Jim's twisted arm. He steered him toward the entrance of the Tipsy Frog. Jim moved along at his side, offering no resistance. He knew he was no match for Paul's superior strength. I watched the two of them disappear into the gloom of the night, then resumed my watch over Walt and his remaining team.

Walt turned to me, his voice a whisper. "See what you can find out, EZ. I'd love to know who the blackmailer is, kick his ass," he said.

"I'll see what I can learn, Walt," I whispered back.

Bob broke the silence. "Now that your campaign is official, Walt, if only amongst us for now, I need to call the Secret Service and let them know they have a new candidate to watch over."

"That's right," agreed Walt. "Once they're in place, these threats should go away, and EZ and Paul can get on with their lives." He pulled out one of the chairs at the table and sat. The remaining members of his team followed his example.

I sat with my back to the pond. I could see into the lounge and watch for anyone posing a threat. Meanwhile, Bob searched his phone's contact list and made the call. Nobody spoke. Stunned silence prevailed. I could hear an occasional word from Bob's lengthy conversation. "Three threats." "Two dead." "Two bodyguards." Then "Sure. Hold on." Bob leaned towards me, his phone held out to me. "Secret Service wants a word with you, EZ."

I took the phone, said, "EZ Kelly. That's capital E capital Z Kelly," I added, then listened.

"This is Special Agent Alan Cottrell, Miss Kelly. I'm in charge of assigning agents to protect presidential candidates. Robert Hixon told me you were chosen to act as bodyguard to General Walter McKelvy and you've encountered three threat assets. Two ended up deceased and a third is in custody. Is that correct?"

"That's mostly correct, sir. I've had help from a recently-discharged Special Forces soldier named Paul Miller," I said.

"He kill the two downed assets?" asked Special Agent Cottrell.

"We took turns, sir. I took one out, and he took out the other," I explained.

"Where'd you get the skills to carry that out?" he demanded to know.

"I served two tours in Afghanistan in Special Forces, sir. And my dad taught me everything he knew," I added.

"What'd he know?"

"He was Special Forces, too. When he saw where my name was going, from Esther Zane to EZ, he figured I'd better know how to take care of myself. I learned well, sir."

"Anyone else out there who can vouch for you?"

"Sure. You got a pen and paper handy?"

"I don't need it. Go."

A fellow eidetic. "Okay. Call Special Agent Rick Brophy at the FBI Field Office in Miami. Then try Special Agent Lou Menendez at the FBI Field Office in Atlanta." I recited both their phone numbers to Cottrell. "Got all that?" I asked, to confirm.

"Got it," he said. "So you know, we'll get a detail together to protect General McKelvy, should be at your location by noon tomorrow."

"Sounds good, sir. We'll be here, waiting."

"I'll call Brophy and Menendez, confirm your story."

"Yes, sir. Give them both my best."

"Will do, Kelly." The line went dead.

I handed Bob his phone back and said, "Changing of the guard tomorrow at noon," loud enough for all to hear. Relief showed in all five faces surrounding me. I felt it, too.

"Let's not forget what brought us here," said Walt.

"Hear! Hear!" said Tony. "All this excitement's worked up a powerful thirst." He was doing his part to defuse the situation.

Walt stood and waved his arm at a passing cocktail waitress. She scooted unerringly through the crowd and up to our table. "Ready to order?" she asked, her smile showing off perfectly formed dimples.

There were six of us, counting me. Walt surprised me when he ordered coffee. I followed suit. The four team members ordered beers.

When the waitress left to assemble our orders, I leaned in and asked Walt if he drank anything besides coffee.

"Sure. I tossed back beer and whiskey with the best of them. One morning I woke up feeling terrible, and that was it. I stopped all alcohol, and I don't regret it for a moment. That was, let's see, nine years ago," he said.

"Now that you can pay the bills, when's the big announcement coming?" I asked.

"Tony, Kim, and Peter are getting that set up to take place in Topeka. Since I was born in Kansas, it seemed appropriate. Tony's handling the scheduling, Kim's doing the publicity, and Peter's in charge of notifying the media so we have TV and newspaper coverage. They think they can get it set up for the first of next week."

"Kansas, huh? Seems like I remember hearing about another general from Kansas who made it to the presidency," I said.

"General Dwight David Eisenhower, better known as Ike. Yeah, he was raised in Kansas, but did you know he was born in Texas? His family moved to Abilene when he was two, so he spent most of his young life there, and most people think of him as a Kansan," said Walt.

"I didn't know that. Born a Texan. Who knew?" I said with a shake of my blonde ponytail.

Bob's cell phone trilled and we turned towards him, wondering who it might be. He answered, spoke softly a moment, then looked my way, his phone held out to me.

"It's Secret Service, Special Agent Alan Cottrell on the line. He wants a word with you, EZ."

I took Bob's phone, said "This is EZ."

"Miss Kelly, I've spoken with both of your FBI contacts and they've confirmed your identity for me. I can't believe you're a travel agent," said Special Agent Cottrell.

"I don't understand, Sir."

"Hell, Kelly, with your skillset you should be in law enforcement."

"Are you offering me a job, sir?"

"It's not my position to do so, but from what your contacts told me I'd be more than happy to work side by side with you."

"You honor me, sir."

"Give it some thought. On another matter, seems like we have a small glitch."

"What's that, sir?"

"Well, because of the threats already sustained by General McKelvy, we're waiving the time frame restriction on providing him protection. He does need to officially declare his candidacy, however," said Cottrell.

"He told me he and his team are setting up a date for declaring his candidacy in Kansas," I said.

"When will that be? We can't offer protection until then," said Agent Cottrell.

"Hold on. Let me find out." I turned and asked Walt's team for their opinion. The consensus was it'd be another week before everything fell into place. That meant Paul and I would need to continue providing security until then. The prospect was daunting. I told them so.

Kim spoke up. "We could set up a press conference right here, invite the local media, whatever that turns out to be, and get Walt's campaign launched as early as, say, two days from now. Then we can do it all over again in Topeka, consider the announcement a dry run, work out the kinks." His hands gave away the excitement he felt as they danced around in front of him.

"That's a great idea, Kim," said Walt, resting his hand on Kim's shoulder for emphasis.

I got back on the phone with Agent Cottrell. "Did you hear any of that?" I asked him.

"Two days," he confirmed. "That'll work for us. I'll get a detail together, have them there by the end of the day tomorrow so they can get the lay of the land before the announcement."

"That's more than generous, sir. Will you be coming?" I asked.

"I always come for the establishment of new duty rosters, so yeah. I look forward to meeting you, Miss Kelly."

"Once we've shaken hands, you'll have to call me EZ," I said.

"Once we've shaken hands, you'll have to drop calling me 'sir,'" he countered.

"Deal," I said, unable to stifle a smile.

I returned Bob's phone, announced that a detail would be here by tomorrow afternoon. Four beer glasses were raised in a toast. Our drink orders had come while I talked. I found my coffee and raised my cup with the rest. Nobody in the bar took any notice of our group, I was pleased to see. We were six resort guests kicking back and relaxing, is all. If they only knew…

I slurped my coffee—it had grown tepid long before it reached us—and gazed out at the still waters of the pond. I could see no floating frog carcasses, or anything else for that matter. The stillness was soothing after recent events.

"Drink up, everyone," said Walt. "We've got a few details to work out before my announcement, and I know you all want me to get it right."

Glasses were upended and set down, and we filed out of the Tipsy Frog in the same way we'd come in, minus two members. I was anxious to see what Paul had done with Jim Bennett. In Paul's absence, I alternated between leading and following to make sure we weren't someone's target. We made it back to my suite without incident.

Once everyone was settled, I called Paul's cell. He picked up at once.

"Everything okay? Where are you?" I asked.

"All's well. I'm in my suite," he said.

"Is Jim secured?"

"He is. The roll of duct tape I picked up at the PX at Fort Bragg worked wonders on him. I turned out his pockets and removed two little buttons. They have an actuation switch built in. It needs to be flipped on to respond to the detonator. Pretty sophisticated little gizmos. Can't wait to hear what Secret Service thinks of them. Maybe they can be traced to the source," said Paul.

"Maybe. We're all back in my suite next door to you." I filled Paul in on the details of the Secret Service calls and Walt's planned announcement here at El Mar Placida so Secret Service could take over our duties.

"You mean, we might be able to tread water together within forty-eight hours?" he asked.

I got a mental picture of his eyebrows doing the fandango. Then, I got a second picture of Paul swimming towards me with his bathing suit draped over his head and I got the giggles.

After the last several days of tension and violence I couldn't help myself. It was a soothing tonic to my frazzled senses. I had to remind myself there could be another assassin lurking out there, waiting for the opportunity to collect. It remained up to Paul's and my watchfulness to thwart such an attack until Secret Service relieved us of our duty.

"What?" asked Paul, hearing my giggle.

I sensed irritation in his voice. I told him of the image that came to me. His laugh exploded into the phone. He got it. We laughed together. He paused to say Jim was staring at him in disbelief. That triggered another round of laughter. Jim, of all people. I was glad he was immobilized, no longer a threat.

"I'll tell Walt and the crew that Jim's all tied up," I said when our laughing subsided.

"Good one, EZ. Tell them that he's going to stay that way, too."

"I will. And you stay the way you are," I said, the image of him swimming towards me with his bathing trunks perched on his head still fresh in my thoughts.

"And you as well. Talk soon."

"Talk soon."

I set the phone down and heard Walt trying out his acceptance speech. I listened, not wanting to interrupt. He began by saying he was a graduate of West Point. I didn't know that. He went on to summarize his long military career. He said military leaders needed to be politicians when dealing with everyone, from the men who were sent into battle to the ones who sent along the orders, and everyone in between. A good analogy, I thought.

Walt went on to explain how he felt about the state of politics in the country at the present time, and how he felt he could be an effective leader by taking the middle ground, offering himself as a mediator between the dysfunctional main political parties. He said that he was just what the country needed, a man to step up to the plate and work to break the impasse that had developed. He went on to say that the negotiating skills he'd developed over his years in the military were what the country needed to move the needle, get the House and Senate working together once more.

"So, what do you think?" he asked everyone when he'd finished. His team responded with vigorous applause. I joined in.

Walt held up his hand and the clapping dwindled. "Thanks for your enthusiasm, everybody. I know there's a lot I can say to make it better, but what I said is pretty much my main point," he said with a glance that took in everyone.

Kim was first to break the silence. "From my perspective, publicity, I think you're dead-on, Walt. It's a fresh, new approach. I think you'll appeal to a lot of voters by offering that solution to the logjam that exists between the political parties today."

"I couldn't have said it better myself," said Peter, a subtle smile teasing the corners of his mouth.

"You're right, Peter. You couldn't," spoke up Tony, which brought more smiles to their faces.

"I'm putting my money on you," said Bob as he rubbed his thumb over his fingers in the universal gesture for money.

"Your money, or *our* money?" asked Walt, and the laughter rolled on. It acted as a gentle cathartic, soothing away all the problems of the last few days. I could feel the team relaxing, letting the built-up tension slide away. I secretly wished Paul could have been in here to share in it. He'd moved from one war zone into another without any time to process any of it. I remembered the time it had taken me, transitioning from Afghanistan back to home. It hadn't been easy, I recalled. Two different worlds. One filled with violence, uncertainty. The other filled with love, comfort. One difference. Paul had come back to a world of love, comfort, but for now it included violence, uncertainty. I mouthed a silent prayer that the violence was over or would end soon.

The house phone trilled, and I scooted to pick it up. "This is EZ," I said.

"Miss Kelly? Ramon, here at the Front desk. I have spoken with the police, and they have cleared suite 10 for occupancy. Everything is as it was before," he said, his voice reassuring.

"Did they tell you what happened? What the explosion was?" I asked him, doing my best to sound like a curious bystander.

"No, I am sad to say. They informed us that their investigation is ongoing, and they still have several tests to carry out before reaching a conclusion."

"But it is safe for Mister Boucher and Mister Spaulding to return to suite 10?"

"The police have assured us, the staff, that there is no further danger, and I pass that assurance on to you."

"Then I will pass your message on. Thank you, Ramon."

"You are most welcome, Miss. I wish you and your friends a good night."

I replaced the phone handset and turned to face the five expectant faces staring at me. I relayed the message that all was well once more, and that Peter and Kim could go back to their suite. I heard sighs of relief.

"We're done here for the night," said Walt. "Breakfast at seven at the Oceania work for everyone?"

Everyone agreed.

I checked my phone clock and was surprised to find it was already past ten. Breakfast in less than nine hours. No doubt about it: the man ran a tight ship.

"Any thoughts on where you'd like to spend the night, Walt?" I asked, considering the options.

Walt thought for a moment. "How about Bob and I go back to our original quarters, suite 6? They say lightning doesn't strike twice in the same place," he added, his face breaking out in a smile.

"Why not? We'll do like we did before. You and Bob in the bedroom and me on the couch," I said, all serious.

"Now that we've seen three attacks, and three was the number Soldier Bill came up with, don't you think I'm safe?" asked Walt, his steely eyes locked on mine.

"You've made a good point, Walt. But what if someone along the kill chain can't count?"

"You've made a better point, EZ. Better safe than sorry."

"Better safe than dead," I amended.

"That, too."

The team members went about collecting their belongings. They filed out two by two, except for Tony. He would be spending the night alone in suite 8, with his roommate Jim tied up for the night with Paul. I accompanied Walt and Bob to suite 6, the laptop in my left hand, my right hand free to access the M9 if needed.

Bob used his bracelet to open the door and all three of us stepped inside.

I glanced around at the restored suite. For all appearances, nothing looked like it had happened. Walls were as before, new furniture had been swapped out for the old, damaged pieces. The carpeting had been replaced. The only thing that even *hinted* renovations had been carried out was the faint smell of new paint. Otherwise, the trashed suite was as good as new.

Bob expressed it best when he said, "Are we in the right room?"

"Looks brand-new," said Walt as he ducked into the bedroom and flicked on the lights.

I flashed back to the explosion, running in to find Paul lying on the floor, my first thought that he was dead, gone from my life forever. Then he spoke to me, and a silent breeze swept away the nightmare that had seemed so real.

Walt came out of the bedroom and the images were further swept away. He was carrying a blanket and pillows for my couch-bed, as before. He passed them over to me with a smile. "Rest easy, EZ. I can't begin to tell you what your being here has meant to me."

"Thanks, Walt. It's a pleasure to work for the next president of the United States." I meant every word of it.

In short order, Walt and Bob retired to their shared bedroom and I settled onto the couch, my M9 resting on the arm rest within reach, the laptop open, displaying the five camera images. I called Paul to tell him breakfast would be at seven and did he think he could leave Jim tied up while he joined us for breakfast?

"I could, but if he got away somehow, I'd never live it down," he said, all serious.

I suggested that I come to his suite after I had breakfast and babysit Jim while he left to get something for himself.

"Why don't I call room service, get breakfast for Jim and me? I don't want to face charges of abuse if we don't feed him," said Jim.

I could sense his smile coming through the phone line to me.

"I like it. Sweet dreams, love."

"Sweet lying awake, love," he said.

I set my phone down and settled in for a long night. I hoped we'd seen the last assault on Walt, but if another one came, I needed to be ready. With the constant change of rooms, I felt pretty safe as long as the bad guys weren't capable of calling in a drone strike on the whole line of suites. That could be a serious game changer.

A noise from the patio area, splashes maybe, reached my ears. I threw off the blanket and hurried to the patio door. With the lights off, the room dark, I turned the knob and rushed out, my M9 leading the way.

I swept the area right, left, right again.

Nothing. No one.

Then I heard low voices, murmuring, coming from the canal. I strained to hear. A woman's low voice said what a Godsend it was that they were able to enjoy this time together, away from kids, family, commitments. I heard a man's grunt of agreement.

Threat level low. I slipped back inside and silently eased the door closed, not wanting to break the spell the couple in the canal had created.

Chapter Five

Friday, January 27th

Iglanced at my phone clock after I heard wakeup sounds coming from the bedroom. Six-thirty. Walt was on the move, so that meant Bob was, too. I hoped they'd come out with time for me to use the bathroom before we set off for breakfast.

Tony, Peter, and Kim were waiting in the hallway when we stepped out. I felt a swell of pride, being part of such a well-oiled machine.

We pushed through the Oceania's entrance a little past seven without incident. Not surprisingly, there were scant occupants. Families with kids occupied three tables, and a couple sat at a fourth. Despite the size of our entourage nobody paid us any attention.

Walt led the way to the same table we'd occupied before, and he picked the same chair. I commandeered the one next to him. He leaned towards me to ask how Paul was coping with Jim.

I told him of our conversation from the night before. "He's getting breakfast through room service for them both. Said he didn't want to face abuse charges."

Walt's wide grin summarized everything. "Yeah, in this day and age of frivolous lawsuits, he doesn't need that," he said.

The same waiter greeted us and passed out menus, then took beverage orders. Coffee all around. Easy for Ramon. I didn't bother opening the menu. The fresh fruit was perfect last time.

Kim tapped his water glass to get our attention and said, "It's time to choose a campaign slogan so I can order signs, bumper stickers. You know, 'I like Ike' or 'A chicken in every pot.' My suggestion is, 'Win with Walt.'"

A silence surrounded us while everyone considered Kim's suggestion.

"I think that's perfect, Kim! Go for it," said Walt. Period. End of discussion. With the silence broken, the other members voiced agreement.

Kim beamed. "I'll find a print shop after breakfast."

"While we're making announcements," said Bob, "two more pledges came in overnight. We're now over one-point-five million."

"That's great," said Walt, "and I haven't even said anything to the public yet."

"Let's hope that doesn't stop the pledges," said Peter, a lopsided grin on his round face.

Walt looked askance at him, then broke the spell with a full-face grin.

"Hah! Gotcha!" said Peter, with a poke of his finger at Walt.

"Thanks for that, Pete. Good preparation. I think I'll get a whole lot worse from the media and the public in the days and months ahead," said Walt.

Peter turned serious. "Yeah, I'm afraid you're right. By the way, who's setting up the press conference for my announcement tomorrow?" he asked, looking at the circle of faces.

"That'll be me. It'll be my first scheduled event," said Tony, his expression serious, all business.

Further comments were interrupted by the arrival of our breakfasts, and once set on the table, attentions turned to breaking the fasts we endured since the evening before. I munched on my delicious fresh fruit plate, enjoying the subtle differences with each selection I made. Pineapple. Mango. Papaya. Banana. Star fruit. Each had its own unique flavor and consistency. It seemed as if each new bite challenged the one I'd tried before. I'm glad there wouldn't be a quiz following the meal, because I'd fail. I was loving every morsel. There was no clear winner. My final bite left me clamoring for more.

I looked up from my vacant plate to find five pairs of eyes watching me. My focus had been so complete I'd ignored the other diners. Hell, ignored everyone, everything. I'd dodged catastrophe. No one had come at Walt while I indulged myself. A sweep of our table showed everyone had finished breakfast and silently waited for me to finish.

Walt, observant as ever, said, "If everyone is finished, I suggest we return to the war room and get on with the business at hand."

Everyone responded by standing up. I took up the rear as we filed out and into the morning heat. The scent of blossoming flowers filled my senses. *Tough duty.* I thought of other past duties far less pleasant, where the scent was of human waste and garbage and God knew what else. Flowers weren't featured on the menu in Afghanistan unless you considered poppies.

We returned to suite 6 without incident, and after everyone was safely inside, I called Paul.

"Good morning," he said, avoiding making any references to our close relationship with Jim close by.

"Hey, love. How was your ordered-in breakfast?"

"Good, if you like cold eggs and warm juice," he said.

I decided not to mention my breakfast after hearing about his. "Did Jim eat hearty?" I asked.

"When I pulled the duct tape off his mouth, he grumbled and groused a good five minutes, then asked for a fruit plate and coffee. Room service couldn't screw that up."

I agreed. I reviewed with Paul everything that had been discussed and decided upon at breakfast, then volunteered to watch Jim while Paul stood guard over Walt. Change of scenery, change of pace.

"There's a problem. Jim's got a prostate issue and he's in the bathroom every couple hours. You ready to take that on?"

I got a picture in my mind.

"Guess I'll pass," I said.

"Thought so. Thanks for the offer, though."

We said our good-byes and I set down my phone as Kim headed for the door and a cab ride to a print shop nearby. He told everyone that he wanted a first-hand close-up inspection of everything he was getting.

"First impressions are everything," he said, summing up his thoughts.

Tony made a call, spoke to Miss Haversham about setting up a press conference and announcement of Walt's candidacy. Her excited voice came through the receiver. Tony arranged to meet with her at ten to go over all the necessary arrangements, including notifying the local press and media, and getting word out to all the guests.

"How will you dress?" I asked Walt.

His face went blank for a moment as he considered the question.

"Huh. I never thought to bring a suit, or a sports jacket, for that matter," he said.

"Nobody else is going to wear anything fancy, certainly not your audience, Walt. My suggestion is that you wear your nicest trousers and sports shirt. You'll fit right in. A coat or suit would make you stand out like, I don't know, a bull in a china shop," I finished lamely.

"Are you saying I could be a raging bull plowing my way through a china shop?" he said, his head cocked to the side, a sly expression dancing over his craggy face.

Seeing his expression, I knew he was well on the way to handling what lay ahead for him.

For the remainder of the morning, Walt worked the bugs out of the speech that would announce the start of his candidacy, and he and Peter discussed possible questions he might get from both the media and the assembled guests.

Tony came back from his meeting with Miss Haversham looking like he'd scored the winning goal. He regaled us all with the arrangements. The announcement would take place tomorrow at two in the afternoon. All the guests would be sated with lunch, and anyone who went on a morning trip should be back by then. She knew from her many experiences as a hostess that it was the optimum time for Walt's announcement. She also agreed to contact the local TV and radio stations, as well as give a heads-up to local journalists. She expressed her glee at having the announcement take place at El Mar Placida, said the publicity alone would attract hundreds of people to the resort. Maybe thousands.

We all congratulated Tony on his success.

I got through the morning with no guns drawn, bombs thrown, or explosive devices planted on Walt's shirt. A success, no matter how you looked at it.

At a quarter to twelve, Kim returned with sample posters, buttons and bumper stickers. He'd done well. The colors were true to the red, white, and blue of our flag and everything he ordered bore a nice professional touch. 'Win with Walt,' not 'Wine with Walt' or some other accidental variation. Kim got a well-deserved round of applause for his successes.

When the applause died down, Walt took charge. "Let's all go get a nice lunch, celebrate. Anyone have an objection to Fruit of the Sea? I didn't think so," he said without pause.

He led the way to the door, but I cut him off so I could have a looksee before we headed out. The hall was empty, so I motioned for the team to proceed. Then, walked amongst them to provide maximum protection. They had grown accustomed to my ways, accepted it with grace.

Fruit of the Sea's lunch menu was to die for. I spotted a seafood salad and fell in love instantly. It had shrimp, mussels, fresh tuna and a local snapper all laid out on a bed of lettuce and fresh vegetables, to be topped off at the table with a cruet of balsamic vinaigrette. I sipped at my iced tea in anticipation.

The table conversation included fundraising by Bob, scheduling of tomorrow's kickoff announcement as well as the one in Topeka next week by Tony, a recap of Kim's trip to the local printers, and Peter's efforts to provide maximum media exposure, starting tomorrow. Bob also said he had put feelers out to find a replacement pollster to fill Jim's shoes.

Walt suggested he find a female to fill the position, help balance out the team. Bob was quick to agree, saying it made perfect sense.

Walt followed up by bestowing his blessings on each and every team member for all the hard work that had been done, as well as for the work in progress. No question about it. Walter McKelvy was sounding more like a polished politician with every passing moment.

I jumped in during a lull in the conversation. "Don't forget, we've got the A-team arriving sometime this afternoon." Everyone knew the A-team was Secret Service.

"I don't know why we need them. You and Paul have handled everything perfectly," said Walt, his beaming smile directed at me.

That triggered a "Hear! Hear!" and beverages raised to me. Embarrassing, but nice. I felt my face flush with the attention.

Mercifully, lunch arrived to intervene. Everyone dove in and silence ruled. I thought of Paul, stuck in his suite, babysitting a man who tried to kill Walt while I feasted on an incredible seafood salad. I set down my fork and called him.

"Hey, EZ. What's up?"

"Do you want me to bring you and Jim something from Fruit of the Sea for lunch?"

"You feeling guilty? I'm glad you are. Yeah. What looks good?" Paul asked.

"Everything. I'm having a seafood salad with shrimp, tuna, a chunk of local snapper and a sprinkling of mussels," I said.

"You *are* feeling guilty, aren't you? No need to answer. Hold on." I could hear him ask Jim if he wanted seafood for lunch. I couldn't hear Jim's reply, but Paul's laugh came through loud and clear. "He says he's allergic to seafood. Last time he ate there he had a plain salad," said Paul, still chuckling.

"I'll bring a seafood salad and a plain salad. Stay well," I said, then set my phone down.

When Ramon did a sweep of our table, I ordered the two salads to go. Done, I turned half my attention back to my incredible salad, while the other half continued to monitor the room and the other diners for any threats.

Nearly everyone had finished when Bob's phone rang. All eyes turned in his direction. He spoke quietly a moment, then disconnected. "That was Special Agent Cottrell. The cavalry has landed at Punta Cana, and they'll be here within the hour. I told them to come to Walt's suite once they'd checked in," said Bob.

"All the pieces are falling into place," said Walt. "You guys do incredible work. I'm proud to have you running my team."

More faces flushed. Bob said, "Speaking for myself, I'm proud to be a part of your campaign."

The other four responded with two 'Me, too's,' and two 'So am I's.'

"Thank you, one and all. Now let's get back to work," said Walt, standing.

We all got up. I scooped up the two salads in my left hand and led the way, my right hand free to access my concealed pistol if necessary.

Mercifully, it wasn't necessary.

When we were all safely back in Walt's suite, I realized I had a problem. I couldn't take the chance of leaving Walt unattended while I delivered the salads to Paul. I glanced at the four team members, assessing each one. Kim was the logical choice, I concluded. He'd procured the buttons and signs. I approached him, asked him if he'd take lunch to Paul. I left out Jim's name on purpose.

"Of course I will. Suite 14, right?" he promptly replied.

"Yes. Let me call him to give him a heads-up," I said, as I keyed my phone. Paul picked up and I explained.

"You're good to go, Kim. Knock once. That's your signal," I said.

Kim left with the salads in hand. He was back in less than five minutes, salads delivered. One more mission accomplished without a hitch. Hooah!

Walt and his team huddled together, their chairs in a circle, while I kept watch over them.

Sometime later, a loud knock on the hall door startled us. I leaped up, motioning everyone to stay put, and rushed to the door. Standing to the side, I asked, "Who's there?"

"It's Cottrell and my team," came the reply through the door.

Was it really? Or could it be a trick? The voice was Cottrell's. Question was: is he with us, or against us? Time to find out.

I swung the door wide, my pistol held in front and leveled at Cottrell. In my periphery, I saw four other young men, dressed casually in shorts and sports shirts, shirttails loose, I guessed to hide weapons. Surprise lit up every face. "I.D.s, everyone," I said.

"You must be Miss Kelly," said Cottrell, extending his hand to me.

"I.D.s first," I said, my eyes locked on his, the muzzle of my pistol inches from his chest.

"All right, all right. Gentlemen, show the lady your I.D.s," said Cottrell, while he took out his wallet and flashed his own.

I had a good, long look at it. If it was fake, it was a damned good one.

Each of the four young men held out I.D.s for me to check. Until I'd examined them all, I held the muzzle to Cottrell's chest wall. They were all great I.D.s. Everything fit.

I relaxed, tucked my M9 behind my back again. "Sorry for the inconvenience. I've learned to be cautious," I said to all the agents.

"No hard feelings," said Special Agent Alan Cottrell, extending his hand to me once more. I shook it, pleased with his solid grip.

"Come in and meet the next president of the United States, gentlemen," I said with a sweep of my hand. The five men stepped inside and I closed the door. Walt stood to greet them. The other four stayed seated, in deference to Walt.

Cottrell closed the gap between Walt and him in two strides, his hand extended. Walt surrounded Cottrell's hand with his own. "Pleasure, General," said Special Agent Cottrell.

"Likewise," said Walt. Short, to the point. By both men.

The four agents stepped forward and shook Walt's hand as well. I watched each of them make their assessment of the man they were willing to give up their lives to protect. I sensed that each came away with a favorable impression. Good start.

Cottrell set the example of shaking hands and getting introductions from each of Walt's team members, and the four agents followed suit. Then Cottrell turned back to face me.

"Your reputation precedes you, Miss Kelly. Both of your FBI acquaintances spoke highly of you. You've no doubt been a valuable asset to General McKelvy."

"You've no idea," said Walt, overhearing.

"I'd like to hear what's happened here prior to our arrival," said Cottrell.

"That'll be you, EZ," said Walt, with a wave of his hand.

I beckoned Cottrell and the four agents to follow me to the far side of the room where we wouldn't be interrupting or distracting Walt's team from their preparations. The five men formed a loose circle around me, though I sensed that a part of every agent's attention was focused on guarding Walt. Professionals.

I began by telling them what Walt had said about forces in Washington who didn't want independents, outsiders entering the presidential race without their backing. Then I reviewed what happened when the man surprised me in my suite and took me out to my patio to kill me. I added that I figured it was a way of sending a pointed message to Walt: give up his plans to enter the race or expect to pay consequences.

"How'd you get out of it?" asked one of the agents, a solidly built Hispanic man.

I took out my lockback knife and held it out for all of the agents to see. "I buried this in his temple," I said in a matter-of-fact voice, while my eyes checked in with each agent.

Eyebrows were raised as opinions of me changed. Cottrell said, "I didn't hear that and none of you did, either." Heads nodded in agreement.

Next, I told them of the bomb attack on Walt's suite, with Paul, not Walt inside, followed by a review of Soldier Bill going to the hospital to kill Walt and finding Paul. I explained to them how Paul had surprised him, and that Soldier Bill told him there were three attackers but didn't know their identities. Before letting him go, Paul got a sworn oath from Bill that he wouldn't try again to kill Walt, but that didn't work out so well for Soldier Bill.

I went on to say we'd taken the third assailant alive—Jim Bennett, Walt's pollster and team member, who had planted an explosive on Walt's shirt during a celebratory get-together at the Tipsy Frog. Paul caught up with Bennett and brought him back to the group. A search of his pockets revealed two more button explosives. They didn't detonate because they had a built-in activation switch on them.

"Paul will see that you get them. Maybe you can trace them back to their origin, nail the jerks responsible for all this," I said.

"That's one hell of a story, EZ," said Special Agent Cottrell with a shake of his head.

"Yeah, well, let's hope there aren't more assassins waiting in the wings."

"Agreed. Where is Jim Bennett now?" Cottrell asked.

"Paul's holding him in his suite. He's got him duct-taped," I said.

"Let's go see him." Cottrell spoke quickly to the four agents, directing three to stay with Walt and his team and indicating the fourth agent was to come with us.

I called Paul, told him what was happening and to expect company.

"I'm ready for a little company. This guy is starting to drive me up the wall," he said.

I led the way to Paul's suite, relieved to leave Walt being guarded by the Secret Service.

Paul opened the door to my knock, and we stepped inside. Jim sat in one of the padded armchairs, his wrists duct-taped together so he had limited movement of his hands. He glanced up at us as we entered, his expression flat, detached.

I introduced Paul to Special Agent Alan Cottrell, and Cottrell introduced us to his agent, Harry Fowler. Handshakes were exchanged.

"I understand you've taken possession of a detonator and a couple of exploding devices, is that right?" Cottrell asked Paul.

"That's right. I took them off Bennett after he tried to kill General McK-elvy. I've got them right here," he said. He reached in his front pocket and removed them, then held them out to Cottrell.

Special Agent Cottrell took them and examined them closely, his eyebrows raising in surprise. "These are top of the heap devices. I'm guessing they originated from CIA or a similar organization. Rest assured, we'll discover their origin," he said. He put the two explosive devices in one of his pockets. "You said there's a detonator, too," added Cottrell.

"There is, but it's in the pond at the Tipsy Frog bar." Paul explained how it ended up there.

"We can get a team there, find it. It could add more teeth to a case against the Washington elite," he said.

Cottrell then turned his gaze on Jim Bennett. "So, Mister Bennett, I understand you've been a very bad boy. Why would you want to bite the hand that's feeding you?"

Bennett stared at the floor, avoiding eye contact, and sat mute, unresponsive.

Cottrell knelt in front of Bennett and reached out to lift his head. When Bennett made eye contact, he said, "We could make things a lot easier for you if you talk to us, you know."

Bennett stayed silent.

"As an example, instead of facing charges of attempted murder of a politician that could net you twenty years in a federal penitentiary, we could modify the charges you face so you'd end up with a brief stay in a state prison, with time off for good behavior. I'm sure you're capable of good behavior, aren't you Mister Bennett?"

No response. His eyes stared vacantly at Agent Cottrell.

"Tell us what you know, Mister Bennett, and I'm sure we can work with you," said Cottrell.

"They'll kill me." The words spilled out of Bennett in a whisper.

"Now, how could they do that? You'd be in our protective custody," said Cottrell.

"They'd find a way," he croaked.

"You want to know something, Mister Bennett?" Cottrell leaned in, forcing Bennett's attention. "If they threatened to kill you if your attack failed, you might as well consider yourself already dead. When they find out you're in custody, they'll automatically assume you've spilled your guts and they'll come for you."

That found its mark. "I don't know anything! No names, no faces, nothing that could help you," said ex-pollster Jim Bennett, his voice rising.

"How did they contact you? How did you get the exploding buttons, the detonator?" pressed Cottrell.

"Phone calls, with something that changed the person's voice, made it sound high-pitched like a woman's, but I don't think it was," said Bennett in a rush of words.

"How much did they offer to pay you?"

"A hundred thousand, at first, but I told the voice it wasn't enough. He or she went to two-fifty in a heartbeat. When I said five hundred, the voice laughed at me, said take the two-fifty, that was the best they'd do. I thought a moment. Two hundred and fifty thousand dollars would go a long way with me. So I agreed."

"What proof did you have they'd come through with the money?"

"They told me to check my bank balance. When I did, there was two hundred and fifty thousand dollars sitting there in my account, out of the blue. They said it'd be there when I completed the assignment, is how they put it. Then the two-fifty disappeared from my account, poof! Just like that. I believed them. Who can do that with money so easily?" said Bennett.

"Who gave you the buttons, the detonator?" pressed Cottrell.

"I don't know. They sent me a key for a locker in the bus terminal. The detonator and buttons were inside, with a typed note explaining how to use them."

"What happened to the note?" asked Cottrell.

"At the bottom it said, *Memorize these instructions, then tear up this note and throw it in the trash bin.* It even told me where the trash bin was."

"Think a moment. Is there anything you remember that can help us find these people?"

Jim Bennett lowered his head, his eyes staring at the carpet, and sat silently a moment, thinking hard. Then, he slowly shook his head side to side. "Nothing. They're pros. They covered all their tracks."

I listened to the entire conversation between the agent and the assassin. In the past, I'd stepped in and applied a little force to the subjects, threatening to kill them if they didn't answer my questions. If they said something dumb like, 'I've got my rights,' I'd tell them I wasn't the law, I didn't need to follow the rules, and maybe push my knife blade into their neck for emphasis. It had worked well. I'd gotten good results. But here? I decided I'd be wasting my time. Bennett's story wasn't going to change. A knife to his throat wasn't going to open any doors. I agreed with Bennett. The guys behind the attempt to kill Walt McKelvy were pros.

Cottrell had heard enough, too. He told Fowler to stay and watch over Bennett so Paul could take a break. That was considerate of him. My impression of him hitched up another notch.

Agent Cottrell, Paul and I left the room and closed the door behind us. I wondered how Agent Fowler would handle Bennett's frequent bathroom breaks. A giggle escaped me.

Paul heard, his eyebrows raised in question.

I smiled and shook my head, mouthing 'later.'

Back in Walt's suite, the three agents had deployed effectively. We had passed one agent loitering unobtrusively in the hallway. Inside Walt's suite, one was positioned in one of the chairs away from Walt's team, while the third agent had staked out the patio. All the bases were covered. It was good to have them on board. I felt an invisible weight lift off of me. A glance at Paul confirmed he was feeling lighter, too.

Walt looked up when we came in. "Learn anything?" he asked, his eyes on Special Agent Cottrell.

"Negative, sir," he replied. "But we'll get there."

"Best of luck," said Walt, before turning his attention back to his team.

Paul and I huddled with Cottrell. "It looks to me like you've got things covered pretty well right now. Paul and I have been a little sleep-deprived over the last couple days. Any chance we can cut away and close our eyes?" I asked, my voice pitched low, not wanting to disturb the working team.

"Hell, yeah. We got things covered. Unofficially, you understand," said Cottrell, offering up a rare smile.

"Unofficially?"

"Yeah. Until Walt announces his candidacy tomorrow, we're not officially on the clock," said Cottrell.

"So you're doing Paul and me a favor by standing guard while we sleep?"

"I couldn't have said it better. Look at it as our way of learning the General's habits so we're ready when we officially take over tomorrow."

"Thanks for offering us your break-in period. Paul and I are grateful. I'll leave the laptop with you so you can monitor the camera feeds," I said, with a gesture at the computer. I checked my phone. It was just past two-thirty. "We'll be back here for dinner. Walt breaks promptly at six."

"See you then," said Cottrell.

Paul and I hurried out and down the hallway to my suite.

Once there, Paul drew me in close, whispered in my ear. "You have such wonderful suggestions, EZ." He nibbled on my earlobe. It took every fiber of my flagging resistance to parry the temptation he was suggesting.

"Let's sleep first. It'll make our lovemaking even better after," I whispered to him.

"Huh. Just when I was thinking you have such wonderful suggestions," he said, his voice pouty. His smile gave him away, though.

We moved together to the bedroom and shed our clothes before crawling under the covers. I reached out and rested my hand on Paul's shoulder. He made an unintelligible sound and was asleep in a heartbeat. I followed him down the beckoning dark tunnel and was soon out.

A loud crash brought me fully awake. Paul heard it and woke, too.

"That sounded like it came from next door," he said with a glance towards me.

Next door. Jim Bennett. Agent Fowler!

Paul and I leapt from bed and hurriedly dressed. He got to the door first, with me right behind. We rushed out and I used my purloined passkey to open the door to Paul's suite. Paul went in low, gun drawn, and I followed right behind.

Jim Bennett turned to see us, his hand clutching a pocketknife he was using to cut away the duct tape securing his wrists.

"Drop it!" shouted Paul.

Instead of dropping it, Bennett turned the knife in his hand, preparing to drive it into his neck and end his life.

I got to him before he drove the knife forward, my clenched right fist driving into his left temple with a loud crack. Bennett sagged into himself, the blade dropping harmlessly to the carpet.

I scooped it up, folded it closed and tucked it into my capri pocket.

Meanwhile, Paul raced into the bedroom. "Fowler's in here," he yelled. He and Fowler walked out to the living area. It was clear the man was shaken. Paul set him down in a chair next to Bennett.

"What happened?" asked Paul.

I noted a red, raised spot on Fowler's forehead.

"I'll never live this down," wailed Fowler.

"We all make mistakes. It makes us better at what we do," said Paul.

I kept my eye on Bennett's inert form. We didn't need a repeat of the previous scene.

"The prick said he had to pee. I walked him into the bathroom, and he fumbled with his zipper. I turned away slightly, giving him his privacy. When I turned back, he head-butted me, knocked me out. Stupid, stupid!" said Fowler.

I dug the pocketknife from my pocket. "This yours?" I asked him, holding it up.

"Yeah. Prick must've picked my pocket while I was out," he said, anger in his voice.

I handed it back to him. "We were next door, heard the commotion. Bennett was going to stick the knife in his neck when we burst in on him. So, all's well that ends well. This'll be our little secret," I told Fowler.

"You mean you won't mention this to Cottrell?" asked Fowler, an incredulous expression overcoming his face.

"What's the point? Bennett's still with us and you're older and wiser. What more can we ask for?" said Paul, his words backing me up.

"Gee, thanks, both of you. You won't regret this," said Fowler.

If I had to guess, Paul was mimicking my thoughts: *I'm sure we won't.*

We left Fowler, fully awake and alert, watching over Bennett, who was showing signs of returning to consciousness.

Back in my suite, I checked the time: five forty-five. We'd grabbed about three hours of sleep, and now we were literally shaking off the effects of our combined adrenaline rush, which is never any fun. Trembling, heart rates up, all our senses keyed to their highest despite our having put the challenge in the rearview mirror. Time to come back down.

Paul and I hurried into the bathroom. We each grabbed a glass, filled it to the brim with water from the sink and drank greedily. We both knew from experience that it helped dilute the adrenaline sensation we were feeling. We refilled our glasses and returned to the living area where we sank into padded armchairs, facing each other.

"Hell of a scene," said Paul between gulps.

"Happy ending, though," I said, holding my glass in front of my mouth between sips.

"One Fowler won't forget," said Paul.

I knew what he meant. He wouldn't make that mistake again. "How are you doing?" I asked.

Paul held out his left hand, his right gripping his glass. He eyeballed his fingers. I saw the faintest of trembling.

"Not bad," I said, then held out my left hand. The fine tremor imitated Paul's.

"Guess we're good to go," he said.

I nodded in agreement.

'Good to go' meant meeting Walt and his crew for dinner. It was now six and they'd be on the move. Since we'd eaten at La Placida yesterday, I guessed they'd be going somewhere else tonight. Paul and I left my room and headed down the hallway. I called Walt's phone. He answered in two.

"Are you at La Trattoria?" I asked. We hadn't had dinner there yet, so it was a safe guess.

"How'd you know? You got spies out?" he said in his deep, amiable voice.

"No. I'm psychic," I fired back.

At La Trattoria, we found Walt and his team already hunkered down at a table for seven. They'd saved seats for Paul and me. A glance around the tables showed Cottrell and his three agents had deployed at two separate tables, two agents per table, each table positioned strategically on either side of Walt's. They had him covered. I loved seeing their learning curve in action.

Walt saw us coming and stood to greet us. We exchanged pleasantries. "Looks like the sleep did you good," he said with a wink and a nod.

"It did," I said, answering for both of us. I noted with satisfaction that my adrenaline tremors were ancient history.

"Grab a seat. We were about to order," said Walt.

Paul and I sat and scanned the menus set in front of us.

With four Secret Service agents surrounding our table, I relaxed and enjoyed my dinner. I knew that they weren't officially on the job, but their presence alone allowed me to focus more on my dinner than on searching the room for trouble.

My meal was not only beautifully presented, but it was a delicate treat as well. I made a mental note to mention it to my tourist customers back home.

A thought came to me. Does the waiter, noting my unique wristband, tell the chefs which one is my order so they can embellish it further, knowing I'm a travel agent? Paul had ordered the same dish, and I scrutinized his plate for any differences. I could see none. He was enjoying his as much as I was. He'd had to brown-bag it for too many dinners.

The mealtime passed without incident. Walt kept his eye out, and when the last fork was laid to rest, he stood, prepared to lead us back to his suite. We all stood with him.

Two Secret Service agents got up and led the way, their eyes busy searching for threats. Our group followed them, and the second detail of agents took up the rear with frequent glimpses behind. We made it back to Walt's suite without so much as a hair out of place.

It occurred to me that with the Secret Service on scene, Walt and his team had no further use for Paul's and my services. I said as much to Walt.

"That's not true," he said with emphasis. "Secret Service doesn't officially take over protection until I give my commitment speech tomorrow. It's true they're here, but it's unofficial. Agent Cottrell told me they're here to learn my habits, how I move, stuff like that, and I guess they'd act in my defense if trouble happened, but they may not be on it as fast as you and Paul would be. Bottom line is, you and Paul are still my main defense line until my speech tomorrow." That put an end to any further discussion.

"When you start your speech or when you finish your speech?" I asked, wanting clarification.

"Good question. Let's ask Cottrell."

Together we went to Cottrell and Walt asked him when exactly Secret Service would take the reins.

"When you declare in your public speech tomorrow that you are officially a candidate for the Presidency of the United States, Secret Service assumes the duty of protecting you," he stated, his face serious as he quoted chapter and verse.

"There you go," said Walt, turning back to me.

"Okay. As before, I'll camp out on your sofa in the living room while Paul guards the patio area," I said.

"It's worked so far, so stick with it. No sense messing with success," said Walt, going back to his team.

I told Paul we weren't off the hook yet and he'd be the patio sentinel. He nodded to me before he hurried out onto the patio and eased the door closed behind him.

When the agents said good night and left the suite, I wasn't surprised. Cottrell had made it clear. Anyway, they deserved a good night's sleep before they took over tomorrow. I assumed they'd split into two teams, changing out every twelve hours. An easier duty than the one Paul and I had done.

I got the pillow and blanket from Walt's bedroom closet and set up shop on the sofa, my M9 pistol set within easy reach, the laptop open within view. I listened to Walt going over his speech one more time, with Bob his critical listener. I could tell from the tone of his voice it was coming together, that he was pleased with his efforts. Practice was making it perfect. I settled in.

It's never easy to stay awake, alert to possible threats when the world around you is sleeping soundly. Walt and Bob had long since retired to their shared bedroom. The sound of their intermittent snoring came through their closed door in the silence that surrounded me. I focused on it, using it as a stimulus to keep me awake. If the snoring stopped, it meant I'd lost the battle and had fallen asleep. And that could spell disaster.

Chapter Six

Saturday, January 28th

Six-thirty, by my phone clock. Thin daylight seeped in through the glass panes of the patio door and Bob and Walt began moving around in the bedroom. Walt's habits were fixed. He and Bob would be dressed and ready for breakfast just before seven.

Showing consideration for me, they swung open the bedroom door and greeted me at ten of seven. That gave me unfettered access to the bathroom for a quick ten minutes. I used the time well. I looked at the shower longingly first, but instead rinsed my face and hands with water, followed by a rearrangement of my straight blonde hair into a neat ponytail. Five minutes, total.

I scooted back to the living room and swung open the patio door. Paul, waiting, ducked inside and did his even quicker five minutes in the bathroom. He didn't sport a ponytail, and his close-cropped hair didn't need a comb, all of which gave him an edge. We were both ready to move at seven.

When I swung open the hall door, three Secret Service agents stood waiting, their faces serious, all business. Cottrell and the fourth agent watched over Jim in Paul's suite, I guessed. I turned to Walt. "Where to?" I asked him.

"Oceania," he replied at once.

I repeated it to the agents, and we filed out as before: two leading, then me, then Walt's team, then Paul and the third agent trailing. The desk clerk gave us a cheery "Good morning!" as we passed, and we all waved to acknowledge her greeting. We were suddenly a force to be reckoned with. Five armed guards surrounding Walt and his team. The veritable size of our entourage was guaranteed to draw curious stares. All we needed was a couple of Kim's placards to complete the picture: WIN WITH WALT. They'd arrive soon from the print shop.

Oceania, as expected, had few breakfasters at that hour. Walt led the way to the same table we'd used before and the agents took tables on either side of us, two and one. The sudden influx brought forth two additional waiters with menus, one for each of the agent's tables and Ramon for ours. Menus were distributed all around with a flourish, and beverage orders were taken. Silence prevailed while all our eyes turned to the menus. The prospect of food was in charge. I already knew what I'd have. I was fast becoming a loyal fan of the tropical fruit plate.

Conversation was centered around the announcement of Walt's candidacy. Tony confirmed it would take place at one o'clock in the lobby. He said it was the best time. Guests would be finished with lunch and Walt's announcement would occur before they got involved in afternoon activities. Peter said he'd already put the word out to all the local news media with hopes they'd post the news on all the major networks. Kim said the print shop would deliver the posters and a big banner, plus leaflets outlining Walt's career by ten o'clock. He would oversee getting the banner up and place the rest of the materials in strategic locations for the expected guests to see and pick up. Paul and I agreed to be "supporters," waving signs and saying positive things about Walt to get the anticipated crowd involved.

Walt cut to the chase. "How many people will show up?" he asked as he glanced around the table.

Tony jumped in. "The manager, Miss Haversham, said just over three hundred guests are here at present. If we can get a third of them to come, that'd be around a hundred. Not bad," he said, smiling broadly.

"Not bad at all. Let's hope at least that many show up," said Walt.

Breakfasts arrived and everybody turned their attention to their disposal in relative silence. Soon, we were filing out of the restaurant in our orderly fashion.

Back at Walt's suite the three agents deployed as before, with one in the hall, one on the patio and one inside the suite. Paul and I huddled together. "Six more hours to go in our commitment to Walt," I whispered to him.

He nodded.

We both stayed in the room with Walt, prepared to defend him to the end.

At a little past ten, the room phone rang. The print shop delivery had arrived. Kim left to sign for it and get the banner hung up. I told Walt I'd give him a hand and Walt waved at me to go.

I caught up with Kim, glad to be doing something.

He turned back, hearing me, and beamed at the sight of me. "You coming to help?" he asked.

"I am. I think Walt's safe enough without me," I said.

We walked together to the lobby. The print shop delivery man stood waiting at the check-in counter with two large boxes set in front of him. He smiled, seeing Kim. I could see no signs of a threat.

After he made a cursory exam of the boxes' contents, Kim paid for the materials. The delivery man thanked Kim as he backed toward the entrance and was gone.

Kim picked up one box while I took the other. He led the way to the far corner of the lobby. I watched him assessing the room as he went, deciding on the best place for Walt to give his speech. He chose the near corner. From there, Walt could face all the expected participants, both media and resort guests.

Kim removed the felt banner and unfolded it. It was approximately four by six feet, with red, white, and blue waves rolling over it. In the center, 'WIN WITH WALT' dominated.

"It's perfect," I said.

He acknowledged my compliment with a broad smile.

Together, we secured it to the wall so anyone passing by would see it.

That done, Kim removed two-by-two placards bearing the same message, plus a bundle of informational brochures touting Walt's accomplishments and his goals as president. He set them on a nearby table. Last to come out was a bundle of bumper stickers with WIN WITH WALT emblazoned on them.

It occurred to me that some of the spectators might want Walt's autograph and I asked Kim if he had a pen Walt could use to do the signing.

"Good point, EZ. I'll make sure he has a pen and maybe a felt tip pen, too, in case someone wants a cap or a shirt signed. You never know," said Kim with a wide gesture of his hands.

Although we were done in short order, I was surprised to find it was after eleven on the lobby clock. Less than two hours until the announcement and I knew Walt would want some lunch before his big speech.

Kim and I hurried back to the suite, and I used my passkey card to unlock the door. I opened it to find a pistol pointed at my face.

"Sorry, Miss," said the embarrassed agent, as he secured his pistol. It was Fowler, the agent who got head-butted by Jim. He was making up for the momentary lapse of his guard.

"You did right, Agent. No excuse needed," I said after I drew in a calming breath.

"Hey, EZ, Kim. Everything set?" called Walt.

"All set, Walt," said Kim.

"Then let's all get an early lunch so we aren't rushed," he suggested.

"Great idea," said Bob. "We should be back here by twelve-thirty to deal with any last-minute details."

"We'll do the La Placida buffet, be in and out quickly," said Walt.

It was a speedy lunch, as promised. We were back in Walt's suite at twelve-thirty. Bob's prediction of the time turned out to be right on.

Paul and I stayed out of the way during the last-minute shuffling of papers and checking of lists. Our eyes and ears stayed focused on the task of protecting Walt.

At ten of one, two of the Secret Service agents left the suite and headed for the lobby. Then I led the way, with Bob, Tony, Peter, and Kim following behind me. Walt came next, then Paul and the other agent took up the rear, covering our six. Halfway there, I turned to look back at Walt. He was striding along like he was leading his troops, confidence bubbling out of him in silent waves. He was feeling it. He was fully in command.

When we turned the corner into the lobby area, the size of the crowd surprised me. There were easily a hundred people waiting for us, for Walt. All eyes turned our way, expectant. Bob strode to the corner where the banner was on display, drawing all eyes, and began to speak, his voice brimming with enthusiasm.

"Good afternoon to all of you. Thank you for sharing your time with us at this historic moment. General Walter McKelvy, now retired after a long and illustrious career in the U.S. Army, is here to announce his candidacy for the president of the United States of America. Without further ado, I turn the floor over to General McKelvy."

While he spoke, Kim handed out the placards that said WIN WITH WALT to anyone wanting one. He quickly ran out. Paul and I managed to grab two and we held them high for all to see.

Walt stepped forward and delivered his extemporaneous speech. He spoke of being an independent and of uniting the Democrats and Republicans, who seemed more willing to disagree with one another than get things done. I watched the crowd as he spoke. They were listening, weighing, considering.

Walt finished by saying, "I am officially entering the race for president of the United States of America, and with your support, I *will be* the next President of the United States."

Then, the crowd erupted with cheers and whistles. A TV cameraman caught it all. A throng of well-wishers surged forward to get Walt's autograph. There was no doubt about it: Walt's first speech was a huge success.

I caught sight of the Secret Service agents. They stood facing the crowd, their eyes everywhere at once, their right hands held loosely in front of their jackets. I smiled, imagining the lethal firepower hidden underneath their coats.

Several people in the gathered crowd stepped forward to ask Walt a question or to wish him well. The agents moved in to create a barrier in case one of Walt's new fans tried anything. Walt ignored the agents and responded to his admirers. He was relaxed, at ease.

I was feeling relief at having brought him to this point without injury, or worse. At the same time, I felt fatigue wash over me from all the hours of wakefulness I'd endured. I glanced at Paul. The shadows under his eyes reflected his own level of exhaustion.

When the last well-wisher had drifted away, I stepped up to Walt, my hand extended. He took it, pulled me in and gave me a warm hug. "Thank you, EZ. I couldn't have done it without you." His words rang with sincerity.

"I was glad to do it. You are worth protecting. I think you'll be a fantastic president," I said.

"I've got a long way to go, but thanks for your support. By the way, we'll be on a plane out of here this evening. Come by my suite after this, you and Paul, so Bob can pay you. You both deserve every penny of it," said Walt, his warm smile adding to his kind words.

Paul had joined us while Walt spoke and now offered Walt his hand. Walt took it, then drew him close and hugged him tight.

Walt turned to follow his team back to his suite, the three Secret Service agents in full command of his protection. Paul and I stood watching them go, Paul's arm held loosely around my waist. It felt perfect there. I rested my hand on his arm, feeling his warmth, his strength.

"I don't know how you feel, Paul, but I'm ready for a nap," I said, looking up at him.

"You tired? I'm bubbling over with excess energy!" he replied through a sleepy smile.

"Uh huh. How come your eyes are at half-mast?" I said. I stroked his nose with my finger.

"Well, maybe I could use a *little* nap," he conceded.

"Let's go collect our paychecks first," I suggested.

We strolled together hand in hand, not a care in the world, to Walt's suite. An agent stood at the door, alert, on guard. Seeing us coming, he turned and tapped on the door. The agent posted inside swung the door open for us and we stepped through.

Bob and Walt, busy packing their belongings and briefcases, looked up to see us.

"Hey, you two," said Walt. "I'll forever be in debt to you. Bob, do you have their envelopes?"

"Right here," said Bob. He handed one to me, the other to Paul.

We took them, tucked them into our pockets, not bothering to check them. If we couldn't trust Walt and Bob, who could we trust?

Walt watching, said, "You both deserve those," meaning the contents of the envelopes. "If it hadn't been for you, I'd be a statistic instead of a candidate."

"It was an honor and a privilege protecting you, Walt. We'll be following you every step of your campaign." I spoke for both of us. Paul nodded in agreement.

"If I'm anywhere near you during my campaign I hope you'll come see me," he said with warmth.

"We will," Paul and I said in unison.

Walt's warm smile sealed the deal. "Now go catch some sleep, you two. You've earned it," said Walt.

We said our final farewells to both men, asked them to say good-bye to the others for us, and left the suite.

"Your room or mine?" asked Paul, as we shuffled along side by side.

"Whichever comes first," I said, knowing his did.

Inside, we found everything neat and tidy. All traces of Bennett were gone. I guessed that Special Agent Cottrell had transferred him into the legal system for would-be assassins. Paul had the foresight to put out the *Do not disturb* sign. We stripped slowly, our weary eyes feasting on each other's bodies as we did so. Then we crawled into bed and lay facing each other, arms loosely laced across each other. Relaxed and contented, sleep swept us away.

Hours later I awoke and stretched, feeling alive, alert, refreshed. Paul's caressing hands showed he was awake, too.

I brushed his lips with mine, signaling I was in the mood to play.

Together, we climbed to the top of the mountain and cascaded down the other side, clinging to each other, not wanting to let go. It was worth all of the anticipation we had endured.

After we recovered from our shared intimacy, Paul declared he was starving.

"Me, too," I whispered, as I playfully nibbled on his ear. I reached for my phone. It was after eight. We'd slept for a much-needed six hours. I felt alive once more but being close to Paul had a lot to do with it.

We showered together, barely resisting the temptation of more intimate contact. Paul stepped out first and dressed in his khaki shorts and navy polo shirt. I took a moment to wash my hair before I turned off the water, wrapping myself in a plush towel before putting on my yellow capri pants and pale yellow blouse.

The forgotten envelope Bob had handed me dropped from my pocket as I stepped into my capris. Curious, I tore it open and pulled out the bills. All hundreds. I counted. Twenty-five of them! I couldn't remember holding so much money at one time, and then I remembered: the mansion in Valdosta. I shook off the memory, stuffed the bills back in the envelope and tucked it in my pants pocket.

Meanwhile, Paul had checked his envelope, came up with the same total. "I was here one day shy of you," he said. "Walt overpaid me."

I reminded him that he was put on the payroll the evening before he arrived at El Mar, so no, it wasn't a mistake.

"More than generous," he said, pocketing his envelope.

"Where to?" I asked, knowing already what he'd say.

"El Gaucho!" he said, confirming my thoughts. The last time he'd tasted El Gaucho's fare was when he'd put up with takeout. I knew he was looking forward to hot and fresh off the grill. We left the room hand in hand.

El Gaucho's at eight-thirty was crowded, but the maître d' spotted my wristband and had us at a table in a flash. As a special treat, we shared a bottle of cabernet, which paired beautifully with our steaks.

Paul made ooh and aah noises as he cut his way through his T-bone steak, and my tenderloin had me humming softly with each tender bite. We thoroughly enjoyed applying our full attention to our meals and each other. Having to scan the room for threats was behind us. It felt like we were on vacation. Hell, we were!

After we finished our steaks, we had a cursory look at the extensive dessert list, but our meals had been more than enough for both of us. We took a rain check.

When I asked the waiter how much the wine was, he pointed at my wristband and said, "It is all included, Miss." Recalling the admonition against tipping by travel agent guests, I quietly asked Paul to leave something for Ramon. He smiled and did so.

We took our time getting to Paul's room, detouring through the botanical gardens where the mixture of tropical flower fragrances filled our senses.

"That's my dessert," I murmured to Paul, inhaling deeply.

"It's nice," he said, smiling. "But I have other ideas."

"What?" I asked, not catching on.

"Let's go back to our rooms and get into our bathing suits."

Then I knew.

I giggled all the way back, leaving Paul at his door, moving on to my own room next door. I hurried inside, found my bathing suit in the bathroom, and changed into it, leaving my clothes in a heap on the bathroom floor.

I could feel my pulse quickening as I opened the patio door and stepped out. A few short steps later I was at the canal door, and then it was open, and I was through to the landing as I pushed the door closed behind me. My eyes swept the canal waters to my right, and there was Paul, or I hoped it was Paul. His bathing trunks obscured his face from where I stood.

Without a thought, I leaped into the canal, then tread water while I took off my bathing suit bottom and draped it over my head. A giggle bubbled out of me. I couldn't help it.

Paul swam up to me. There was no mistaking him now, despite his suit concealing part of his face.

We merged together, our arms encircling each other, our mouths sealing the bond. I could feel his swelling passion pressing against me and I opened myself to him. With our bodies joined as one, the rest of the world faded away. We were alone, treading water and climbing a glorious mountain once more. The journey to the top took longer, which made it all the sweeter. We reached the summit together in perfect unison, and clung tight to each other during the memorable descent.

As the last waves of passion ebbed, we dropped together to the bottom. When our feet made contact, we pushed ourselves off from the bottom of the canal and broke the water's surface.

I became aware that my bathing suit was gone from my head. I looked at Paul. His was gone, too. My laughter rolled down the canal, but no one was there to hear it.

Paul patted his now-bare head and joined in my laughter. "I'll have a look for them," he said, then turned and porpoised below the surface.

For the next several moments he swam underwater, searching, and then returned to the surface for a breath before diving again. The sight of his bare bottom flashing in the moonlight each time he dove had me in stitches.

He never found them.

We swam back to our patios with a pledge to meet in my room. Paul climbed out at his suite, the pale moonlight washing over his naked butt as he climbed out.

I giggled and waved at him, then paddled to my patio door. I was aware of my own nakedness as I climbed out, but the only observer, as far as I could tell, was the pale moon overhead. I would remember forever the incredible swim with Paul in the canal.

I took a quick shower to wash off the salty canal water. With a plush towel wrapped around my dripping head and another around my body, I padded into the living area. I was halfway across the room when I heard Paul's knock-knock-knock at the door.

As I reached for the handle, alarm bells went off in my head. Paul knocked *once*. It was our agreed-upon signal.

I dashed into the bedroom and retrieved my M9. I drew back the slide far enough to confirm a round in the chamber, grabbed the suppressor from my suitcase and moved back to the door, mounting the suppressor as I went. I heard a second knock-knock-knock as I approached.

"Sorry! I was showering," I said in a loud voice.

Silence came back at me.

I dropped to one knee, positioning myself slightly to the side of the door, and with my M9 gripped in my right hand, reached with my left hand for the door handle. I hauled down on it and yanked the door inward.

Paul stood in front of me. Standing to his right was a man I'd never seen before. He had a pistol in his hand. It was pointed into the room beyond me, not at Paul. Stupid mistake.

My first round, fired upward from a kneeling position, entered just below the man's chin and ploughed through his brain. He collapsed like a puppet with his strings cut, his pistol dropping silently onto the carpet. I didn't need to take a second shot.

The only sound came from my M9's slide cycling back, then forward as it powered another round into the chamber. The CLICK-CLICK sounded loudly in the silence of the hallway, followed by the unmistakable stink of cordite from the expended round. Nobody was witness to hear or smell the death scene except Paul and me.

Paul caught the man's collapsing body. I leaped to my feet and grabbed his limp legs. I kicked the dropped pistol into the room and bumped the door closed with my butt, then together we hauled him out to my patio. We dropped his inert body on the tile floor.

"What happened?" I asked Paul, searching his eyes.

"I'd finished dressing when I heard a knock at my door. I thought it was you. I opened it to find this creep holding a gun aimed at my face. He rushed into my room and pressed the muzzle against my head. It happened so fast I didn't have time to react. He kicked the door closed, then spoke in a whisper. Told me not to move or he'd shoot me where I stood. I believed him.

"He said he was sent to teach me and my lady friend a lesson, that it would send a message to General McKelvy to give up his run for the presidency. Then he opened the door, checked to make sure the hallway was empty, and forced me down the hallway to your room.

"'Knock on the door. No tricks,' he whispered in my ear, his pistol muzzle pressed against my temple. So I knocked three times, hoping you'd realize it wasn't me since we'd agreed to a single knock. You didn't respond, so he told me to knock again. Then I heard you saying you were sorry, that you were showering, as you came towards the door. When he heard the door opening, he swung his pistol in your direction. You surprised the hell out of him by kneeling," said Paul, with a glance at the dead man.

"I nearly opened the door after your first knock-knock-knock but remembered our one-knock signal and ran to get my pistol. When you knocked the second time, I was ready," I said, positioning my towel around me more snugly.

"You done good, my love. You saved the day," said Paul. He encircled me with his strong arms and gave me a comforting squeeze. It sent warm tingles down my spine. Considering what had just happened, Paul's words and hugs helped to wash away the ugliness of the moment.

"Let's check his pockets. Maybe we'll find something," I suggested.

Paul bent down, turning out his front pockets and tugging a wallet from the guy's right rear one. The front pockets had a set of car keys, a handful of loose change, and a typed piece of paper. Paul picked up the folded paper and handed me the wallet. He read it while I examined the wallet.

I found a D.C. driver's license in the name of one Howard A. Smith. I committed the information to memory. Nothing else in the wallet except for a wad of twenty-dollar bills and three one-hundred dollar bills. I guessed the total at somewhere over five hundred, give or take. I set it aside. Howard A. Smith's need for it had come to a bloody end.

A glance at his hands showed he wore an inexpensive digital watch on his left wrist and a resort band on his right. He was a registered guest at El Mar Placida. *That was a start.*

Paul spoke up, interrupting my thoughts. "This paper lists our room numbers and a general description of each of us. At the bottom it says, 'When the job is done, present this paper to claim your payment.' It doesn't say where," said Paul, holding it up for me to see.

"His wallet has a driver's license in the name of Howard A. Smith, with a D.C. address, plus around five hundred bucks in cash. The big find is, he's wearing a resort wristband. If we can find his room, we might learn more about him," I said, my eyes on Paul's.

"Do you have a big plastic bag?" asked Paul.

"There may be a plastic clothes bag in the bathroom closet. I'll go check," I said, guessing at what he had in mind.

Sure enough, there was one. I hurried out to the patio, the bag clutched in my hand.

Paul took it from me. He grabbed a handful of the dead man's black hair to raise his head off the patio tile and slipped the bag over his head. Then he tied a knot in the bag at his throat. Any additional blood leaking out of him would be trapped in the bag. It would make our cleanup chore far easier later on.

I used my lockback knife to carefully cut off the man's wristband and held it up for Paul to see, a grim smile on my face. "Let's go see what door this opens," I said.

"You may want to change out of that outfit," said Paul, a playful smile working its way across his rugged face.

"Good point," I said, the towel my only cover-up. "Give me a sec."

We went inside and closed the patio door. I changed back into my capris and blouse while taking deep breaths in and out to clear the adrenaline from my bloodstream.

Paul picked up the man's pistol where it lay on the floor just inside the door. He held it up so I could see it. It was another government-issue M9 with a suppressor, identical to the one I'd taken off the first assassin and used to shoot the late Mister Smith. "Somebody out there doesn't like us, EZ," Paul said grimly.

We left my suite ready for anything, Paul with the man's M9 behind his back (minus the suppressor), me with my M9 in the same position. I held Mister Smith's wristband in my left hand. We moved down the hallway, pausing at each suite door so I could run the wristband by the lock, then move on to the next when I got no results.

We located the suite in the third hallway. When we heard the suite door lock click open, Paul burst inside, pistol held in front of him, and I followed behind with mine held ready. No one was there. The suite was empty.

I closed the door and flicked on the lights so we could search for anything left behind by the late Mister Smith.

The living area gave up nothing. We moved on to the bedroom and found a suitcase open on the floor. Paul knelt down to search it.

I glanced around the room, saw the house phone on the table by the bed. By it sat a small pad of paper and a pen. I stepped closer, looking for something written on the paper. Nothing. I leaned over it, staring intently at it. Then I saw it. No visible writing, but I could see impressions left on it by a pen. The page with the writing on it had been torn off, leaving behind the impressions from the pen on the page below. *Maybe something.*

Paul stood, shaking his head. "I've never seen such a sterile suitcase," he said in a low voice. "It could have come from a store display. Absolutely nothing personal about it," he concluded.

"I may have found something," I said, pointing at the pad of paper.

"What?" he asked.

"There are indentations made by a pen. Worth checking it out," I said.

We made one more careful search through Mister Smith's suite but found nothing more. I picked up the notepad, cradling it in my hand with care, and we left the suite. We played the casual lovers as we made our way back to my suite.

Once inside, I got my mascara kit and with the fine brush in hand, I swept it gingerly over the notepad. A number emerged. A phone number. Area code 202. Could be something. Or nothing.

Paul watched me closely, smiled seeing the number. "Let's call Cottrell," he said.

I did, calling up his cell phone number from memory. He answered on the second ring.

"Agent Cottrell," he said, all official.

"It's EZ," I said.

"My caller I.D. gave you away. What's up?"

I briefly told him about the man who came to kill Paul and me, about his demise and our search. I gave him the driver's license information, then recounted our finding his room, the search, and the notepad. "It may be nothing, but it's a D.C. area code," I said.

"Worth checking. Give it to me."

I recited it to him.

"Got it," he said.

"Where are you?" I belatedly asked.

"At the local Dominican police station. I brought Mister Bennett here for safekeeping until we can extradite him back to the States to stand trial," he explained.

"Any problems?"

"At first. But when they learned he tried to kill the future president of the United States they had a change in attitude."

"Did they ask you what you knew about the two deaths here?"

"Yeah, and I played dumb. I don't need to get caught up in their investigation. I have enough to do without adding that mess to my appointment book."

"Well, there's going to be a third one when Paul and I find out if the dead guy can tread water," I said.

"I'll be long gone by then. You two should be, too," Cottrell said.

"We're out of here first thing tomorrow," I said.

"Good. Stay safe," he said, before ending the call.

Paul had overheard what Cottrell said so there was no need for me to rehash it. We turned our attention to the unpleasant task of cleaning up after Mister Smith.

The plastic bag had done its work, holding most of the blood that had been leaking from his head. I had a thought.

"What if we weighted down the body so it sat on the bottom of the canal? It won't be discovered as quickly," I said.

"Hmm, yeah," said Paul, thinking. "What could we use?"

I had an idea, but it meant going back to Mister Smith's suite. I told Paul my thought.

"That'll work," he said. "You know, his suite is only a couple hundred yards to the left, along the canal. I could swim there, grab the toilet tank lid from his bathroom and be back with it in no time."

"I'll start cleaning up the blood left behind while you go for a swim," I said.

I had enough peroxide left to do a thorough job. There were a couple droplets inside the front door on the carpet that vanished with a little white foam. I spotted my shell casing and picked it up. Then, I followed the path we'd taken to the patio door and found a few more scattered droplets. They disappeared under the peroxide bath.

Out on the patio, the biggest mess was where Mister Smith's head had rested. I blotted the thickening blood off the tile with toilet paper and used the peroxide to make the rest go away. I'd do a final inspection and clean-up when Mister Smith was busy holding his breath underwater.

I heard small splashes from the canal and opened the door to find Paul was back. He gave me a thumbs up. I saw that he'd substituted a pair of shorts for his lost bathing suit.

After he scanned the canal in both directions, he mouthed 'all clear,' then set the lid on the step and climbed out. Together, we manhandled Mister Smith's mortal remains into the canal. Paul jumped in and loosened the man's belt enough to slip the toilet lid inside, then cinched the belt tight. The body dropped rapidly below the surface with the added weight.

The rest was up to Paul. He towed the body slowly, painstakingly, in the direction of Mister Smith's suite after he untied the plastic bag from his head and pulled it off. I could see a cloudy area in the water from the sudden release of blood, but it rapidly dissipated as the current swirled it along.

I lost sight of Paul for a time before hearing him swim back, breast-stroking to make minimal noise. He climbed out and I shut the canal door behind him.

"Hell of a night," he whispered to me.

"All's well that ends well," I whispered back, holding him close.

I'd finished cleaning up the gore and flushing the blood-soaked toilet paper down the toilet before Paul returned from his swim. I watched him sweep the area.

"You do good work," he announced to the stillness surrounding us.

"Thank you, kind sir," I said, putting a seal on my statement by planting a kiss on his mouth.

"Your place or mine?" he whispered.

"Yours. I've had enough of this one."

We retired to his suite, took a mutual shower that transitioned into more lovemaking, and fell into his bed, exhausted but satisfied. For the time being…

Epilogue

Sunday, January 29th

Paul moved first, or so I thought. Light flooded through the high bedroom window. A new day had dawned. I stretched, feeling my nerve endings tingling and reached for my phone. It confirmed the birth of a new day: seven-thirty in the morning. I rolled towards Paul. "You hungry, lover?" I whispered.

"Mmm-hmm," he murmured, moving against me. "But food can wait."

He was right.

After the long wait, I swear my appetite was stronger.

We breakfasted at La Placida, piling our plates high with all things scrumptious and filling, not knowing when we'd eat again. We could hear no whisperings or mumblings amongst the other diners, so we assumed Mister Smith was still undiscovered. Good.

After breakfast, we strolled through the botanical gardens, breathing deeply of the incredible tropic fragrances. I remembered one more errand I had to make and dragged Paul with me to the gift shop. The scarf I'd picked out before, that screamed Holly's name, was still there. I had them gift wrap it and I paid cash. One of my hundred dollar bills covered it nicely.

On the way back, my phone trilled. "This is EZ," I announced to the unknown caller.

"Hey, EZ, it's Agent Cottrell. I have some news for you and Paul," he said, his voice matter-of-fact.

"I'm all ears and Paul's right here beside me. What's up?"

"We've got a lead on the crew that attacked you and the General. It's one of the most convoluted organizations I've seen. Its tentacles go everywhere, from congressmen and senators, even to members of the presidential team. It's going to take time to unravel it all, but I wanted you to know we're on it, and we're involving FBI, NSA and every law enforcement agency out there."

I held my phone so Paul could hear Cottrell as well. He was first to speak. "Good work, Agent. That's great news. We had one more visitor after you left, wanted to take us out to show Walt how vulnerable he was. He failed."

"I hate to say so, but you may have more like him paying you a visit. There's people out there who don't appreciate the help you gave to General McKelvy," said Cottrell.

"Thanks for the heads-up, and thanks for keeping us informed. We appreciate it," I said.

"With your warning, we'll continue to watch our backs," said Paul.

"No problem. Stay safe, you two."

Back in our rooms, I quickly packed while Paul did the same in his suite. I had an M9 semiautomatic pistol with a suppressor to deal with in addition to my own. I chose to take a chance with the Punta Cana baggage people and dropped it, wrapped in clothing, into my check-through bag. Holly's wrapped scarf went in with it. As for my lockback knife, I hated to be without it, but on the other hand the thought of losing it in a scan of my backpack was worse. I settled for putting it in with my keys and wrapping strips of tin foil loosely around it. An x-ray machine might miss seeing it for what it was. Time would tell. My fingers were crossed. It's how I always packed it so chances were good it would work again.

Done, I dragged my suitcase and shouldered my backpack out to the hall and to Paul's room next door. He had both duffels on the bed, an array of firearms on display. "I have a plan," he said, smiling at me.

"Whatcha gonna do, soldier boy?" I asked.

"Don't call me boy, girl."

I quickly got his point. "What are you going to do?" I said, chastened.

"I'm putting all the ordnance in one bag and checking it at the airport. I'll contact Bragg, send them the key and tell them where it is. It's government property, after all."

"An excellent plan."

Paul finished packing, with one duffel for his personal items, the other loaded with the M4 carbine, pistol, and assorted loaded magazines, all wrapped securely in a handful of his shirts and shorts. I doubted if they'd make it back to the PX shelves in their current condition. We left his room behind and made our way to the reception desk.

Miss Haversham was there, her hand full of memos that needed her attention. I told her what a wonderful time I'd had, and I promised to send many travelers her way in the future. She gushed with delight.

"It's been a pleasure having you here, EZ," she said as she grasped my hand in hers.

If she only knew.

I introduced her to Paul, and she shook his hand warmly, too.

"I called for the limo, EZ. It should be out in front momentarily," she said, her face beaming.

"Oh, that's not necessary. We're perfectly fine taking a taxi," I protested.

"Nonsense! It is a part of our promise to you," she said. She placed her well-manicured hand on my shoulder for emphasis.

What could I say? I smiled and accepted her gesture with grace.

We said our farewells and stepped outside into the mid-morning heat and humidity. The limousine sat idling at the curb, the driver standing by the rear door. Seeing us, he swung it open, inviting us to step inside.

I went first, Paul following behind me, and the driver closed the door. The air conditioning swirled welcoming cool air around us.

The drive to the airport was uneventful. We climbed out into the humid heat and retrieved our bags from the trunk. After we both thanked the driver, Paul held the airport entrance door for me and followed me inside. He spotted a wall of lockers and tucked his duffle of armaments inside, then pocketed the key. We moved together to the check-in counter.

With our pockets full of cash, we booked seats in first class to Atlanta. Once there, Paul would board a plane for Columbia, South Carolina and his parent's welcoming committee, while I took the short flight to Valdosta and Holly's welcoming committee.

I sighed with relief when my backpack made it through screening unscathed. I love that little lockback and I'd miss it terribly if it was confiscated. We had a history that goes way back. It's saved my skin more than once.

When they announced boarding for our flight, I was pleased when they called for first class passengers to board first. I was accustomed to being one of the last ones on. We stepped into the plane and attendants surrounded us, assisting us with our bags and asking us if we wanted to hang up our coats. The perks of first class. With my purse, backpack and jacket stowed above, we took our plush, wide leather seats while an attendant asked us what we'd like to have to drink.

"Is the fruit juice fresh?" I asked.

"It is, Miss. We get it delivered every time we land here."

Paul and I both opted for a huge glass of Dominican fruit juice, no ice, no rum.

We sat sipping our chilled juice while the cattle class passengers filed by. Some pointedly ignored us while others stared with envy. I couldn't begin to recall how many times I filed by like them. Now I knew how it felt to sit and watch them pass by.

The cabin door was closed, and I felt the plane being towed backwards from the gate. Then the engines came to life. We were running on our own power, taxiing to the departure runway. I felt the plane brake to a stop, then the engines revved to a crescendo. Brakes were released and the plane lurched down the runway, gathering speed as we went.

I reached out and grasped Paul's hand. Takeoffs have always done that to me. The moment of truth when the plane breaks away from the runway and struggles to gain altitude has always been a nerve-wracking time for me. I felt the nose of the plane point skyward and the cessation of vibration told me we had lifted off from Punta Cana and the Dominican Republic.

A short time later, the plane leveled off and the engine noise softened. I released my death grip on Paul's hand and peered out the window at the turquoise waters below. There they were. Clumps of dark shadows within the clear water. I speculated once again if they were sharks. Déjà vu.

I held my half-empty juice glass up to Paul and he clinked his glass against mine, a contented smile spreading across his broad face.

A loud voice cut through our reverie. "Attention, all passengers! The Federal Liberation Front has taken control of this aircraft! You will remain in your seats and you will not be harmed!"

I turned around in my seat to see a short, swarthy man dressed in casual clothes. He looked like so many other passengers on the flight. He held a female flight attendant tightly against his side, a weapon clutched in his right hand. Knife? Box cutter? I couldn't tell what it was from where I sat, but the terror on the flight attendant's face said it all. The man stood just beyond the first-class section curtain, facing the rear, the tourist class.

I turned to Paul and whispered softly to him. "Here we go again."

Acknowledgements

I wish to thank the members of my Author Book Club for their support, as well as for their thoughtful critiques of my work. All successful authors in their own right, they are Dallas Hembra, A.L. Mundt, Katharine Nohr, Flo Parfitt, Simi K. Rao, and Callie Trautmiller. Check out their novels. Thanks also to Brittiany Koren, my editor, publisher, and the head of my cheering squad. And thank you to Ed Vincent for the fantastic cover.

My acknowledgements wouldn't be complete without sending out a big round of thanks to all my loyal readers, both current and future. I'll continue to do my best to please you all.

About the Author

Charles M. DuPuy collected a bountiful supply of experiences as a young man, and now he's using them to round out his novels. He's traveled through most of the United States, including a drive up the AlCan Highway to Alaska with a buddy, traversing Canada from east to west en route. He's snorkled from Florida to Hawaii and served two years in the Peace Corps in Africa. He's been a teacher, a real estate broker, a salesman, a farmer, and the managing editor of a Vermont outdoors magazine. In his early forties, he studied to become a physician assistant. His assignments ranged from pediatrics to geriatrics, and from substance abuse treatment to the maximum security unit of the New Mexico State Penitentiary in Santa Fe.

Retired now, he spends much of his day at his computer where he blends fact with fiction, adds dashes of romance and humor, and concocts the suspenseful mysteries he's so well known for. He shares his life with his beloved wife, Janet, their two cats and a wonderful Westie named Jack, somewhere in the Great Southwest.

www.ingramcontent.com/pod-product-compliance
Lightning Source LLC
Chambersburg PA
CBHW030402200726
48286CB00015B/2553